FETCH !

(THE JOURNEY CONTINUES)

Harvey Price

Publisher: Harvey L. Price, Jr

Hoquiam, Washington

ISBN: 978-0-9819220-2-7

Library of Congress Control Number: 2008906885

Manufactured, printed and bound in the United States of America by Minuteman Press, Olympia, Washington; and by Phil's Bindery, Seattle, Washington.

FOR

STEVE, BEN AND JUANITA

Greg

Photo courtesy of The Daily World/Macleon Pappidas

FOREWARD

This second travelogue is a companion to its sister volume, "Speak!" It also catalogs the mishaps and adventures of the same, oddly-mixed posse that eventually found refuge by the end of the first book in the Hoh Rainforest. Soon, in this second account, new recruits are added to their band, and the story evolves into a worldwide cruise of reform and transformation. It is, by all accounts, an odyssey, which takes place in the future. But its many locations and present day conflicts are familiar to all of us in the here and now.

Again, the narrator is Greg, the now moving-on-past-middle-age, Blue Healer, who, as before, seems to get overly involved in complicated situations or, sometimes, to make them so quite easily.

International intrigue and the collision of ideals emerge as the Wagoners sail into five regional, trouble spots across the world. The likelihood of their saving the planet, despite earlier success, is not guaranteed, nor is it even quite likely. Oftentimes, their mission appears doomed. To give them the slimmest chance of success, they try to insure that most of the world's creatures are allowed to have a voice in the centers of government and to contribute their unique talents to preserve and to enhance all life. Without their help, the Emissaries will win after all, and the world will be doomed.

DUTY CALLS

ONE: ED AND IRIS

But wouldn't you know, the days of relaxation and endless conversations with these magnificent, Hoh River Rainforest trees and assorted, local, newly- acquired friends had to change. It was a little over four months from when our odyssey ended that Bernie came up to me, while I was sunning on her grandmother's, luxurious front porch, and gave me a delightful scratch behind each ear, but then uttered those now famous words, "We have to go now, Greg."

Immediately, feeling that old, on-the-road-again dread returning, I replied, rather sharply, "Why?!"

"Because our work is far from over," she answered quietly. "My grandfather-Walt's centuries'-in-the-devising-and-implementing plan to rid this world of the Emissaries was successful, but, as we both know, it tragically ended at the expense of his own life. And our grief over his loss will probably never lessen. But if we do not follow up on your cross-country plan and grandfather's worldwide one, which has only just begun with the elimination of the Emissaries, all we have done up until now will have been for nothing. He confided in me during his last days with us that we had to resume our mission, once we were rested enough and had time to see what the initial effects of our journey together across America had been. From what he explained to me, it was time now to address the second major obstacle to global peace and good will, the evolving likelihood of obsessively homicidal individuals, groups, dictators and governments in haggard and war-torn countries beginning assemble everywhere."

"Gulp," was all I could manage to whisper. There's no sense trying to fool you, I was crest-fallen by Bernie's appeal. She didn't have to make demands or play on my patriotism or humanitarian leanings. She just had to ask a favor of me. She and Wally, along with Sophie, Frank and Willa, were my dearest friends. If they asked me, I'd attempt to swim upstream, the length of the Hoh River. Or even if they requested that I try to cook a Thanksgiving meal or stifle my herding and barking behaviors or get a haircut and perm, I'd do my best to make it happen. I would do about anything for them, but asking me to leave this place was almost too much.

Besides, I had made a couple of new friends, and I had finally convinced them to come over that evening for dinner. At long last, I had won their confidence, and they agreed to meet my extended family. And, come to think of it, probably right about now is as good a time as any to fill you in on how I met them. Describing those chance encounters will help reduce the sadness I experience, even now, as I remember that day when Bernie made her request.

So first, let me tell you about my meeting Ed. It all started one early morning in October, about a month after we first arrived at Willa's. As was my custom, I had begun to wander around in the early morning, before everyone was awake, and Jennifer was just returning from her nightly prowls. And going down to the river was becoming a pattern during my morning walks. It just drew me to its banks. The fall rainstorms had recently started and the river was beginning to rise. This seasonal pattern of nature begins to beacon the salmon upstream for spawning. It is a rhythm of life that absolutely amazed me. I could stand on a rocky outcrop for hours, looking down into a shallow area and watch those huge fish sweep by. Their speed and determination convinced me that they knew exactly where they were going and what they were doing. It was hypnotizing.

Now, THEY had a story to tell! TALK ABOUT JOURNEYS! They travel throughout the world's oceans, denied the privileges of motoring on paved highways, having covered rest stops along the way, stopping at fully-stocked grocery stores, or resting in recreation vehicles. On our trip, our only hazard was being hit by an occasional, reckless driver and, of course, being vaporized by the Emissaries. These mighty fish, on the other hand, had to chart their own course hundreds, if not thousands, of miles out from this river and back, constantly hustling for food, all the while dodging nets, hooks, seals, sharks, bears, hawks and eagles. Talk about your unsung heroes.

There was no way I could touch or somehow influence one of them to talk, I knew that. They were too fast, too big, and probably totally uninterested in any of my leftover magic or conversation. Besides, Walt's alterations of me had probably, by then, run their course. I felt most of my extraordinary abilities were, no doubt, spent. Or at least that's what I sincerely thought.

But on this particular day I found one of these mighty fish gasping for breath, lying along the river's shoreline. Unsure what to do, I cautiously walked up to it and lightly touched it. There was no thought in my mind that anything would come of such a gesture. It was simply born out of pity at my seeing the obvious distress this wonderful creature was in.

"I'm sorry to see you in such a way," I muttered quietly, as I gently stroked its flank. "I can't imagine what you have been through, and I sincerely wish I could help you."

But to my absolute shock and amazement, sputtering and wheezing, the fish replied, "Can't say I'm too happy about being in this condition myself. I was sideswiped and then made too high a leap to avoid another collision and landed here. And now I'm pooped, trying to catch my breath. I can't even remember the last time I had a good meal, and from the looks of things I'd guess I'm about to become someone else's. This cycle of nature, as they call it, just isn't what it's cracked up to be. If you know of anyone involved with recycling life forms or who does reincarnations for creatures like us, would you put in a word for me. I'd rather be a land-lubber my next time around, if that should be the way this creation business works out. And while you're at it, could you nudge me over a little further into deeper water. I'd sure like to finish this trip back where I was born, but I still have about five more miles to go before I reach my destination."

"Sure," I stuttered, in a state of shock at listening to a talking fish. Nervously, I added, "Let me push you out further into the water with my nose."

Once she was into deep enough water where she could be upright, she stuck her head out and called, "Hey, thanks... By the way, do you have a name? You've just made it possible for me to deliver hundreds of potential fish like me to my own birthplace upstream from here. And I'd like to thank you personally for that."

Still unsure whether I was dreaming all this and by now feeling more than a little silly talking back to a fish, I shyly answered, "It's Greg."

"Then 'Greg' it is, and please know how sincerely grateful I am for your selfless act of kindness. You saved my life... at the end of it."

To which I could only manage to reply, before she interrupted me, "It only seemed the right thing to do..."

And then I was interrupted with her yelling, "Look out! There's Big Trouble swooping in for the kill! I'm not sure whether I'll be able to escape his deadly clutches... Do something Greg! Look overhead! HELP ME!"

Quickly looking around me, I saw nothing. Then as she instructed, I glanced overhead. Making a supersonic dive was absolutely the biggest bird or object I had ever seen in the sky. It was headed straight for the fish I had just met. Instinctively, I spun around, and was able to just barely straddle my hind legs around her head. There wasn't much room left once I assumed that position. She was one big fish, and, as you already know, I'm not a very tall dog. Then looking skyward, I issued forth one of my more authoritative series of barks, with a few snarls thrown in, which was very uncommon for me. But I wasn't sure at that moment if it was doing any good, because that huge thing coming towards us seemed to be gaining speed. From the size of it, I figured he could probably carry us both off and have a two-for-one-dive in breakfast.

It was only when he was about five or ten feet away that he veered off and circled toward Willa's house. And as he made that maneuver, the fish under me raised her head, striking me on my underbelly. I leaped straight up. This wasn't like one of my usual, serene, morning walks, and I was a little tense by now. Spinning again, in midair, I landed with a big splash next to the fish.

"Sorry, Greg, but I really have to run now. And that's the second time you've saved my life. I wish I could repay you in some way, but there is no time. Maybe someday you'll meet some of my offspring. Look for them in about three to four years at this same spot. And take care of yourself. I think that big bird is probably a little miffed and is coming back for another try. Good luck to you. So long…"

And with her saying that, she spun around, and before I could hardly focus on her, she had shot into deeper water, joining other salmon migrating toward the smaller streams closer to the nearby, snow-covered mountains. I didn't even get a chance to say "good-by". And soon my morning was to become even more complicated.

I saw that the mammoth bird, which now I could verify as such by his outstretched wings, was heading straight back towards me. Getting colder as I stood in the water, I quickly hopped up on the rocky shoreline and faced him straight on. My only instinct again was to crouch down in a defensive position and bark. I wanted to yell something like, "Listen you jerk, you lost that round! Make like a flat tire and hit the road!" But instead, I just barked.

Typically, I had forgotten in all this excitement how Rita's influence could easily have spread over this region as well. So, equally shocking to me, as this huge bird filled my field of vision and then stretched out his seven foot wingspan to land effortlessly in front of me, he commented with some testiness, "Nice move, Slick. You're heroics have prevented me from catching a feast for myself and the family. If you weren't so scrawny I'd take you instead."

As this stunning creature landed, I could see that I was dealing with someone almost twice my size, at least when his wings were outstretched. And he stood head and shoulders above me, looking down at me with eyes that blazed with fury. It wasn't until later that I realized he always had that determined look. Also, at that moment, I observed that he was one, handsome specimen. His head was pure white, as were his tail feathers. His other feathers were black as Willa's potbelly stove. His beak and HUGE feet, or talons as I later learned they were called, were a bright yellow. I tried not to be speechless, but honestly, I was scared witless. And I have to confess, I did a little wee.

Mustering up some very marginal courage, I managed to say, "I guess this just isn't your day. The fish was under my protection, and I am not interested in your attempts to intimidate me. You are, after all, on private property." I made up that last bit, thinking it might throw him off. Plus, I hoped my speaking might at least add more confusion to our confrontation and buy me some time.

"WAIT A MINUTE!" the bird then shouted. "Not only are you squirrelly looking, an unwelcome obstructionist, and an unappetizing option for a meal, YOU ALSO TALK! I'm aware that trees somehow have that ability, as do others who nest or perch on them. But now I find out that you do as well! What's it all coming to? I use to hunt freely, to roam at will, and to roost wherever I pleased. Now I have to ask permission of the trees, excuse myself constantly with the other birds, and hunting is becoming a real hassle. I expect someday soon I'll need to register somewhere and get a license to hunt. And then, there's you! Mercy, this is all just too much." He looked down at that point and shook his head. It was obvious he was discouraged.

8

Seeing this moment as my one chance to gain some bargaining power, I replied "You need to get around more. There are lots of us who speak now. Maybe we should sit down sometime and discuss all this when you're in a more relaxed state. And maybe even a little less hungry."

"You mean to tell me that there are more like you!" he exclaimed. "Does this mean I'm going to have to beg for food? This is my territory. It's where I shop. Are guys like you going to make it more difficult for me to do so?"

"Not in the least," I replied. "It was only by chance that I came upon that fish today. I'm certain that sort of thing won't happen again, unless, of course, you happen upon some bear who is eying the same fish as you. Then you might be in for a lengthy discussion about property rights and food sources in the neighborhood."

"One more, quick question," the large bird commented, obviously becoming more perplexed as we talked. "Did by any chance that fish also talk?"

"Yep," I had to say with a rather, self-satisfied smile. "But that was a surprise to me as well."

"Do you mean to say that whenever I now attempt to catch one, I may have to listen to them try and talk me out of it being my next meal?"

"That could very well happen," I pondered. "Stranger things have been happening everywhere over these last few months. Now, it wouldn't surprise me if that one particular fish should make contact with its associates and passes this trait along to them and to her offspring. Just thinking about that, I can imagine the consternation of people, like sonar operators around the globe. Instead of hearing beeps, whines, whistles and mournful cries, there will be riots of conversations, yelling to one another and singing throughout the seas and oceans. And all of it starting with that one fish!"

"You've got to be joking," the big bird mumbled, with his head slumped forward, shaking side-to-side.

"Maybe, maybe not," I honestly had to say. "Just the fact that you are talking to me now and that you have been hearing and talking to trees is reason enough to start preparing yourself for such an eventuality. And all this is as a result of what my compatriots and I have been asked to do by Walt, our resident wizard.. It was started with him."

"This is too much information. I just wanted some breakfast, not an overview of the most staggering, evolutionary upheaval in the history of this planet. Can you at least tell me something mundane and straight forward, like do you have a name?"

"Sure," I happily replied. "My name is Greg. What's yours?"

"I never thought of having one, to be honest. Recently I did overhear a particular tree introducing itself to another tree, and it said his name was 'Ed'. I kind of like that name."

"Hey, then 'Ed' it is," I said coming forward and reaching out to shake paw with claw. "It's nice to meet you, Ed. What kind of bird are you, by the way?"

"I'm a bald eagle," he replied, lifting his head proudly, and doing a small walkabout so I could appreciate all his finer features. "I'm the national symbol," he then added.

Not to sound too dumb, I had no choice but to ask, "Of what?"

"Silly," he answered somewhat put off, "of everything."

Well, that really impressed me. First, I rescued a talking fish, and now I met a very large bird who claims to be the symbol of everything. Can you have a better day than that, I ask you?

From that time forward, until the day Bernie told me it was time to leave Willa's farm, Ed and I would meet almost daily down by the river. He'd dine on something local, and I would scratch or chew on an odd piece of driftwood while we talked about anything and everything. He was a treasure trove of Northwest history and lore. Between him and his cousins, he had heard of or seen most of everything that had been happening in these parts for years. Finally, two days before Bernie spoke to me about having to leave on our next journey, he and Iris, who you haven't met yet, worked up the courage and agreed to meet everyone. It was to be the night before the Wagoners were to make preparations for leaving Willa's.

But, again, before I get into the events of that evening, I want to introduce you to my next friend. She was someone I met, also by accident, about three weeks after my first encounter with Ed.

As time went on, I had become more brazen about exploring the river and the little side creeks that emptied into it. On this particular day, I had wandered a mile or so upstream from my usual gazing spot, which was in front of Sophie and Frank's family's, newly acquired store. Of course, initially, it was Willa's and Walt's. At that furthest point up river, I spied a perfect place to observe a deep, clear pool of large salmon. They appeared to be resting before making their next run up a series of difficult rapids, immediately ahead of this pool.

To get the best view of their sanctuary, I needed to inch my way out onto a floating log that had snagged up in some branches. They had been caught up in a tangle of downed wood along the riverbank. It was probably stupid of me to do so, but I'm certainly not immune from catching the "what the hell did you think you were doing" bug. And becoming freshly infected with it that day, I crawled out on this perfectly positioned log. All was well and good until I decided the view would be just that much better a little further out toward the end.

It was a remarkable sight, seeing the fish schooled in that deep, crystal clear refuge. I became lost in the privilege of watching them...until the log I was crouched on tipped with my weight on the end and dislodged from its entanglement in the branches. I was soon set adrift, heading downstream.

Have I told you that I don't swim, or that I never wanted to even try learning how to. Howard's bathtub escapades were enough deepwater experiences for me. The only swimming strokes that I knew were ones that might incorporate standing petrified on that log and howling, barking, screaming and yelling, combined with avoiding touching any water, at all costs. Water is to drink. No one in their right mind swims in it; unless they have scales, fins or other underwater attachments. And that's my final word on the matter.

But feeling and saying all that did little to rescue or reassure me. I was heading downstream toward the Pacific Ocean. The log at the beginning did seem to stay upright, not rolling as it began its journey. At least that was a little comfort. But hearing the rapids up ahead wasn't. So I screamed a little louder.

Maybe it should be noted, as well, that it was now November, and the temperature of everything was colder: the water, the fog, the air... my ears. So, to relieve at least one of those issues a few weeks ago, I began wearing my pullover, leather flight-helmet again. And today was no exception. And because earlier this morning it had begun to sprinkle, as they call it in these parts (but anywhere else it would be more correctly called a monsoon), I had also donned my goggles. At this moment they were well secured over my eyes. To anyone standing on the river bank, I must have appeared a little out of place, as I skimmed down the river, pretending to look like some old-time, air ace. And believe me, I sure felt out of place.

It was about the time when I began to realize my options for making a successful venture of this trip were disappearing that I heard a voice cry out to me from overhead.

"Are you ok down there?!" the voice yelled

out.

Sputtering, now that the log was heading into rougher water and splashing waves into my face, I yelled back, "It doesn't feel like ok! In fact, I'm in the market for a little help down here!" I said this knowing that any minute I was heading into the drink. These, most likely, were to be the last words I would utter that didn't sound like I was gargling.

"Do you mind if I suggest something, then?!" came that same, strange, overhead voice again.

"No, as long as you do so quickly," I answered, trying to avoid being too curt and not wanted to sound too impatient with any assistance that might be forthcoming.

"Well, if you're not wanting to stay on that log, I'd suggest you get ready to jump just before it goes under those branches up ahead. What I'd further suggest is that you jump as high as you can when I tell you to, like RIGHT NOW! JUMP!!"

It was like whatever was hovering right over my head had yelled directly into my ear, because the shock of its booming voice scared me so much that I leaped far and high. I was honestly more frightened and startled by that shouting than I was of the water. The result was that I landed in some overhanging branches of an Alder tree, which had been blown over in a recent wind storm. It was a tangle, but at least I was out of the water and a lot safer than I was. Eventually, I worked my way through all the limbs and got back onto firm ground, and standing there at the base of that downed tree stood the strangest looking creature I had ever seen, bar none.

Its head size was hard to estimate, because its face had grown a HUGE, plastic-looking snout, with hooked tip-end. And then, to top that, hanging down from it was a rubbery sack of some kind. The head, itself, was all white and, wouldn't you know, also had those intensely fierce, staring eyes. What's with this? It must be something about me that brings out these looks. I mean I know I stare, but I don't stare with a look that indicates who or what I am staring at is about to be my next meal.

And when it opened its beak to talk the sack underneath it dropped down and formed a bag large enough to fit a week's worth of groceries in it for both Flo and I! My first thought was, "Wow! This guy really knows how to gulp down a meal, or four or five of them, with one swallow. If this flying grocery bag was a guest at some formal, tie-and-tails banquet, he or she would be a waiter's worst nightmare. You'd have to reserve an entire table and dedicate two waiters to serving him or her, just to keep up with the amount of food that would be consumed.

The creature's body was brownish-looking and very big. And its wingspan just before the landing in front of me must have been nearly seven feet across. Between Ed and this individual, I was convinced this area was no place for the petite, gentrified songbirds of my hometown neighbor in Atlantic City.

And then I caught sight of his black legs and feet, and they made me feel much better. His legs were shorter than mine! And attached on the end of them were snowshoe-sized, web feet. I'd walk beside him or her anytime in a parade and not feel at all conspicuous. And to top it off, it waddled when it walked. Perfect. I knew right away that we could become friends. And just then we made eye-to-eye contact.

"Who or what are you?" I asked, short of breath and trying to shake off the water that had splashed over me.

"I'm the one who directed you to jump just now," the odd-looking, almost bird-like, form replied.

"You're the one who saved my life?" I followed up, with some disbelief.

"The very one."

"Are you a bird of some kind? I guess you must be. Your voice came from overhead when I was floating on that log. And you can talk as well. If you're from around these parts, you wouldn't have happened to run into Ed, the eagle, before? He also talks. You don't possibly know him, do you?"

"Yes," she replied, somewhat impatiently, as my string of questions poured forth endlessly. "I am a bird of some kind. I am a pelican. Actually, I am a brown pelican, of the family: Peleconidae and of the genus/species: peleconus occidentalis, if you're someone who likes to dabble in details.

"And obviously, I do talk. I didn't before a few months ago, but some geese that our group ran into got us started. It has caused us no small amount of consternation since then. It's amazing. It seems the more words you know; the more likely you are to get into an argument with someone. When we simply squawked, times were simpler. Now we have to discuss EVERYTHING. And as to your next question, 'yes' I have met Ed. It was a few days later, after you and he first met. He told me about you. And he actually asked me to keep an eye out for you. He didn't think you had too much common sense and thought you might get yourself into trouble. And he was right."

"Well, I am really grateful for your being here," I answered; now feeling like a tenderfoot squatter, way out of his depth. "Do you have a name?"

"As a matter of fact I do. After meeting Ed, he told me about your helping him get a name, and sometime after that I decided to select one as well. So I chose 'Iris'. He said your name is 'Greg'."

"Yep. It used to be Bob. But I changed it before I left Atlantic City, some time ago.

Just at that moment Flo called out from the farm house for me to come in for breakfast. She was still very protective of me and didn't trust my outdoor, survival skills. I swore everyone during that time must have been talking to Ed.

"Upps," I said, "That's Flo calling me. It's time for me to head back home. But I certainly want you to know how grateful I am for your saving me from my probably floating, lifelessly, with the fishes. Maybe we can meet up again sometime and get more acquainted."

"Sure enough," Iris answered. "You seem harmless enough and Ed seemed to vouch for you. You realize, don't you, that Ed is actually the presiding official who represents all of us life forms in this area. At any official function we have now, he chairs that meeting. He's really quite a fellow, a natural leader, as it were."

"Well, no, I didn't actually know that," I replied with some amazement. "And hearing it now, I hope that he and I can also spend more time together. And, of course, anytime we do, you are most welcome to join us, if you happen to be in the neighborhood."

That seemed to please Iris, because she waddled closer to me and held out one of her wings, and I instinctively reached out with my right paw. Our clumsy paw-to-wing shaking seemed to convey to both of us that we'd meet again.

"See you around, then," she called out as she turned. "I don't usually fly up these rivers. Mostly, I just hug the ocean's shoreline. But I enjoy the change of scenery when I come inland. None of the others in my group like to come with me. But that's their loss. Because now I have a friend I wouldn't have had otherwise. I'll catch up with you later. So long for now."

Saying that, she took a series of jogging strides, spread her massive wings, flapped them three or four times and left the ground. It made me envious to see that strange looking, awkward appearing creature, who seconds before stood in front of me, soar so effortlessly and gracefully away. "Dog," I thought, "there's a classic case of not judging a book by its cover."

For the next three months I met with my two, new feathered friends on a fairly regular basis.

They were reluctant to come into contact with humans and the other animals living at my residence. This reticence required that I be patient.

Now, that's a trait that I was certain had to be genetically implanted. If you didn't get some patience genes in those formative moments, you didn't have any, to speak of, thereafter. And by now I was certain I was skipped over when they were passed out. I figured that's the reason I bark. It's my way of saying in certain situations, "Hey! Don't you realize, you bozo, that I'm handicapped and deserve more respect in this matter at hand! After all, I wasn't born with hands that open doors or pick up food dishes to be refilled, or that I have legs long enough that I could drive a pickup truck all by myself!"

But, then, come January 16th, two days before Bernie spoke to me about our having to leave on another mission, both Ed and Iris surrendered to my hounding requests (no pun intended) and accepted my invitation to come to dinner. I was so excited.

TWO: SUPPERTIME- JANUARY 18TH

It probably would have helped matters, if I had given everyone sufficient prior notice that I had invited Ed and Iris to dinner that night. But thinking ahead, like patience, is another of those missed-out-on genes of mine. I'm a "lost-in-the-present-moment' kind of dog. I don't mean to be rude or inconsiderate; it just works out that way, particularly in social gatherings. And on this night I outdid myself.

Even more disturbing for everyone involved, I had also forgotten that I had invited them. I guess Bernie's announcement to me earlier in the day swept my brain clear of any purposeful or sequential thoughts. I had become the classic model of "You naughty dog."

And then there was the usual rush of getting the meal prepared. Everyone always took part in the preparations, cooking and setting of the dinner table. But, maybe I should back up for a moment and give you some idea where this nightly event takes place.

Willa's home was originally the estate of a

local lumber baron. It seems Thomas Nelsen migrated from Maine to the Puget Sound back in the mid-1800's. At that time most logging was still done by hand. It was called, "hand-logging", because there was minimal mechanization involved in those early years. And most of it took place along the shorelines of the ocean, up the mountain sides bordering the mighty Northwest Rivers and around the deep lakes and fiords. Working in these places made it easier to eventually get the logs to market. Building right of ways, with all-weather roads and rail lines, was years in the future. But that was Mr. Nelsen's genius. After some time cutting timber this old fashion way, he knew there had be a more enterprising way to harvest these woods. But to the end of his days, he loved to recount how thrilling it was to watch the logs skid 50 miles per hour down the mountain sides and sound into the deep bays and then shoot skyward, once they hit bottom. To him, they were the glory days of logging.

Years passed and his many lumber mills made him very rich. To try and please his wife, he built an estate up the Hoh River. By clearing acres of land, bringing in livestock, planting orchards, flower and herb gardens, he hoped it would be a setting that would entice her to stay in this rugged and isolated place. But, alas, she would have none of it. The lure of Boston, her home town, was too great. She never spent one night in his chalet.

However, you'd have to say Willa's rambling, two story mansion is not like any typical, Swiss home. It was built by blending a mixture of massive logs with native river rock. There are thirty rooms, with each of the seven bedrooms having their own fireplace, as does the kitchen, den and living room. It was more like an Englishman's manor, with a generous portion of local cedar, spruce and fir decorating and supporting the interior structure.

Willa came on the scene soon after Mr. Nelsen's wife fled the Northwest. She knew the circumstances of her departure and came ostensibly in answer to an advertisement in the Seattle newspaper for a housekeeper. She and Walt had decided this locale was perfect for their future plans, which as you now know, involved all of us cross-country travelers. Nothing romantic was ever reported between Mr. Nelsen and Willa, but he remained infatuated and devoted to her until his death. Sadly, he had no living relatives. As a result, he left the estate to her at his passing.

And so you have a more complete picture of Mr. Nelsen's devotion to her, Willa was, and still is, strikingly beautiful. I think she is actually ageless, even more so than Walt. She is almost five feet tall. Her skin has a rich, pearl-like quality. Her facial features are petite but perfectly proportioned. And her eyes are a sparkling, deep azure. Her voice, to me, has the tone of chapel bells, tolling across a meadow. And the fragrance that surrounds her is always like freshly baked bread. Whenever I'm not wandering down by the river, you can find me resting at her feet. Other than Wally, Bernie and Sophie, she is my hands-down favorite person. Fill the world with folks like those four and you'd have paradise.

Finally, there is Mr. Nelsen's dining room. It, as you might guess, is quite large, with a stone fireplace that easily accepts logs four feet long in the back of the hearth. Once it is fully loaded with firewood, the cracking and popping easily competes with our dinner table conversations. The dining room is off to the left side of a long, wide hallway, leading in from the front door. On the right side is the stairwell leading upstairs. Straight ahead is Willa's kitchen. The living room is to the immediate right side, once you enter the home. My point being is that when you answer someone knocking at the front door, no one in the dining room can see who has just arrived. And finally, in the middle of the dining room is a massive round table, which can seat sixteen to twenty people at once, depending on how close you want each person to sit next to the other. On this night, there was the usual setting for seventeen of us.

I've probably forgotten to mention before that Sophie and Frank's three children arrived one month ago. They are now in the process of taking over management of the roadside market and becoming the straw bosses, under Willa, for upgrading and day-to-day running of the farm. Their oldest daughter, Margaret is married and has two children. Their son, Jimmy, just got married before they moved from Atlantic City. And the youngest daughter, Helen, is unmarried. I have yet to really get to know any of them, but they have shown the same resilience and initiative as Sophie and Frank. What else would you expect?

We ate dinner at 7 p.m. sharp. It was always a rather chaotic dash to get everyone together and arrange all the bowls, plates, serving dishes, chairs, boosters and perches. Everyone ate at the table, me included. Jennifer, Flo and I had our bowls of food and beverage set like everyone else. We just stood on our boosters and leaned over the bowls to eat or drink. Rita, likewise, would often stand on a booster, rather than use her perch, and then peck at her food in a bowl, particularly if it was fruit of some kind. The one inviolate, dinner table rule was: no one was allowed on the table. Can you image? If two dogs, a cat and half-crazed cockatoo took it upon themselves to go for seconds, rather than wait until they were passed. And, mostly due to me, there was also a second rule, even more stringently enforced than the first: there was to be no barking at the dinner table. The humanity of it all! Sometimes I was just so happy to be there with all my friends I just had to bark, howl, wag my tail, scratch, pant or possibly even drool. But they'd have none of it. Actually, I was glad I didn't have to wear a tie; it all seemed so formal at times. But not on this night.

Finally, we had gotten all the food and drinks set up, chairs in place, everyone seated and Frank was about to give the blessing, when there was a loud banging at the front door.

And at that instant, and for the life of me I don't know why, everyone turned automatically and looked at me. "What?" I responded. "Don't look at me," I added. "I'm not expecting anyone…." Then it hit me.

At that moment, Po, who always sat with his back to the dining room door's entrance, also glanced at me, shifted his chair backwards, excused himself and went to the door. And the pounding had persisted throughout all this time. I was beginning to feel sick.

You have to understand that Ed and Iris had never had to knock at a door before, so they felt it perfectly appropriate to both bang their very strong and very large beaks simultaneously on the heavy oak door. I'm certain their knocking was heard for miles, and it didn't let up…sadly.

By the time Po had been able to lunge across our dining room, through the long hallway and up to the front door, he was miffed. Jerking open the door he stared straight ahead and shouted, "Hold your horses! Just who in tarnation are you?" But he couldn't immediately see anyone or anything; that is, he couldn't as long as he looked straight ahead, at his full height of over six feet. Reflexively, as his second option, he looked down, and to his utter and most profound surprise there stood one bald eagle and one brown pelican.

Now you must also realize that when Ed and Iris heard someone shouting to them about "holding their horses", they became concerned. Greg had failed to mention anything to them about bringing horses to dinner. And certainly they weren't holding on to them at that very moment. Confusion was mounting steadily as these events unfolded.

Next came Po's reaction to seeing this odd assortment of birdlife at the front door: "Greg!" he shouted, without any hesitation, knowing as sure as hens lay eggs that I somehow was behind this fast-evolving fiasco. "Come out here! NOW!!"

Well, there I was, realizing I had forgotten everything but my name, and that no place settings had been arranged for these two guests because I had forgotten, no one was aware of their coming, no extra food was prepared, and now I had to try pretend being stately. So, mustering all the savoir-faire I could, I tried to shrug, which had to be a first in the annals of dog life; then I casually glanced around the table and announced, "Oh! These must be our dinner guests for tonight. How perfect they arrived, just as we were being seated."

Jumping down off my bolster, not looking back for fear I would lose all confidence to face what was ahead, I scampered out into the hallway. As I entered it, Po was striding back into the dining room. Passing me, he muttered, "This ought to be a real performance. Nice work, Greg."

Skidding to a stop at the doorway, I came upon my two, possibly used-to-be friends. "Hi," I said meekly. "I'm so glad you really came. I was afraid you might not."

Ed spoke first. "You didn't mention anything to us about bringing horses."

"Huh?" I stammered. Now I knew things were really going downhill. I had the most intense urge at that moment to brush right by them and go out behind a bush and have a quick wee. The tension was just too great.

"No, no," I managed to blurt out. "I'm truly glad you didn't bring any horses with you." My land, I thought, what if they had? How would I ever explain that to everyone? "It was just you two that were to come tonight. Come in, come in, please. It's so great to see you. And how fine you both look tonight. You are a handsome pair."

"Greg," Iris then commented, as she preceded Ed into the hallway, "I'm not sure you would be able to make water travel downhill. I told Ed as we were walking up to this place, I thought it was a mistake our coming here tonight. But here we are, so let's see what you have in store for us."

"Yeah," Ed added. "I'm starved. I haven't eaten in two days in preparation for this meal. I coaxed Iris into coming anyway, despite her reservations. Are there any other guests coming tonight?"

"No, not to my knowledge," I answered. "It's a special occasion when we do have any. You two are actually the first."

"That's even more encouraging…," was all Iris said as we rounded the doorway into the dining room.

I had managed to position myself ahead of my two guests as we entered the dining area, so as to properly introduce them. And hoping to prevent any undue mix-ups, I theorized that by announcing their names simultaneously, as we entered the room; that would work the best. So, in my most officious voice, I called out, "Willa and my esteemed New Jersey Wagoner comrades, let me introduce to you my friends, Iris and Ed."

Upon retrospect, maybe the three of us were traveling a little too fast as we entered the dinner area, but Ed, after all, was hungry. I say this because just after I called out their names, the room exploded with shouts, screams and tipped furniture. Jennifer leaped up onto the middle of the table, hissing and growling, with every hair on her body taut, staring at Ed like he was the Grim Reaper. She was absolutely paralyzed in that pose. Rita, likewise, jumped onto the table, mixing cockatoo squawks, with various disparaging comments about me. She was jumping up and down in place all the while. Flo sat straight up on her bolster and began to howl, like she had just been evicted out of some Nordic igloo for the night. Bernie and Wally were both giggling and pointing at the three of us standing there. Frank stood up immediately, demanding to know what I was up to, bringing total strangers unannounced into our midst. Po just sat there, shaking his head, and continued to eat, with his back to us. And Willa simply got up and went into the kitchen to get more food, calling out over her shoulder as she left, "Po, you and Frank get two more chairs for our guests. Wally, you and Bernie, get two place settings for them and make room at the table for them. And Sophie, bless her heart, came around the table and walked up to them both and knelt down and held out her hand, saying, "Greg has talked so much about you two. We were really looking forward to meeting you tonight." God, I love that woman.

Ed, like me, melted in Sophie's presence. And it seemed to have a quieting effect on Iris to have her kneel down and reach out. Ed spoke first.

"Well, I suppose everyone here knows that Greg is not the most socially adept individual you'd ever meet. And he certainly has spoken to Iris and I countless times about each of you and how important you are to him. You can't help but like him, but, God Almighty is he dumb at times."

Now I've never been the sort that people take the time to talk much about, whether good or bad. So when I heard Ed say those words about me, I felt somehow encouraged by them and didn't know what else to do but smile broadly and nod. Who says that being reliable, dependable and caring means you have to also know and observe are the rules of etiquette and be highly intelligent? I do my best. That's about all I can do.

And in reply, Sophie just laughed and replied, "Yes, we know. But we try to love him as much as we know he loves us." And then she reached over and gave me a nice scratch behind my ears. God bless her.

THREE: NOT AGAIN…?

On the evening of January 20th, it was Sophie who led our two new dinner guests around the table to their respective seats. Ed was to sit between her and Frank, with Jennifer arched in life-ending, petrified panic beside him. Iris was seated, or better described, squatted between Bernie and Wally. These arrangements were Willa's ideas, which, unbeknownst to anyone including me, she had planned ahead of time. Like Walt, Willa had her ways of knowing. And she was prepared for Ed and Iris's arrival.

Calling out from the kitchen, Willa requested that Frank and Po, after arranging chairs for two guests, were to come out there and carry in plates for them; or in Iris's case, a tub. By now, I was in complete shock. My head was dancing back and forth, watching people scurry back and forth, and all with such purposefulness. What utter chaos I had created, they were sorting through and mending with absolute order and decorum. I don't think, as hard as I might try, that I could screw up ANYTHING so bad that this intrepid band couldn't sort it out and then make it right. Talk about having your own back-up. But, throughout all this activity, I did feel so mortified. My intentions were good; my execution was and always is, lousy. With my head drooped, I slinked back to my chair and curled up, and just stared over at my bowl of food that would now be tasteless.

Sensing my despondency, Bernie reached over and petted me, whispering as she did, "You did great, Greg, as always. These are the last two team members we desperately needed for us to do what lies ahead. Don't feel bad. You've done just what I hoped you would. Even though it all appears to have been by happenstance that you met Ed and Iris, you are, in fact, my accidental and most trusted talent scout, just like you were for my grandfather, Walt. So, eat up, you've still got lots of work ahead of you before his decree for us is finished."

Well, her saying that certainly went a long way toward making me feel less like a toad, but to also hear that we had more in store for us didn't actually sharpen my appetite much. Looking at Flo, sitting beside me, I saw her staring at me, her face filled with mixed emotions.

"Are you ok?" I asked, knowing deep down she wasn't. As much as she liked living here, and being close to the snowfields of the Olympic Mountains, our company and this location didn't completely satisfy her deepest desires.

"Something is missing, Greg," she replied. "I see all this activity and hear rumblings of our possibly heading off on another journey somewhere, and I'm not keen on pulling that bloody wagon thousands of miles again."

Her comment really touched a nerve in me. As I mentioned much earlier, I don't have much of a memory. And I had completely lost the brain file, entitled "wagon pulling". After Flo's remark, I was jerked into the full realization that I, too, was not ready for another towing job. "You're right, Flo," I answered. "If there were dues that we needed to pay, I think we paid them on that last trip. I'm with you. Maybe they'd better go without us, if there is another venture like that in the works. I know you initially wanted to eventually finish up our journey from Atlantic City somewhere in the arctic, closer to your relatives. I got my wish, just being here. My part of the bargain with you was to get you there. Let's wait and see what Bernie has to say later tonight, and then make up our minds what we want to do next."

"Ok, Greg," she answered. "I'm glad you understand. And by the way, your newly arrived guests sure look like they have big appetites. Look over there!"

As I looked where Flo nodded, I watched as Frank brought in a mammoth plate of cooked salmon for Ed. It would have fed the entire lot of us. And for Iris, both Frank and Po brought in a 25 gallon, galvanized tub of herring. They set the tub down behind Wally and instructed him and Bernie to hand Iris the fish, or more specifically to drop them into her gapping, wide-open mouth. We later learned that her stomach easily held a gallon of food but her beak-pouch could hold over three gallons...! Talk about carrying around your midnight snack or something to munch on in case of an emergency, that pouch was the answer. I wished I had one too.

Soon the dinner settled down to the sounds of eating, slurping and lapping from all the various species represented. To my ears, it all began to sound something like a barnyard bacchanalia. If a total stranger had walked in on this scene at that moment, I'm sure it would have altered, thereafter and forever, his or her grasp of reality. Here was a still-arched cat eating daintily while being ever-watchful of Ed, knowing full well she could be his dessert at any moment. Then there was Ed merrily munching away on his platter of fish. He'd glace up every now and then at me, as if to say, "nice spread, Greg," Wally and Bernie were giggling as they took turns dropping herring into the gaping cavern of Iris's open mouth. And I might add, it appeared she had her eyes closed, as if she had just arrived at heaven's doorstep. Sophie and Frank were busily eating, while discussing some business matter with Jimmy and Helen. Rita, bless her heart, appeared to have had a stroke. I know, deep down, she wanted to ravage me for dragging her all the way out here from her roost on The Steel Pier. In my defense I have to add, however, that over the next few months she, Iris and Ed formed a trifecta that was the vanguard of our missions overseas. But, at this moment, her yellow crest was perfectly erect, and she was breathing heavily. I knew to keep my distance for now. Po, for all his long-suffering, simply kept eating whatever was passed his way. I think he must be related to Iris, except it's his stomach that can hold three gallons. And finally, there was Willa, who out of the corner of my eye, I could see was quietly and expertly guiding the rhythm and direction of this meal. She, like Walt, was a master of managing us earthlings. I often wondered what the anteverse was really like, to have produced such amazing folks like Walt and Willa.

And so it went, until I noticed Willa nod briefly to Bernie. It was as if it was a signal of some kind. And following that, Willa called out, "Ok, my dearies, that will do it for tonight. I think everyone, including our guests, has about had all the dinner that's being served this night. We can adjourn to the living room for some sweets and a hot drink after Bernie addresses you. So, Helen, Jimmy, and Margaret would you three mind helping me clear the table? Just give us a few moments, Bernie, and then the floor is yours."

Bernie and Wally then, taking Willa's cue, got up and rearranged their chairs so that each of them could stand on them, and placed them far enough away from the table that everyone could easily see them. After the dishes were cleared and everyone was seated, with their chairs, bolsters and perches facing Bernie, she began to address us.

"My dearest family and friends, just before my grandfather left us, he sat Po, Wally and myself down in Willa's study and gave us his final vision of the future. He then gave us his perception of what was and is presently happening to the so-called leaders and citizens in particularly troubled spots around the world.

"To summarize, for the sake of getting

quicker to the reason all of you were asked to come here tonight, let me say that what is now taking place within this country has mischief makers the world over banding together as never before." And looking specifically at Ed and Iris, she added, "And let me emphasize right now that I do mean all of you. They see this time of America's turning inward for renewal, as a golden opportunity to forge ahead with their simmering plans of conquest and terror.

"Walt commissioned Po, Wally and I to form a plan and again enlist each of you gathered here to execute it."

And for the record let me note, it was Ed and Iris who, at that moment, then stared at me with disbelief at what they just heard. You could tell they were rapidly becoming agitated and disenchanted with how the evening was evolving. This was obviously nothing they were prepared to hear or to volunteer for. And besides, they were still hungry.

Sophie and Frank's children and family members were beginning to look like they'd just arrived at the wrong address, for a function being conducted by assorted vampires and broom-riding beings. What their parents did, crossing the country on tricycles, was their business. And the fact that somehow, nationwide, birds, animals and trees were now discussing stock market fluctuations and national politics were things they could accept as "what do you expect? It's all part of this global warming business". They weren't selfish or unaware, but like most citizens of this land, or the world for that matter, they were content to make a living, to nurture and watch their children grow and then hope to enjoy a few other unexpected pleasures in life. Bernie's introductory remarks didn't fit in any of those categories. Each of them began to look at each other, and around the room, like any minute grotesque creatures were going to start circling overhead. They looked scared and bewildered. And, naturally, I had to stifle one or two howls myself.

Sensing this, Bernie sidetracked from her prepared remarks to say, "I need to add that not all of you will be directly involved in the next journey we have ahead of us. Some of you will need to stay here and tend to our home and to Willa."

Well, that perked me up! I wanted to immediately run over and cozy up to Willa and be the first one in line to comfort and protect her. Besides, I knew there was nothing further I could do on some international rescue mission. I didn't have the credentials or a dossier for being Diplomat Dog. After all, I was just a silly-looking guy from Atlantic City, who occasionally barks. And while living there, I took pride, as did most of my associates, in knowing as little as possible about worldly events. On second thought about this time, I did acknowledge to myself that our recently completed cross-country trip was eye-opening. But if you put a world map in front of me or asked me to name three countries outside this one, I couldn't tell you where I was or what country was where. And I wasn't alone in that feeling. I could tell that Bernie's last remark had eased the tension for

Sophie and Frank's families and for Ed and Iris as well. Bernie and Wally sensed all this but chose to say nothing to confirm my relief or the others.

"I'm not going to go into detail as to what is going to happen once we are on our way, but I do need to give those of you who are to go an idea where and how we will be traveling, at least initially, and what we need to take with us. And, of course, we will be letting each of you chosen to go know who you are.

"We will be traveling to five different regions of the world. In each region there will be a conclave of self-named leaders from multiple nations. These meetings are all being convened without the other's knowledge, but unquestionably for the same purpose and, more ominously, within the very short period of just a few months. The first one is scheduled for three weeks from now, and it is being held in Shanghai, China. It will have representatives from China, Russia and North Korea attending that meeting. From there, we will travel to Karachi, Pakistan; then to Nairobi, Kenya; Cairo, Egypt; and finally to Caracas, Venezuela. I will fill you in on the details of each meeting and what we will be doing prior to our arrival at each destination.

"As to how we will be traveling these extended distances, for Sophie, Frank, Flo, Jennifer, Rita and Greg, I can relieve each of you by saying not by tricycles or wagons. We are going by ship most of the way."

Let me pause here, because, of course, there was a double whammy in what I had just heard, and I could feel a long series of barking howls build from deep inside me. FIRST, I WAS GOING AFTER ALL! I felt like the step-child of all miseries. What had I done wrong to deserve this fate? AND SECONDLY ...BY BOAT! WHO ARE YOU KIDDING? I COULDN'T EVEN RIDE ON A FLOATING LOG in the Hoh River. I'm as seaworthy as a herd of elephants. I got seasick just looking at some of those old war movies I watched at Howard's. If I see ripples in my water bowl, I become nauseated. Transoceanic travel is for dolphins and whales. Dogs belong on terra firma, the firmer the better. And as I looked at Jennifer, I could see she was including cats in that category. Forget about Flo. She was eying the door, getting ready to start hitch-hiking north. Rita, for once, looked rather aloof from what was just described. That worried me as well. She had a plan, and I didn't have any idea what it was.

All I could do was blurt out, "You've got to be kidding! Bernie, this is really a funny act you and Wally dreamed up. You both have gotten to be such jokesters. Now can I help with getting our dessert treats and a round of hot drinks for everyone? I know our guests are probably getting tired and will need to be heading home soon..."

"Sorry, Greg," Bernie said, interrupting me. "This is no act nor is it a joke. And it's not going to be brought to a vote. It's urgent business, as much so as our encounter with the Emissaries. Our country is critically vulnerable at this moment, as are all decent, living beings the world over. The shroud of death that was to be brought down upon us by the Emissaries will be no different than what the schemes and dreams of those meeting in these five locations will bring. Walt made this absolutely clear to us, both by what he described would surely happen unless we intervened and by what new powers he then instilled in Wally. Unless we eliminate the threat posed by these upcoming gatherings, freedom and life will disappear forever from this world, as surely as if the Emissaries themselves had caused it. Like Wally and I, those of you chosen will have no choice. You will come."

"Gulp," was all I could manage to mumble. Maybe other folks, under these same circumstances, mustered their courage from their heart and/or brain. I had found that over this last year or so, it was my bladder that was the seat of all my courage. And right now it was about to pronounce this meeting adjourned.

"And we will leave from the Port of Seattle in three days on a U.S. Coast Guard vessel. They are preparing for an extending tour of duty but, as yet, the Captain and crew have no idea where, exactly, their orders are taking them. And they certainly have no idea we will be going with them."

This should be something interesting to watch, I thought to myself. Maybe this trip won't be any longer that a nice drive to Seattle. Because I can just imagine the Captain and his crew gazing down from the deck of their mammoth ship, looking out over an odd assortment of animal, bird and human life forms and being told by a seven and eight year old that they were now going to be diverted to violently unstable regions of the world, ferrying the sole rescuers of all life on this planet. Seems to me like this could be something a little hard to swallow all at once. I don't wish anything embarrassing to happen to my dear friends, Wally and Bernice, but come on! Is this something that you would be interested in doing? And I can just bet that the ship's Captain will have some choice phrases that I'll have to try and explain to the two of them as we drive back to Willa's after this aborted mission. So, "what the heck", I thought. Let's just ride this out.

"Next," Bernie continued, "I need to let you know what we will and will not be taking with us. As previously mentioned, our cross-country equipment is not going to be needed for this mission. For some of you, you need to pack some warm clothing for our first stopover. However, the remaining stops will be in warmer climes, so pack for staying cool, but pack lightly in any case. For the others of you, packing clothes is not an issue.

We won't have much room for storage on board the ship. It's not what we take with us this time that determines the outcome of this next journey. It's only what we say and do that matters. And soon enough, you will realize how important and grave that is.

I tried to let that last remark about clothes pass, it simply being an unintended, discriminatory remark. Even Bernie was going to have to learn that a new inclusive way of conversing was going to have to become fully integrated into the new world order she, Wally and Walt were recreating. Just because I don't wear clothes doesn't mean I wouldn't like to. Look at Jennifer. I bet she'd give anything to be able to wear a nicely tailored pastel-blue, pantsuit outfit, along with a shiny pair of mauve stilettos. And I'd be mighty proud to sport a bomber, flight jacket, whenever I wear my leather helmet and goggles.

But give her time. New standards of socially acceptable references, titles and comparisons take some adjusting to, even by the most liberal-minded amongst us. Maybe even some day I could be addressed as "Mr.", by someone other than Wally. That seems unlikely, though, after tonight's, dinnertime fiasco.

"Finally," Bernie concluded, "Wally will discuss with you who needs to go and a few details about what happens once we get to each of the five destinations."

At that point Wally, who had been sitting quietly, but had appeared to me to be toying with some toy-like object, quickly turned his head towards Bernie and cried out, "Oh, goody, it's now my turn to talk, is it Bernie?"

To which Bernie, taken somewhat by surprise at his gleeful outburst, replied in a rather officious tone, "Yes, Wally, if you will please."

He then spun around and carefully climbed onto the wooden box Po had made for him; that done, he turned back to face each of us sitting around the table. Immediately, I was impressed that he didn't seem like the usual Wally who I spent so much time with on our cross-country journey. The truth is that I hadn't spent any time with him since we arrived at Willa's. He and Bernie seemed removed from the day-to-day activities, occupying the rest of us. And, of course, I had to take my daily investigative trips down to the river and up into the woods. But I felt both children were well cared for, and I gave their absence, except for meal times, no further thought. But Wally seemed somehow different. And as he began to speak, he appeared nervous. Most surprising of all, he began to stutter.

"Hi, everybody," he began. It's exciting to...to see all of you here. I...I am so glad y...yo...you are here tonight. I know our two new gue...guests are quite nervous about what has be...been said by Be...Bernie so far. I want to try and ca...calm you."

If that was his plan, I thought, his stuttering wasn't helping that much. I was beginning to nod my head at each stutter, in hopes of helping him get the words out. I was flabbergasted at what I was seeing and hearing. I began to think that I needed to spend more time with him after tonight.

"And to d...do so," Wally continued, "I want to perform a little de... demonstration."

As he finished saying that, he took his wand out of its sheath and raised it in front of him. It was an act that didn't make me feel any more at ease. As sensitive as that device was, I couldn't imagine what might happen if he trembled or shook it while going through the necessarily strict and formalized hand motions. I had to close my eyes for what might happen.

I later learned that, sure enough, he did have a nervous tremor while holding the wand outstretched. And when he pointed it toward Ed and Iris and wiggled it, as he muttered something, THEY EACH DISAPPEARED...!!!!! When I opened my eyes at everyone's cries of surprise, I was aghast. What a perfect climax to their evening of surprises, I thought. And it's always been so hard for me to make new friends...now what? I thought to myself that the rest of the dinner party probably thought this was a party trick of some kind. I knew differently. Wally had goofed. And now, there was no telling where my two friends were off to. I wanted to throw up.

"Upps," Wally mumbled. "I think I made a little mistake."

That eased my mind. "What happens to you if he makes a big one?" I asked myself. If disappearing is a "little mistake", then for a real show-stopper, I guess you have to burst out in flames and soar off into the heavens. I wanted to say to Wally, "Give me that wand! I may only transform the world into dull life forms like me with it, but at least you will still see them."

So then, as he appeared to recover his composure somewhat, he waved it in a counterclockwise circle and, blessedly, they reappeared. Now, don't get me wrong, both Iris and Ed, upon their reemergence from whatever realm they had just visited, were just a little edgy as to what their next trip was to be like. But, oddly, they seemed more becalmed than I would have been in that circumstance. I swear, as hard as it was to tell, given Iris's rather inflexible beak and pouch, she appeared to be smiling. And Ed, for all his temperamental attributes, looked at me with a kind of serenity.

I couldn't help myself, after all, they were MY invited guests, so I blurted out, "Are you two ok? What happened to you?"

"I have no idea what happened," Iris replied. "But, and I don't know about Ed, I just visited the most wonderful place. It was filled with light, and circulating around it were the sounds of hauntingly beautiful music, amidst fragrances that were sublime. And you felt you were in the company of your closest relatives and friends. Flashes of scenery of beautiful vistas came and went, some familiar and some, it seemed, were in the heavens, surrounded by shimmering stars and galaxies. And you felt completely at peace."

As Iris described this, she looked at Ed and he was nodding his head in agreement. And then they both looked at Wally like they would pay him in hard cash for another ride through that wonderland.

Instead, Wally said in a most contrite manner, "I am so sorry. All I was trying to do was to wave my wand to lessen your fears and put you at ease with what is ahead for you as members of our team. I certainly hope I didn't cause you any harm."

To which, both of the guests shook their heads and said they were just fine. And that if he'd promise to send them back that way again sometime, he had their assurances that they would travel with our group. You could see Wally was so relieved, but very embarrassed at his gaff. Still unsure what to do next; he looked down at Bernie, who just shook her head. Then he looked over at me, and I winked and smiled. That seemed to give him the encouragement to go on with his speech.

From that moment on, his list of who was going and what would happen when we got to our five destinations was briefly outlined. Basically, he acknowledged that none of Sophie and Frank's extended family was to travel with us, but that the two of them were needed, as was Po, and the rest of us, assorted bird and animal life. Like with Walt, he did not want to divulge what roles we each would play in the course of our next journey. That was ok by me. I'd only worry that I'd get it wrong if he did. And all he really said about the five regional destinations was that each one would involve our having to accomplish significantly different objectives.

THE FINAL JOURNEY BEGINS

FOUR: U.S. COAST GUARD ICE BREAKER, "POLAR WIND"

Despite all the surprises and announcements, the dinner at Willa's appeared to end with relative calm and resoluteness. Wally took me aside immediately afterwards and expressed his deepest desire that I accompany him on this most-important mission. And seeing his vulnerability with speaking before everyone I couldn't say "no". He, beyond anyone else, was my best buddy and friend. So, in retrospect, I awoke the next morning with a renewed sense of purpose. If saving the world from immediate disaster doesn't inspire you, what will?

But I can't say the same calm extended out to Jimmy, Sophie and Frank's son. By 8:30 a.m. the next day, when he had finally finished breakfast, he lunged out the front door of Willa's homestead, mumbling to himself, "How in the world do they think I can get this bus ready in time to go all the way into Seattle? It was absolutely crazy for me to leave Atlantic City in the first place. Now I'm cooped up with a crazy bunch of hallucinating children, toddling geriatrics and assorted birds and animals that argue with me. Where's the fairness in all that? .....I just wanted to have a little store, like they promised me before I left to come here and later maybe develop a tourist, bus business. They're just asking too much. I can't get this bus ready in time for tomorrow's trip!"

If you're wondering how I know all this private conversation took place, it was because I was taking an early morning break on the porch when Jimmy came out the door. He did glance over at me, and muttering something else like, "...And YOU, YOU'RE the one who started all this!!!" From that outburst on, I'll just have to explain what I witnessed firsthand, because it has some significance for what happened the next day.

Sure enough, Jimmy did ply himself and soon after arriving at the Hoh Ranch, he was able to line up a second-hand, tour bus. But, and this was most important to him in the search for one, it had to be new enough to have those very large, side windows. As much as possible, he wanted his customers to have an unobstructed view, when he escorted them to the venues around the Olympic National Park and Forest. The one he found was perfect.

And he had worked like a colony of leaf-cutter ants since then to get it ready for the start of the upcoming tourist season, come April. In particular, he had ordered and installed three new windows on each side. Now they were eight feet long and five feet high, none of which had any vertical divisions throughout that eight foot span. He thought having these might hamper a tourist's view of the breath-taking scenery. He had to construct extra-heavy supports elsewhere along the side of the bus to compensate for this unobstructed viewing. Then he had hand-built beautiful eighteen inch wide sills underneath these side windows, the entire length of the bus. It allowed people to place their cameras, drinks or snacks in front of them. Still to be completed were the bench-style seats on both sides. He had finished and installed them on one side, but not on the other. What he apparently didn't understand was that there wasn't an army of life forms going to Seattle the next day. The one side of seats was enough for all of us. We could store our luggage and carryon's, those that had any, on the one side where the other bench was to be built.

But I felt it best to just keep quiet and let someone else enlighten him. And by nightfall, he had cleaned out the shavings, screws, bolts and mill ends and seemed to have reconciled that the bus was roadworthy enough for us to travel in the next day. I think Bernie spoke to him around lunch time, giving him a clearer picture of what was needed and congratulating him on his handiwork. But I don't think that changed anything about his opinion of me. To this day, he still calls me, "You".

Come 7:00 a.m. the next morning, after we had all but finished a final meal with Willa and the folks staying behind, the next surprise happened. As we were having our last cups of coffee, warm milk, cocoa or tea, Willa disappeared and took

Sophie with her. Coming back into the dining room, the two of them were carrying two large cardboard boxes.

Then with uncharacteristic relish, Willa said, "Your attention please. I have gotten these items for you to wear on your upcoming mission. I wanted you to have a uniform, of sorts, when you came before the various bodies of leaders and despots. I felt that by your wearing such, you would be given more credence and that you were an official-looking body. And I'd like for you to wear them today, to signal to the officers commanding the ship you are about to board that you are important envoys. Sophie, will you help me hand these out please."

I had never seen such clothes before, except maybe during some high school or college football game halftime show. Willa brought out all-weather, fleece-lined, Mackinaw jackets. Except, rather than having a plaid pattern, they were each a rich, dark green, but with a gold, inlay strip across both shoulders. And to go with that, Sophie brought out straw-gold, Fedora-style hats, with a band around the base of the hat, just about its brim, which was the same dark green. The brims had been reshaped, to have the front edge sloped lower and the back edge angled higher than the sides.

Obviously, those items were for the two-legged, non-feathered, less hairy members of our party, which meant that Sophie, Frank, Po, Bernice and Wally each had their own set. As a consolation prize, the rest of us got a set of ribbons, one with each of the above colors. They were to be tied around our necks and were crossed and folded in front in an inverse "V".

Sophie had the box with the jackets, and Willa had the one with the hats and ribbons. Each of them took their time checking the names attached to each article and then passed their around. As we were each fitted with our properly sized article, I glanced over at Ed, as Willa put his ribbon on. For the first time in my life, I had to giggle. He looked so forlorn with it on. It reminded me of a ceramic bird I had seen in a pawnshop window back in Atlantic City. But to even the score, when he saw me with mine on, he tipped his head back and let out a series of boisterous cries that only birds that fly at great heights have. "Touché," I thought. That taught me a lesson about manners and quick judgments. And I had to admit that the jacket and hats, once fitted on Bernie and Wally, were nifty. Even Po, with his great size, looked official. The rest of us animals and birds looked more like we'd won a prize at the county fair, but be that as it may, if it made Willa happy, I was ready to go with it, particularly if it was only for official events.

Then, with little fanfare, once we were dressed in our uniforms, Willa instructed us to get our suitcases, musical instruments and assorted sundry items together and go outside. While we were off doing that, she told Jimmy to drive his bus up to the front of the house for us to board.

Actually, I had had no opportunity to see the inside of Jimmy's bus, until we began to board it. And once I did, it was thrilling! I loved the huge windows and the great ledge to lie or stand on.

He'd even cut holes in the ledge for anyone to hold their drinks secure and attached a railing on the front of it, for anyone to hold onto if standing behind it. The benches were also all hand-built. Sophie, Frank, Po, Bernie and Wally set their luggage behind them, and the kids excitedly stood on one and waved out the window at Willa. Everyone agreed Jimmy had done a great job getting it ready. There were cheers all around, and he seemed quite pleased with the recognition. His wife, Diane, sat in the jump seat, immediately behind him, which he had securely attached to the floor and wall of the bus.

Quickly, we all said our good-byes, shared hugs and kisses and took off. Maybe none of us, aside from Wally and Bernie, had the foggiest idea what we were heading into, but there was no question at that moment that it all seemed like a circus ride. We squawked, meowed, barked, giggled, laughed, and scurried around like we'd been in solitary confinement for ten years. Eventually, however, by the time Jimmy had driven us as far as Forks, we settled down. All of us, comprising the animal and bird kingdom of this entourage, found our respective lairs on Jimmy's very fine ledge. Wally and Bernie wiggled and shoved their way to secure a spot right in the middle of us. They sat on the very edge of their bench, resting their chins on the ledge, eagerly studying the scenery as we bounced along. Meanwhile, the adults were happy to settle back on the benches and began to doze. Po actually lay completely out and took a nap. I swear that fellow will stay asleep even as Gabriel is blowing his horn and the heavens are undergoing their final collapse.

And yet, lurking in each of us poised on that ledge, there was almost a telepathic message being transmitted between us. And it sounded something like this: "We've got to be naughty when we come to the first city." And as if in answer to our prayers, within the next two hours we were pulling into Port Angeles. It was ideal.

Almost on cue, as Sophie, Frank and Po were fast asleep, and Jimmy was driving us slowly through the bustling, main streets of town, we launched into our performance. Flo, being by far the largest of our lot, mooned everyone. Rita began her rolling over, jumping up and down routine. Ed hung upside down, clinging onto the luggage rack, swinging side-to-side, while suspended. Iris opened her cavernous mouth wide enough that Jennifer climbed in and out, pausing once inside it to wave at passersby. And I did my lying-on-my-back-scratching-routine, all the while grinning broadly, with my head turned to the gaping residents. Wally and Bernie kept their chins on the ledge and waved frantically, probably giving everyone the impression they were being held captive by a band of rabid animals and odd-acting bird life. It met all our highest expectations.

People pointed, some ran alongside the bus, others shouted, many laughed; and I think I saw someone get violently ill. The shock of it all must have been too much. And what's more, we got away with it. Jimmy was busy driving and impressing his wife. Sophie, Frank and Po were unaware and way too trusting.

And so it went, through crossroads, by passing cars, in and out of small villages and up to the time we parked, waiting in line to cross the Puget Sound on the ferry. At that moment we were caught, but not before we had impressed many of the other waiting vehicles that this was not your ordinary tourist or city-transit bus. There was something unhinged going on inside this one, at least until Sophie awoke and saw us.

"What in the dickens do you all think you are doing?" she shouted. "Look at you! Stop that! Flo! Greg! Get up! You both look obscene! Get down from there Ed! You've got better sense than that, or at least I hope you do! And Jennifer, GET OUT OF IRIS' MOUTH! I can't believe it! And Wally and Bernie, you just let this happen and didn't wake any of us! Shame on you!!"

"YEAH!" all of us, covered with hair and feathers, cried out in reply, "it was their fault..."

Then everyone started rolling around laughing. Finally, even Sophie and Frank had to join in. They knew we were hopeless. And, of course, Po kept sleeping.

Once we were directed to our designated parking spot on the ferry, it was apparent we were located next to the exit, where the drivers and passengers of the cars and trucks climbed up the stairwell into the ferry's, inside cabin area. It was up there you could get refreshments, read or sightsee. Frank suggested that while people were getting out of their cars, trucks and buses that we should open the multiple escape vents in the top of our bus, get out his accordion and Sophie's fiddle and begin to play and sing some songs for the passengers as they headed up the stairwell. That seemed like a great idea to all of us. Besides, we'd never heard Ed or Iris sing. Within minutes of Jimmy turning off the bus' engine, we were all singing. The effect on the ferry passengers was electric. Instead of going up to the ferry cabin and staying, most either never made it up or, if they did, quickly returned and stood, sat in their vehicles or on the stairs and listened, with many eventually singing with us.

The trip from Bainbridge Island to Seattle passed quickly, and as we docked, the other passengers clapped excitedly for our performance. Soon we were driving off the ferry landing and down to the docks a few blocks to the U.S. Coast Guard's terminal. It was at this point I began to have butterflies in my stomach. This journey was about to take its first, serious turn. Playtime was over.

Bernie and Wally got up from their chin-resting position on the window ledge and walked towards the front of the bus, as we drove onto the waterfront roadway. Just before reaching Jimmy, Bernie turned and announced, "Po, Frank and Sophie, Wally and I need you to reach down and unlock the pins in the benches and turn them to face the middle of the bus. Then please relock them in place. Next, we need each of you to sit down and face the front of the bus at an angle, but with Sophie, Frank and Po up front and Flo and Greg at the rear. You are to be serious; there is to be no joking or singing. And, most importantly, you are TO BE QUIET! DO YOU HEAR ME, GREG?"

Given the way she yelled that out, I could only nod that I heard her. And then, to top that off, everyone, even Jimmy and Diane, looked at me, as if to say, "Yeah, Greg, see what you did! You've made the rest of us look bad. Bad dog..."

So, what else could I do but slink to the back of the bench, climb up on it and sit there. Flo ambled back behind Rita, Jennifer, Iris and Ed and crawled up beside me, shaking her head.

"Looks to me," she muttered, "like we've got a long boat ride ahead, if this is the way this trip is beginning."

But before I could answer her, Jimmy was pulling the bus into a driveway marked:

"STOP!! ALL VEHICLES AND PASSENGERS ARE SUBJECT TO INSPECTION. PULL AHEAD ONLY WHEN THE GUARDS SIGNAL YOU TO. U.S. COAST GUARD STATION."

By now, both Bernie and Wally were fully poised and positioned at the front door of the bus, when Jimmy was given the ok to pull forward to the guard house, with a heavily reinforced gate behind it.

As Jimmy opened the front door on the bus, there were two U.S. Coast Guard sentries waiting there to board it. And while they were about to climb on board, there were two more who began a detailed inspection around and underneath it. But in neither case did I see any other member of this four-person team, until the first two had entered the bus. The fifth member was a rather, sleek-looking, beagle dog. And she had boarded the bus ahead of the two guards. I overheard one of the guards ask the smallest member of their team, "Ok, Sparkie, go ahead and check to the back of the bus. We'll be following you."

Now, at this point, it is probably best to back up a moment and explain a timeline that will amplify the events that soon followed. Unbeknownst to me, or to all the rest of our party, neither the four guards nor "Sparkie", had been anywhere near the continental United States throughout our recently completed, cross-country journey. They had not heard of, nor experienced any of the life-altering events associated with Walt, the Emissaries or us, for that matter. They had all been on an emergency deployment to Antarctica. This front gate, inspection team were all crewmembers of the U.S. Coast Guard's ice breaker ship, "Polar Wind", the newest and fastest of its kind in their fleet. And, further, they had just gotten back to the Port of Seattle two days ago, just long enough to restock supplies and equipment. They had been working non-stop since their arrival, twenty-four hours each day, for another emergency deployment, this time to the Arctic Circle. They were to depart as soon as possible. And if the Capitan could push them hard enough, it would be sometime this very night. It was not a happy crew, nor one that was particularly interested, at this very moment, in any outside disruption or interference.

You'd have to say that the first part of our bus' inspection went quite smoothly. Both guards entered, sweeping past Bernice and Wally at the doorway, checking Jimmy and Diane's identifications, asking them about the two children's ages, relationship to everyone on board and the purpose of the trip. But before the explanation for that last question could be fully explored, Sparkie had taken the opportunity to venture further down the aisle, past Po, Frank and Sophie.

It was at this point that I got my first look at her. She was wearing a very fine, grey-colored, blanket saddle, which was draped across her back and down her sides. On both sides of it were the beautiful slash insignias, seen on the bow of all Coast Guard ships. The saddle was cinched under her belly, so it flowed smoothly with her walking. She was truly handsome and official-looking. But, what can I say, that can only go so far with me. After all, I'm from Atlantic City. There, all the finery and gloss will get you only so far. From there, you've got to show us what you've got. And now it was time for this team's point guard to show us just that.

It was very clear to me that Sparkie was not expecting to see the assortment of animal and bird life that was staring down on her from that bench. True, as Bernie had warned, none of us had said anything, at least up to that moment. You could tell, however, that ole Sparkie was getting somewhat over-extended with her perception of what reality usually was. She had never been so close to or so intensely stared at by a cockatoo, an eagle, a pelican, a calico cat, a Siberian husky, and finally by a portly, middle-aged blue-healer. At least, as far as she could remember, this had not all happened at the same time. She was getting nervous. But it was the constant sniffing that she had to do that just confounded me. She sniffed everywhere, everything, anything and anyone. It was too much. I finally had to break the silence.

"Nice job, Sparks!" I couldn't help but say. And it was at just the moment I said that when she sniffed, ever-so-lightly touching her nose to Flo's tail. And BINGO! Sparkie, the Sniffer from Seattle, as we came to call her, was welcomed into the transformed ranks of speaking life forms.

"I sure wish I could get a job like that, don't you Flo?" I then added.

Flo, realizing what changes were inevitably occurring within ole Sparkie at that moment, replied, "No thanks…" But she never got to finish that remark, because the ever-dutiful Sparkie spun around, facing her two guard handlers and yelled out, "They're right. I hate this job!"

The two guards, now completely abandoning their official duties bound down the aisle toward Sparkie, justifiably bewildered at what they saw and heard. Calling out to their two companions inspecting the bus on the outside, they yelled for them to come in quickly to also check on her. In an instant, fearing there might be some explosives on board, the other two rushed inside the bus. Now the luggage area, across from our bench, which all of us new arrivals were sitting on, was filled with frantic Coast Guard personnel and their now-talking dog.

Fred, the ranking guard, leaned down, gently petted Sparkie and quietly intoned, "It's ok, ole girl, we all heard your moan. Are you sick? Did someone here hurt you? Oh! How I wish you could talk to us and tell us what's the matter or who did it."

"Then all you have to do is listen," came the reply from the newest edition to the speaking world. "I repeat. I am tired of sniffing for a living. I sniff things you folks wouldn't go near. And the smells....ou'vay! You need to try just putting yourselves in my paws for once."

Looking around at each of us, the guards became increasingly agitated and alarmed. "What's going on?" Fred shouted at us!

It was Rita who spoke first. "I think it is fairly obvious, isn't it. You're friend here just resigned her commission as Chief Sniffer."

"And I certainly can't blame her," chimed in Jennifer. "It's absolutely indecent for anyone to have a job like that. Good on ya', Sparkie!"

Finally, Bernie realized that things were heading in a direction that could end up creating total chaos. Shuffling past Wally, she ran back to us, exhorting all of us to be calm. "Please, everyone, stop! Listen to me! Just stop! Let me explain what is going on. It's obvious you've not heard of the changes that are occurring throughout America right now."

But Bernie's exhortations went unheard. All the guards were now leaning over their team member. It appeared to me it was like they were administering her the last rites, as if her speaking meant that she was about to take her last breath. It was dumbfounding. What people get used to, and then what happens when a variation of the routine happens. It's like the sky is falling.

So, into this burgeoning fracas strolled Wally. I say stroll because of everyone now in the bus, all of whom were either in midst of a swoon, a stroke or a loud shout, it was Wally who appeared the calmest and almost appeared prepared to deal with the matter. I say, "Almost" because I still had a memory of him stuttering last night after dinner and being reticent and unsure of himself. But, as I looked up to see him approach the edge of this madhouse, he glanced at me and winked. That gesture reassured me somewhat. It reminded me of the look he gave me when we were standing together on that battlefield in Oregon many months ago. Right away I knew that if the guards thought reality had just taken a rather sharp left turn with a few spoken words from Sparks, they should brace themselves for a steep drop-off immediately ahead. Their lives' were about to undergo a radically new, charted course.

Up until now, it hadn't been since we were in Oregon that I had seen Wally with his wand, either in its holster or with him holding it. But, just after his winking at me, he pulled it out from behind him and gave it a sharp upward movement. It was directed solely at the guards, all five of them. And immediately each of them became mutely frozen in place.

"I... I...I'm sorry had to do that to you," Wally began, still stuttering. "B...Bu...But it was necessary to stop your panic and g...gi...give us time to sort out some matters with you. None of it will make too much sense right away, but with my bringing you to a standstill, y...you...you can better listen to what I have to say. Also, your bodies and minds will feel refreshed and re...renewed after I return you to your previous activity level. As you now know, you are able to hear and understand everything I say. Bu...But let me be brief, because we need to hurry on to your ship b...be...berthed at dockside.

"I...I am going to leave you in your present condition until j...just before we drive on from here and park by the gangplank to your ship. T...to be as brief as possible, those of us on board this bus will be accompanying you and your crew on your upcoming deployment, with the exception of Jimmy, our driver, and his wife. However, you will definitely not be going to your original destination. All that will change, and the reasons for that will be explained later.

"Y...Yu...You are under no threat and n...no harm will come to you from us. Our m...mi...mission, like yours, is to rescue. Th...the only difference is that our rescue will be on a little larger scale than yo...yours that was originally planned. And you...your new destinations are going to be much different. But th...that's all I ca...can say for now. I...I have to leave you and open these gates so we can d...drive through. Ju...Just close your eyes and rest. You'll be released from your p…pa…paralysis soon."

With that, Wally, Hoh River's stuttering, poster child for the idyllic country boy turned around to continue on with his wizard-like transformation duties and walked back to the front of the bus. He awkwardly climbed down the steep bus steps and out the doorway. Once more, while facing the gates, he again waved his wand, and they slid open like their tracks were newly greased. He then turned and waved for Jimmy to drive through. As the bus passed by, Wally then motioned with his wand and the gates were closed, sealed and remained so until the ship's return to Seattle in mid-April.

Meanwhile, Bernie, the Anteverse and Universe's sole remaining Herald, turned around from seeing her brother exit the bus' front door and demanded, looking straight at me, "WHO and WHAT got all this bedlam started? Whoever and whatever it was has possibly jeopardized this ENTIRE MISSION!"

Of course, the five newest travelers on the bus couldn't answer her question, unless you could follow and translate their darting eyeballs. I could tell at least four of them were not accepting their new status well. Maybe Wally was right that they'd have a new outlook of life, with renewed vigor, once he removed his spell over them. But, and this was just a guess, right now his magic hadn't taken its full effect. Just the same, I'd have to say, looking at her, that Sparkie, on the other hand, did appear quite docile and serene. That encouraged me somewhat.

But the silence continued to thicken. No one spoke up in answer to Bernie's question. So she prodded more. "Sophie?... Frank?... Po?... Did any of you see anything?" But they just shook their heads in reply.

Then, wonder of wonders, out of the cosmic dust that created all goodness and beauty, it was Ed who finally spoke. "It was all of us, Bernie," he intoned. "Each one of us recognized the servile position these guard's fifth team member was languishing in, and we had to say something. We all contributed to this situation. But my guess is that it will have a good outcome. Our intentions were good at the outset; therefore, I would expect that the result should be more than acceptable."

Bernie then looked at each of us and responded, "Is that true?"

And like schoolyard chums, we all twisted our heads, looking at each other, smiled and nodded that it was. I knew then our team was coming together again. And the last gesture of that affirmation was when Ed glanced at me and winked. I began to experience anew that strange and wondrous feeling of Walt's magical presence and that it may still be at work amongst us.

It took a few minutes for Jimmy to drive the bus out to the dock and park it adjacent to the gangway, which led up into the "Polar Wind's" cargo hold. Naturally, by this time, Jimmy and Diane, not having had the benefit of our recently concluded months' long travel cross-country, were stretched a little thin by all these assorted magical feats. Both of them were ready to deposit us and seek shelter back at Willa's. The clincher of these feelings was when he turned off the engine and opened the front door again and there stood Wally, grinning at him.

Wally came back into the interior of the bus, almost like he was skipping across a school playground, and revitalized the Coast Guard crew with his wand. And, as promised, the four adults were calm and rested. They greeted each of us like we were all just reunited at a long, awaited-for, family union.

Bernie then acknowledged that it was time to notify the ship's captain that we had arrived and for what purpose. And to my further amazement it was Sparkie that spoke up.

"Let me help you out with that matter, Bernie," she said. "It will not be as awkward or suspicious if I board the ship and make my way to the ship's Bridge, where I should be able to locate the Captain. Let me go get him, if you will."

You could see this request surprised both Wally and Bernie. They looked at each other and whispered something. Then they turned to the nodding, four guards, who by now would probably have agreed to grant everyone on board a year's leave in the Bahamas, they were so becalmed. I'm sure they would have eagerly agreed to any plan suggested.

Seeing them respond like this, Bernie then turned around and replied, "Thank you, Sparkie". "We'd be grateful if you would help us. Simply say to the Captain and his Executive Officer, if present, that they are urgently needed by the individuals in the parked bus, parked dockside."

Nodding his head, it was only a matter of seconds and ole Sparks was winding her way through the crowded bus, out the doorway and up the gangplank and disappearing into the ship's hold. It wasn't until sometime later, in my talking to her, that she related what happened once she found the Captain.

It's pretty safe to assume that he and his Executive Officer, pouring over tide tables, navigational charts and recently received orders were quite busy when the ship's mascot rushed onto the Polar Wind's Bridge. As I understand it, Capt. Jules Shriver and LCDR Marcia Steele both acknowledged Sparkie's entrance by mumbling something like, "Hello, Sparkie, what brings you up here? Aren't you supposed to still be on duty at the Gate House?" Of course, they were not expecting any reply and probably, if pressed, thought she was snooping around for some handout or snack. Besides, they were extremely busy and harried. This back-to-back deployment had pushed them and their crew to the edge. There was a lot of tension in the air, not just there on the Bridge, but throughout the ship.

So, try and imagine their surprise when an 18-pound, rather fit and well-groomed beagle dog replied, "There are a group of dignitaries in that bus down by the gangplank that urgently need to speak with you."

Looking at each other first, then at the two doorways into the Bridge, where they confirmed there was no one in there besides themselves, and finally as a desperate last resort, down at Sparkie, they both shouted, simultaneously, "WHAT?!!!..."

"Like I said," she repeated, "you both need to immediately go down dockside and see what these people want. It's urgent."

It probably wasn't too clear to either of these often-decorated officers whether they should immediately leap overboard, cling desperately to each other, kneel in prayer or do exactly as they were instructed.

"Why are you talking, Sparkie?" the Captain asked in a quaking voice.

"Because I can."

"Oh, that's reasonable... Has it been going on for long with you?"

"No, for only about fifteen minutes is all," Sparkie reassured them.

"I see," the Captain said, nodding, as he tried to keep uppermost in his mind he was still supposed to be in command, but desperately wanting to burst into tears. "And who did you say wanted to see us? Are they, by chance, the same people that make you talk?" And it was at this point, just having to ask this question that reinforced to the Captain that it was his bounded duty, even if it was his last duty, to find out immediately who or what was behind the impossible transformation of this animal at his feet.

"Yes they are," was all that Sparkie said in reply.

Without saying another word, both individuals rushed out the door, through the narrow corridors, down steep stair wells, and out the gangway to the front door of the bus. Arriving there breathless, the Captain shouted, "What is the meaning of all this silly business?!! What kind of robotic mischief are you up to, sending a mechanical dog to our quarters and demanding we come down here to see you?!! And where are my guards who are supposed to be at the front gate?!! What are they doing?!!"

It was at this point the Captain glanced up into the windows of the bus and saw his intrepid Guardhouse staff grinning and waving at him. He began to feel sick. "I need answers right now!!" he demanded, in a somewhat more muted tone of voice.

Greeting him at the front door of the bus was Wally. Obviously, that, too, did not add much, in the way of reality, to the situation. If this was a renegade band of terrorists, it didn't seem likely that a seven year old boy would be leading the charge

.   It was Bernie who then appeared in the bus doorway and cordially greeted him, "Thank you Captain. We sincerely appreciate your coming down here straightaway. There is a critically, urgent matter that has to be discussed with you, as Sparkie no doubt mentioned to you. Your deployment to the Arctic will have to be altered to allow us to complete our own mission. But, in the interest of time, you will be filled in just before we get underway later tonight."

"I beg your pardon, young lady!" the Captain snorted. "Enough is enough! You and your busload of...can..." However, stopping in mid-sentence at this point, the Captain took his second look inside the bus and now saw, to his growing horror, not just his grinning guards, but other adults and the most bizarre assortment of animals and birds...all smiling and waving at him. "Err, uh...you are not doing anything of the kind," he finally stammered. Seeing and hearing all this, he was beginning to realize his Coast Guard career was likely in its concluding moments.

What happened next is still the stuff of legend, but I need to insert some background information ahead of the actual event. Unbeknownst to me, and everyone else, including Bernie, Walt, just before his passing, had issued Wally another magical device. It was one that Walt, himself, had never had the opportunity to use. As a consequence, he was not able to provide Wally with enough of the very vital background information one might need for it to be fully functional and appropriately used. Particularly, if that someone was seven years old and had just recently begun to stutter and seem a little more nervous and hesitant than usual.

The device was a collapsible staff. It folded neatly into the palm of Wally's hand. When it was unfolded, this required only the slightest movement on his part, and it extended well beyond his full height. And, interestingly, as Wally grew, the staff maintained that same proportional length: it grew too. He held it, when it was fully extended, about a third of the way from its top. And, yes, it had a slight curve at the top end.

Now apparently, as I later learned in much greater detail from Wally, there are two simultaneous acts that accompany its use. One is that he has to bang it against the ground a certain number of times and the other is that he also has to say a designated word or phrase, while doing the banging. The staff is somehow preprogrammed to respond only to his voice and only to a particular set of words or phrases that he repeats. Supposedly, it's some kind of safety measure. Right...

Except, this afternoon, as we were parked by the U.S. Coast Guard's finest Ice Breaker, Wally was not entirely sure of himself. He seemed to lack some self-confidence. As a result, he did at least two things that would leave future accounts of this day open to some discussion.

In response to the Captain's objection, Wally asked if the Captain would mind stepping aside momentarily, and let him get down off the bus step. Moving a few paces away from the Captain and the Executive Officer, Wally then, for the first time, proudly extended his never-before-used staff and struck the ground one time, while incanting, "t...to...tomato soup." To the shock, horror and disbelief of everyone, either standing at the bus' door, sitting in the bus' driver's seat, perched on the benches, standing in the isle, or having a wave or two, the gangplank, the mooring lines, half the adjacent pier and the "Polar Wind", disappeared.

FIVE: MAKING AMENDS

"Uh...Uh, Oh," Wally stammered, looking toward where the huge ship and dock used to be. "I did a bad thing. All I wanted to do was rock the boat."

"NOOOOO!!!!," Capt. Shriver squealed, as he stared dumbfounded and petrified out into the open water of the Puget Sound, where two seconds ago his magnificent ship and crew were berthed and busily getting ready to launch. He and his Executive Officer slumped down the side of the bus, falling prostrated with both legs straight out in front of them and their arms straight down at their sides. They could never have imagined anything this terrible, something this sudden and so devastating happening to them and the crew in this place, at this time.

I was momentarily dazed myself after witnessing this awesome display of Wally's new device and was, likewise, spell-bound. But before the remaining crew and passengers on the bus could gather themselves, I leaped off the ledge and skirted in and around everyone in the isle and dashed out the bus door to Wally.

Seeing that Wally was transfixed, not moving or hardly breathing, I realized something had to be done, and quickly, or there was going to be drastic consequences for all of us. Particularly for Wally.

"Wally, Wally, look down. It's me, Greg! Look at me!"

Peering down at me, with his head moving slowly like the mechanical arms of an old grandfather clock, he replied, "Oh, Mr. Greg, I...I made a big mistake, d...di...didn't I?"

"Well," I answered, "I've probably made worse. But I'd have to say, with this effort, you are coming pretty close to my all-time best effort. Do you think we can reverse what you did?" I asked that with a progressively more uncontrollable tremor in my voice. If he couldn't, it was the dog pound for me and much worse for my dear buddy, Wally.

"I...I don't know. I had never used the stick or said those words before. And I forgot the way I was supposed to do it. I think I banged it too many times on the ground."

With growing desperation, I then suggested to him, "Then why don't you try banging it the same number of times, but just reverse the words you spoke. Maybe that will reverse the spell and return them from the Alternate Universe where you've airmailed them, along with various nearby objects. At least it's worth a try."

At this point the door of the bus was filled with hysterical remnants of the New Jersey

Wagoners. And Bernie was leading the charge. Even Sophie had a look of horror on her face. That, most of all, really scared me.

"Hurry, Wally!" I begged him. "You must do something now, before all these people and assorted, rabid wildlife descend on you."

And in that instant I felt the ground at my feet shudder three times, as Wally struck it with his staff, and I heard him announce, "…eciuj otamot" However, he said that garbled phrase, not just once, but three times, in cadence with his hitting the ground with his staff each time.

And before Bernie had come squarely in front of the two of us, there was an overpowering sound of creaking wood, snapping rope, scraping metal, lapping waves, and blessedly, before all of humanity and the animal kingdom, there stood the "Polar Wind", complete with all the pier, mooring lines, gangplank and crew.

And it was at about that same moment that the ship's two commanding officers, still slumped at the side of the bus took what they thought would be their last look at anything before sinking into a death spiral, and witnessed the reappearance of their vessel. Watching it disappear was terrifying enough. To witness its reemergence was possibly even more so. It affirmed that this was no fantasy, no nightmare or dream, no trick of memory or slight-of-hand. Before their eyes, there were two, distinct events, as none other could, that proved to them that animals and birds could and do wave and wink at you, that small dogs do talk, that very small children do cause mighty ships of sea to suddenly disappear and them reappear, and that this was their new reality. And Capt. Jules Shriver, at that moment, wondered sincerely and deeply, why he'd stopped drinking heavily a few years ago. He knew at that moment it had been a bad decision.

As everyone was swooning and celebrating the return of the ship, I turned to Wally and suggested that maybe he might get out his wand, while slipping the staff back into its vault for safety, and then go over and give the Captain and his associate the same treatment he gave the gate guards. I felt sure they needed some down time. Wally concurred and quickly administered the wand sedative. And within a few minutes he revived them as well, and they were as refreshed as their guards. Interestingly, so was all the crew aboard the ship. Wherever Wally had shipped everyone off to, allowed them to become refreshed, renewed and the ship to be fully re-supplied.

During later conversations, I learned that everyone who had been transformed by Wally compared their venture in exactly the same way. They were enveloped in an aura of brilliant, but soothing and restful light, the same description that Iris and Ed had given us at the dinner table two nights ago following their cosmic sojourn. Again, I couldn't help but feel that Walt was lurking in the shadows. Old Wizards never die, I thought. But they do have to watch over stuttering, younger ones and keep in line bumbling, out-spoken dogs. It was so comforting for me to sense this, particularly on the eve of our having to depart on Bernie and Wally's mission.

And it was only a matter of minutes when everyone on board the ship was at its side rails looking down at us; and all of us on the dock, assembled at the gangplank, were looking up at them. And within the time it took for Wally to do all this disappearing and reappearing, the Captain, his Executive officer, and the four guards were rushing over to eagerly hug and welcome our band of transformers. Everyone had, by then, poured out of the bus. And within seconds of this happening, the gangplank was filled with the ship's crew pouring out to do the same. It was like Wally (...or Walt?) had given all of them a potion of happiness-combined-with-where've-you-been-all-our-lives pills that filled them with relief and the urgent need to touch and reassure us. We all became like family within those brief moments. I was dumbfounded by it all, as I know Iris and Ed had to be.

While all this was going on, Jimmy and Diane busily unloaded the various suitcases and boxes we'd packed and stacked them all by the gangplank. It was clear that this entire episode had been too much for Jimmy. He kept muttering to himself throughout all this shuffling and transferring. I could tell, more than anything, he wanted to be somewhere, anywhere else, than right here. And soon he and Diane were closing the bus door, revving the engine and honking the horn as they pulled away. But there was one small problem. Wally had sealed the front gate with a near, lifetime guarantee that no one would enter or exit it until the Polar Wind returned.

I tapped Wally on the leg, as we stood on

the edge of the jovial ship company's welcoming, and said, motioning to the bus, "I think Jimmy has one last disappointment ahead for him. The front gate is secured. They can't get through."

"I know, Mr. Greg," Wally replied. "I knew he'd be anxious to get back home to Hoh, when I sealed it, so I decided to give him and his wife some help when it was time for them to head back."

Saying this, he reached into his front pocket and pulled out that blasted, staff gizmo again. I thought to myself, "Not again....please. Just give it a rest, Wally." But before I could object, he had extended the thing, pounded it one time on the ground, as he intoned, "Orange juice", and the bus was gone. It wasn't like I next thought that he had killed the occupants, but I dreaded to think that maybe they were well on their way to the anteverse or some other heavenly destination. Happily, I was wrong with all my misgivings. Wally had done well. In the time it took for me to look up at Wally and object, he looked down at me and said, "There. They'll be parked at Willa's front door about now."

Once all the embracing and introductions were finished, the representatives of humanity, and of the other species present at that moment, began to migrate up the gangplank into the Polar Wind. Wally and I were at the rear of this procession, for which I was extremely grateful. The very last thing I wanted to do was get on that ship. The ferry wasn't so bad because we were misbehaving or singing all the time we were on the water. Walking up onto the gangway was, to me, a terminal event. I wished I was back on the bus with Jimmy. Wally looked at his watch and told me it was 8:00 p.m. straight up. And for the record, we left port that same night with the high tide, at 12:31 a.m., on January 21st.

SIX: "POLAR WIND" DEPARTS

Ed and Iris hung back with Wally and I, as they sensed my reluctance to get on board the Polar Wind. Probably the only reason I even ventured onto that gangplank was that it wasn't moving. The ship was perfectly still at that moment. The water in Elliott Bay was quiet and calm. If everything could remain like that for this next journey, I'd be fine, I thought. Just travel in a straight, smooth line. No bobbing, weaving, twisting or lurching, and most of all, no rolling. Reluctantly, I crept up into the gangway.

Once inside the ship, members of the crew were strategically positioned to direct us newcomers to our quarters. It was as if they had planned our arrival all along. They all appeared so relieved and rested, and thankfully, they were very helpful. Apparently, Wally's induced foray, into some unknown realm, had infused in them an optimism and sense of purpose, far beyond anything I would have imagined. That, plus their keen awareness of a ship's storeroom full of Walt's special inventory of goodies and supplies I'm sure helped. Of course, I thought it was easy for them to feel this way. They hadn't seen themselves suddenly disappear, nor did they have to jolt Wally into returning them back to earth. I desperately needed to lie down somewhere; it was all becoming a little too overwhelming.

And so I did, once our guide showed Flo and me to our cabin. It was number 518. It had two single beds, one tucked under a porthole window and the other off to one side of it. On the opposite wall was a dresser and small closet, neither of which we needed except for storing our walking gear. Each of us still had our flight helmet, goggles and saddle bags from the first journey. Happily, there was no tack. Our pulling-wagon days were over. And before the nice crewman pulled our cabin door closed, I had jumped on the wall-side bed, not the one under the window. I didn't need any more reminders of where we were. That was ok with Flo. She could sit up and just see out the porthole. It allowed her to dream about maybe heading home to Siberia one day.

Maybe at this point, I should also give you more details about the Polar Wind. Her hull was painted a bright orange-red, with the overlaying, customary white and blue sash about ninety feet from the tip of her bow, emblazed obliquely down each side. She stood at least one hundred feet above the barely visible, all-black, water line to the top of the Bridge. Various antennae, rotating apparatuses, towers, vents and exhaust stacks were atop that. I'd venture to estimate that she was at least 450 feet long and a good 90 feet wide at her beam. There was a large square-shaped, white superstructure, positioned on the topside deck, and about a third of the way back from the bow. It was a good 80 feet long by 80 feet wide by 60 feet high. Inside it were Decks 5-8, which contained the Living Quarters, the Bridge, Radio Room, Auditorium, Offices and Library. She had a draft of about 36 feet, with a cruising speed of around 19 knots, and a crew of 150.

The topside deck had four Zodiac boats lashed onto it, positioned in front of the large white superstructure. And behind the superstructure was the helicopter hanger, with lifeboats lashed in place alongside it, on both the port and starboard sides. At the stern of the vessel was the circular helicopter pad or platform. A crane, retrieval equipment and some armaments were also in the far stern area.

Below the topside deck were three more decks, which included the Engine Room and a mammoth Storeroom. Directly below the superstructure were two Dining Rooms, the Medical Clinic, and the Kitchen.

It was particularly noteworthy to me, but more so to Frank and Po, that the ship was powered by a nuclear reactor. In fact, much of their free time was spent going back and forth between the helicopter hanger and the engine room. I rarely saw them except at meal times or for ship-wide meetings or entertainment. Both of them were fascinated by this equipment. Po, for all his otherworldliness, was a quick learner. And whenever the crew would let him, he or Frank always accompanied the helicopter on a sortie of one kind or another.

Sophie, on the other hand, was the "House

Mother" of the ship. Everyone loved her and came knocking at her cabin door for advice, help, instruction, encouragement or conversation. The women crewmembers adored her. And the crew, as many as she could accommodate, attended her makeshift music lessons for the fiddle, accordion, banjo and singing. It was everyone's goal, eventually even the Captain's, to have a fully trained choir, with musical accompaniment by the end of this deployment. She and Frank had brought along three fiddles, three accordions and two banjos. Everyone hoped enough crew members could be trained to play them by the end of our voyage. It is with some reluctance that I must confess to you that this hope was not fully realized. Our upcoming mission became all-consuming.

All of the New Jersey Wagoners were billeted on the 5th Deck, with all our rooms located on the port side of the ship, each with a porthole window. Sophie and Frank were in Cabin 533; Po was in 520; Bernie in 514; Wally in 512; Jennifer in 516; and Rita, Iris and Ed were in 517. Our deck also had a small library and a lounge, where Sophie gave her music lessons and where we had our many Wagoner meetings.

The 6th Deck was above us, and it housed the ship's Auditorium and the enlisted crew members' cabins, which also included Sparkie's room. However, as you might guess by now, Sparkie pretty much had the run of the ship. Most of her time was spent in our cabin, with Flo and me. And probably I should mention at this point that, like Ed, Iris, Jennifer, Rita and Flo, Sparkie also insisted on a name change once she could freely converse. She chose "Hope". And, all in all, I thought it was a good choice. Throughout the ship, ever after her making that decision, you would hear crewmembers calling out, "Here's Hope!", "Where's Hope?", "Thank goodness, it's Hope."

It gave the atmosphere of the ship a lift. Honestly, it had seemed a little stiff to me at first, but I soon began to realize that my impressions were fraught with bias, prejudice and background luggage that gave them little worth. Life aboard the ship taught me to look closer inside myself. Mostly, it taught me that in order to survive difficult times I needed to open my mind and consider all options. I needed to free myself from my past of rigid thinking and overly emotional responses. I had to quit barking when scared, threatened, irritated or confused. I needed to start trying to think, to prepare myself, and to speak with greater care. There were dangers ahead that I could never imagine, and we were headed right into their throat. Little Hope was to be one of our colleagues in meeting this challenge, and over time I was so relieved she was.

The 7th Deck housed the ship's commissioned and warrant officer cabins, as well as the Captain's cabin. And finally the 8th Deck was where the Bridge and Radio Room or Communication Center was located. I rarely got up to that level. I saw enough of the ocean from our cabin window, thank you.

As an aside, I want to tell you about Rita, Iris and Ed's ocean crossing. They absolutely loved being on the ship. There was a set of outside stairs on the stern end of each upper deck. Our stairway led to a covered walkway beside the helicopter hanger, and eventually it ended at the helicopter platform. And, as you would expect, the walkway had a safety railing. It was on that railing that the three of them sat, conversed, preened, gossiped and launched themselves into the surrounding sky. On a clear day you'd see one or all of them flying above or beside the ship or even perched on the ledge in front of the Bridge or on some equipment at the bow or stern. The crew was always thrilled to see the three of them fly in formation. Rita with her snow white plumage and bright yellow head sash; Iris with her huge brown body and immense wingspan; and Ed with his distinctive black and white markings were a sight to behold.

In addition, it should be mentioned that over the course of our round-the-world cruise, over those next three months, these three birds made frequent bodily contact with other birdlife, e.g. gulls, skuas, albatrosses and terns, and the conversations that resulted were edifying and often quite helpful. Certainly, the ship's radar and sonar helped locate and indicate upcoming weather changes, other approaching craft and potential hazards, but these newly transformed, ocean travelers were an endless source of conformations and first-alerts.

Finally, I need to briefly describe the actual shape of our ship's hull, especially the bow section. You are probably aware, certainly much more so than I was, that a typical boat or ship has a pointed bow. It allows the vessel to cut through the water, and thereby minimize, somewhat, the ship's overall instability and give it a smoother ride. Our new, ice-breaker home did have a sort of pointy bow at the level of the Top Deck, however immediately underneath it, for 95% of the bow; the hull was shaped like a shovel, spoon or a sled, depending on how you looked at it. Ice breakers, you see, break ice. They don't cut through it. What I didn't know, amongst all the other collective knowledge of humankind that escapes me, was that ice breakers ride up and over the ice and then crush it as they lunge or fall back onto it. Now that works great for moving through ice flows, but in the open Pacific Ocean there aren't many of those to be found. So, instead, we had thousands upon thousands of miles of open water, often with swells of 30-50 feet in stormy weather. I swear the Arctic Wind was like riding in a bathtub across the ocean. For whatever reason Bernie chose using this ship, smooth sailing wasn't one of them. But don't get me wrong. She was and is a wonderful ship. She just needs some ice in front of her to show you her best attributes.

Saying all this, once we had been shown our quarters and the various pieces of luggage and equipment were brought up to the cabins, Bernie then came to each of our cabins and asked that the eleven of us meet in the nearby Lounge in 30 minutes. We still had to be introduced to the ship's crew before we sailed that night, and she first needed to discuss with us last minute details of what she'd be saying. Our meeting was held at 5:30 p.m. We ate at 6 p.m. And she and the Captain scheduled the ship-wide meeting with the crew for

2000 hours, to be held in the Auditorium. An announcement of that meeting was broadcast throughout the ship by Capt. Shriver, after we all agreed to the time and place. All of us were about to hear for the first time the gravity of what lay ahead. Even Bernie appeared shaken by what she had to say.

SEVEN: THE FIRST BRIEFING

Ten minutes beforehand, Capt. Shriver called out over the ship's intercom, "All hands report to the Auditorium at 2000 hours." Without exception, all the ship's crew promptly mustered and was eagerly seated by that time. He had felt that with Wally sealing the gates shut, as he did, there was little need to post guards in or about the ship at this point. The Auditorium was filled with nervous excitement. Everyone wanted to know what was happening, both for their own sake and for the sake of their loved ones, who they would tell what they could, immediately after this briefing was finished.

Po and Frank had arranged chairs and make-shift stands on stage for all eleven of us to sit or perch on throughout the meeting. And as a final bit of background, you should know that NO ONE aboard the ship knew ANYTHING about all of us being able to speak. Even with the fracas on the bus and the shock of Hope's (AKA: Sparkie's) debut on the Bridge with the Captain and Executive Officer, the shock of all that was happening had not sunk in yet.   Actually, anyone who saw or heard Hope speak was in denial of it happening.

Plus, it seems that this ship and its crew have been out of commission for over eight months prior to this meeting. They had had to institute radio silence early on in their deployment due to some security issues. Then they were ice-bound for four months in the Antarctic. And most recently, they had another secret mission to go on just before we burst on the scene. Their families knew of what had been happening throughout the country, but no one had had the opportunity to tell their family members aboard the ship.

With this background, you can now appreciate the difficult situation Bernie found herself in as she arose to address the audience. She was, after all, the Herald. And it was only she who Walt had confided in about this upcoming journey and the reasons for it. But, I can tell you at this juncture, he certainly did not know everything, because before it was over we were in deeper trouble than anyone could have imagined. Maybe, if he did know, he chose not to tell her, for fear it would render anyone who knew, immobile with fear. That sure would have been the case with me, for instance.

But, with the wooden box that Frank set up behind the podium and with Po giving Bernie a lift up onto it, she began the briefing. Her initial remarks were to introduce each of us, but beforehand she had given each of us strict orders not to flinch, preen, scratch, paw, bark and most importantly, to speak. She did not want that added element introduced into the meeting yet. She rightly thought it would create an inattentive atmosphere. "Panic" would have been the word I'd chosen.

Anyway, she began the meeting with a brief description of our own Walt, the Wizard. Then she covered some aspects of our cross-country journey that were not too revealing of the animal, bird and tree transformations; about the Emissaries; the Battle of Oregon, as it was now being called, and finally about how all the States were holding elections for new representatives to redefine, restate, reorganize and regain the spirit and substance of what the United States of America truly meant. She summarized that last statement by saying that, essentially, a huge sign was being erected over the nation and at its borders, which said "Closed Temporarily for Remodeling. Due to Reopen in Four Years." And further, that our military branches were now standing down, returning home and becoming home guards, protecting the sovereignty of the nation. We had to isolate ourselves to heal and to rebuild. But, and now this was the main thrust of her having us meet at this time, that the crux of what Walt had revealed to her, was that there were other countries and foreign bodies mobilizing to take control of much, if not all, of the world during this time of our country's rebuilding and absence.

She recounted how the Emissaries had sown destruction and evil throughout the entire world for millennia and how Walt had felt that their final, desperate intentions were now to plant this same drive for destruction inside various rogue leaders, groups and armies, if Walt had succeeded in eliminating them, as he did in the Battle of Oregon. Sadly, he informed her that he recently had confirmation that with the death of the Emissaries, there had been a cascading, and most assuredly, a deadly spiral of attitudes and intentions within these foreign leaders and bodies. Further, but not being able to give any specific details, Walt also believed the Emissaries had another, more sinister plot, that would be initiated if for some reason Walt, and his band of transformers, had succeeded in neutralizing these newest threats. It was these most evil of creatures' final, backup plan. But it was only a hunch on his part. Immediately on the horizon, there were five regions beginning their final plans for an assault on the world for total domination, which would threaten the future existence of a free humanity. And it was at this point that she began a detailed description of the five areas that the ship and its crew would have to take us. From here on I will quote what she told all of us.

"Our upcoming venture will entail going to five separate and distinct regions, each with a varied mixture of governance, or lack thereof, all of which together will put our planet in gravest peril. They stand apart from one another, but at some point they could unite to form an insurmountable obstacle to world peace. And, yet, their presence and motivation does not lessen the responsibility we have to get our own country's house in order. As our group has so forcefully reminded people across this land of ours, during our recent cross-country journey, unfettered consumerism and a devastating policy of rather mindless government and corporate-driven globalism have begun to lead us down a one-way dirt road to ruin. That's one of the reasons why we began, what now appears to be only the first leg, of this two-part odyssey. We wanted to alert our country's residents..." (Aside: Bernie failed, at least for the present, to mention that all animal and birdlife, along with trees, were alerted as well.) "...of our own missteps and failings and to suggest ways we could begin the healing and repair. What has begun happening here in our homeland must now be instituted worldwide. Otherwise, all is lost.

"Now I want to describe in more detail for all of you, including my group, just what is lurking on the horizon for humanity.

"Elimination of the Emissaries, as I said earlier, was the first victory necessary if there was to be a measure of planetary peace. Now we have to face another unpalatable list of 'isms', scattered around the world. Doing so will be our second journey's battle. And each of you has been drafted into this struggle.

"By this second group of 'isms', I am referring specifically to communism, jihadism, tribalism, nationalism and terrorism. Each at this moment is metastasizing and merging together into hideous lesions that are being spread like an almost undefeatable pandemic. They are outmaneuvering and overwhelming peaceful governments' will and ability to combat.

"Menacingly, the subtle attitudes of dislike,

envy, distrust, resentment, and suspicion, can almost overnight be twisted into open hostility and attack, using the excuse of needing to defend oneself. Recorded history, and no doubt the time preceding it, is overflowing with accounts of foreign invasions, destruction and occupations based on the invaders' perceived need to defend themselves. It's what I chose to call the ultimate 'ism', "defendism'.

"Free and well-meaning citizens of this world need help immediately. The innocent, the world over, are suffering terribly at this very moment. Conflicts and diseases are becoming unmanageable. Larger and larger areas of our planet are beginning to evolve into a death spiral. If you listen carefully, you can hear the last gasps of life and hope.

"And to insure that you have all the information I can give to help you understand what is ahead, I am going to try and give you a chronological sequence of how and why these five movements, theories or 'isms' began. It was how Walt described them to me.

"Humanity's first societal entity was the tribe. Significantly, it offered an organized system to protect the family, thus better insuring its survival. Over the thousands of years that followed its emergence, it also came to define one's cultural identity, which for our purposes has come to be labeled, "tribalism". The conflict for humanity then became one of how to blend a tribal member and his or her family into a larger political body, e.g. a state or a nation. To become a democratic republic requires legitimate and equal representation of all the participating tribal entities within that nation's geographical boundaries, and this representation should serve to bind them together in this union. To not accept this trusting, possibly even, sharing identity and responsibility has resulted in national resentments and unrest. And in too many instances these same misgivings have resulted in progressively greater chaos and finally to all out civil war.

"Following closely on the heels of tribal formations, and eventually tribalism, was most likely the use of terror. Terrorism was and is, obviously, a very successful method to coerce and intimidate ones adversaries. Its main objective would have been to create fear, through violence, in a rival tribe. And it allowed a smaller, weaker tribe to possibly succeed over a larger, more menacing one. Over the course of history, however, terrorism has taken a darker, more lethal, turn. Now the almost hallucinogenic and sought-after end justifies any means, particularly if they involve greater loss of civilian life. And the goals that are being sought by this modern day form of terrorism could be quasi-religious or pseudo-cultural. Their claims are false. Their methods are criminal. And their message is bankrupt.

"There then follows a period, both in pre-recorded and in the beginning of recorded history, when the most intoxicating of all the isms began: militarism. The lure of conquest, enslavement and pillaging was just too enticing. Egyptian, Greek, Persian, and Philistine rulers; Chinese dynasties;

Roman and Holy Roman Empires all had a role in creating this new world order. Whether it was offense or self-defense, it led to the same end: humanity's greatest folly, glorifying war.

"Next in this historical lineup arose various kings, emperors, czars, sheiks, dukes and princes, each wanting a taste of conquest. By the middle of the eighteenth century, humanity was gasping for life. Centuries of enslavement, the absence of responsible or mature leadership, the denial of due process, justice, or representative government had reached the limit of tolerance. Revolutions began to occur. And democracy began to emerge.

"This leads us to the third "ism", nationalism, which we will also be facing in the months ahead. While it's true there were hints of this newest social entity during certain periods of ancient Greece and Israel's existence, it did not assume its full-blown identity until much later in history. It, too, was conceived to protect and defend, not unlike tribalism. However, in a particular variant of nationalism, certain demands of its citizens began to emerge. Ones like unquestionable loyalty to the nation, glorification of its existence, loss of democratic principles and a willingness to sacrifice everything to extend its superiority over others. In other words, nationhood got into the conquest business.

"The fourth "ism", communism, did not achieve its fullest recognition until the mid-nineteenth century, and yet it probably had some of its earliest roots in the preceding centuries of czarism. The creators of this social system were reacting to the excesses of the Industrial Revolution, at least for the most part. They saw a widening gulf between the newly created, wealthy class and the workers who created their wealth. They saw that governments were not responsive to this plight and would require that they be overthrown. And beyond ten of these theorists or philosophers most commonly known measures that were to be instituted, they also demanded that communism abolish eternal truths, all religions and all morality. So vast was their indictment, and that of their disciples, that they were demanding full-scale, worldwide revolution over most, if not all, present-day governments.

"That leaves the fifth and final "ism", which we will be facing. It is "jihadism". It represents a willful distortion of Jihad. Jihadism espouses that all non-Jihadists deserve death. On the contrary, however, true Jihad represents someone who works tirelessly, with tolerance, submission and compassion, to gain God's attention and possible blessing. In recent years two groups have found refuge and motivation, within the framework of this distortion, to commit unparalleled, terrorist acts. They are al Qaeda and the Taliban. In their minds jihadism is a holy war. In reality, it is a pathway to oblivion.

"And to help bring our mission into sharper focus, I need to also tell you what will be the combination of these "isms" in each of the five regions we sail to. In Shanghai we will encounter communism and nationalism. In Karachi it will be terrorism, jihadism and tribalism. For Nairobi is will be tribalism, nationalism and terrorism. Cairo will have nationalism, jihadism, terrorism and tribalism. And concluding our journey in Caracas we will find mainly terrorism. However, each of these regional centers will sadly have been affected by the debilitating effects of 'consumerization', along with a failure of global democratization and the inability of all humanity to recognize our absolute interdependence with one another.

"Finally, I don't want what I've just told you to sound like overblown, academic gibberish. All of what I have described is filled with too much human suffering for that to be your impression. There ARE truths that are self-evident. ALL men AND WOMEN are created equal, and ALL are endowed by their Creator with certain unalienable rights. And certainly among them are life, liberty and the pursuit of happiness.

"From our earliest beginnings, humanity has failed miserably to care for itself in a tender and loving manner. Exploitation, conquest and manipulation have overwhelmed the deepest drives in us all to be at peace within ourselves and with our loved ones. This must now change. And we, gathered here in this room, are to be the instruments of that change. It is all too evident that government bodies, everywhere, need help. Democracy is too fragile and will not flourish without our intervention. Our mission is gravely important. And your participation in it is pivotal. You were not chosen at random. And your lives and ours will never be the same. We can only hope and pray the same can be said for the rest of humanity."

As Bernie concluded her remarks, I realized, for the first time in my life that I had broken out into a sweat. I could tell, after hearing all this, that I was going to have to keep my bladder well drained once we made landfall. Bernie scared me.

She then followed up her formal address to all of us with, "Please, bare with me one more minute. I need to speak, briefly, about three other matters. The first is that I will not be taking any questions while on this dais. Just the same, after this meeting is adjourned, you may come up to me or any of our group on stage and ask them anything you'd like. Often, we won't know the answer, but we will give you an honest reply either way. Second, Frank and Po have placed a bench alongside me. Once I step down, Sophie, Frank, Po, Wally, the various animals and birds behind me and myself, will either stand alongside the bench or climb onto it, and you will get a chance to meet all of us. And I sincerely believe once you've had that opportunity, you will have little doubt that stunning events are in progress, and that there are more to come.

And third, Captain Shriver has asked me to announce that all of us have to be at our assigned duty stations at 2100 hours. The Polar Wind will cast off at 0030 hours this morning. Now, I'll let you meet everyone assembled around me."

Looking at each other, we animals and birds were taken off-guard. Bernie had said nothing about doing this, but trusting her like we did; we dutifully waddled, hopped, ambled and pranced up to and eventually onto that bench. Once we were all in position standing on it, looking bewildered at each other, it was clear I'd have to do something. Swallowing with a loud gulp, I began.

"Good evening to you, Captain Shriver, and to each of you, the ladies and gentlemen of the Polar Wind. My name is Greg. And I've been sober for eight years now." I then looked over at Flo and winked and at Bernie and smiled. She just shook her head, as did Sophie. I honestly didn't know what else to say. Everything had been so somber and grave up to this point. So quickly, I added, "And I wish I could say the same for those standing beside me." At that point there began to be some gasps from the audience, then snickers, and finally what I really wanted, some laughter.

"Yes, it's true," I continued. "Each of us on this bench can and do talk. That's been part of what you have been missing during your last deployment to Antarctica. Animals, birds, trees and, most recently I've discovered, even fish have begun to speak; we've all found our own voice. Even now, the few of you who have encountered Sparkie, who now prefers to go by the name of "Hope", can testify to this transformation. But because we don't have much time before the Captain says everyone has to be at their duty stations, why don't all of you come forward and meet us individually and see and hear for yourselves. Let's get acquainted."

And that did it. Between the impact of what Bernie had to say and the confirmation of our ability to speak, the crew rushed down and eagerly pumped each of us with countless questions. And almost immediately, I could tell they were a fine lot.

Most of the crew was surprisingly young and quite eager. It all had a good feel about it. Maybe we were, after all, going to be on a boat, sailing over very deep water, far from land, and I can't swim or float; but they made me feel safe. Bernie (and maybe Walt) had made a good choice. The Polar Wind would do.

THE CROSSING

EIGHT: STORMS AND FISHES

On January 21st at 0030 hours the mooring lines were released, the engine of the Polar Wind was throttled up, and she pulled gently into the ship channel that led into Elliott Bay. It was, oddly enough for this time of year, a clear night, but cold. The night lights of downtown Seattle were spectacular, with the soaring buildings rising almost directly from the shoreline of the Bay. I had positioned myself at the stern of the ship, sheltered by one of the lifeboats. Let's face it, I wasn't 100% sure about this new confidence I had in this ship and crew. Being near the lifeboat was a nice crutch for a dog with absolutely zero courage on anybody's rating scale. From the stern, as we sailed at full throttle out of the Sound toward the Pacific Ocean, I could watch the city lights fade and bid a proper good-bye to the land I so loved. My nostrils became filled with the scent of salt air. It seemed rather sterile after my months enjoying the rich, conifer fragrances of the Olympic Peninsula forests.

I was homesick already.

Dawn was just creasing the eastern horizon when we entered the higher swells of the open ocean. And glancing westward I saw the outlined blackness of an approaching storm, arriving full-strength from the Gulf of Alaska. Maybe it was the contrasts, the brightening horizon of sunrise, against the darkness of the gale ahead of us, but whatever it was, it was ominous. And the crew members seemed to sense it as well. The pace of everyone's movements became hurried or so it appeared to me. Shouts, orders, occasional oaths, and the sounds of running feet filled the air, which was eerily calm over the ocean around us at that very moment.

Unsure what to do, I felt, despite my resolve earlier, the most urgent need to panic. It just seemed like that should have been my bounded duty at that moment. My primordial urgings indicated that my doing so might balance the purposefulness and unnerving, exterior calm of the crew. I would have none of it. If I was going to drown, five minutes after beginning the ocean portion of this voyage, I wanted to display my true self: Mr. scared witless. And so I ran.

Leaping up the staircase to our cabin level, I arrived at that outside door breathless. However, this vessel, as I immediately was about to learn, was not dog accessible. There were no doggy doors. All I could do was pant and wait, and I so needed to wee. Luckily, a member of the crew spied me at the door, peering longingly up at the doorknob, as if I were about to make an offer of sacrifice if it would just turn and open. To my relief, she ran up the stairs to the landing I was on.

"Would you like to get in out of the coming storm?" she asked, in a manner that seemed somewhat in denial of the disaster that awaited us.

"If you wouldn't mind," I replied. "I was just debating starting to jump up and try grabbing the door handle in my mouth, while doing a simultaneous body twist, to see if I could open it."

"Well, would you rather try that?" she asked to my utter astonishment.

"Err…, no ma'am," I answered, trying with all my breath-holding might to remain calm and respectful. "I'd be ever so grateful if you would open it instead." At that moment the thought crossed my mind that the new paradigm of laissez-faire social interactions had gone about as far as it needed to. It was high time us animal, bird, fish and tree life reintroduced some civility and reality into the equation. Dogs need help getting into closed fire doors, pure and simple. People don't. Then people can help dogs. They don't need to waste any more precious time, bladder-wise, asking if various other species would like to do it themselves. We can't. I don't mind being helped. I love courtesy. I embrace magnanimity.

She possibly sensed a bit of this impatience beginning to show, particularly when, by now, I was starting to jump straight up and down. And, thankfully, I became convinced of it when I was in mid-flight and she politely added, "Sure thing, Greg. Here you go." She opened that outside door.

I politely thanked her and made a mad dash to Flo's and my cabin, whose door was ajar. By the

100

time I had done my business and leaped up onto my bed, the ship was struck by the first of the giant waves. And for the next sixteen hours it was one huge wave, after another, striking us. Our room was like being inside a catsup bottle that was nearly empty, and someone was trying to get the last, remaining bit out of it onto his or her scrambled eggs. We were pounded, shaken and hurled side to side. And then sometimes it seemed as if the entire ship was turned completely upside down. Flo and I never left the cabin during that storm. And I can't recall we said one word to each other the whole time. I was scared. She was depressed. ...Happy Trails.

During that storm it was Captain Shriver's plan to angle south by southwest, making a heading toward Hawaii. He hoped to outrun or skirt the worst of it by doing so. I understand from conversations later that his maneuvering did save us from the full impact of it. So intense was the center of that monster that ships, larger than us, had floundered, requiring that their crews be rescued. It seems a major storm from the Gulf of Alaska had merged with another, even larger storm coming up the Pineapple Express from the South Pacific.

It was a good two days after we left Seattle before we sailed into calm waters. And it wasn't until then that I got up enough nerve to wander out to the stern of the ship again. This time Flo and Ed went with me. Both of them had an even more severe case of cabin fever than I did. Besides, I was glad to have the company. My courage was at an all time low.

Finding the spot by the last lifeboat that I used previously, I made myself comfortable and dangled my front paws over the edge of the ship's side. Flo followed suit and Ed hopped up onto the side railing. Once in position, we just basked in the sunshine for a while. The air was brisk and filled our nostrils with the primordial scent of salt air. None of us spoke, at least not until our reverie was broken by an announcement of earth-shaking consequences.

Just at that moment something as big as one of Willa's cows jumped out of the water next to where I was sun-bathing. When it splashed back down, the wave doused both Flo and me. Then an eye, as big as Flo's head, rose up from underneath the waves and when its mouth cleared the waterline, it asked in a deep baritone voice, "Are you Greg?"

Now certainly my life had been full of odd moments and wizard-filled events over the last year, but none of it quite prepared me for this occasion. Maybe it was my being completely relaxed and off-guard that heightened my shock at that moment, but in response to the question I could only stare back and reply, "Huh?"

"I repeat, are you one they call 'Greg'? the mammoth fish asked again. He much later informed me, with some pride in his voice, that he was a Blue Fin Tuna, and that his name was Reg. Furthermore, he noted that he and his kind were the fastest creatures, bar none, in all the oceans of this world. He easily could cruise at 30 to 40 miles per hour, and, if pressed, could sprint upwards to 80 mph! Luckily, he didn't tell me all this initially. It would have been more than I wanted or needed to know. Speed was never my forte. I was always perfectly content, lying on my front porch, cruising very efficiently and precisely at zero mph. And I thought I was pretty darn good at it. But, at this moment, those memories seemed four or five lifetimes ago.

"Yes, I am," I finally answered in a voice barely above a whisper. And by this time Flo had stood, her hackles fully upright, and, given the circumstances, growling almost plaintively. She, too, was overwhelmed at this intrusion. Ed, on the other hand, being the particular specimen that he was, stood his ground and shifted slightly as if making ready to give chase. After all, he already had experience with large bodies of water and had seen the creatures that dwell in them. He, along with Flo, were to become my protectors, like Po was to Wally and Bernie.

"Then lend an ear to what I have to say," the giant, sleek, bluish-silver fish added, as he skimmed effortlessly alongside the ship. "Something strange, and it's my guess, quite prophetic, appears to be underway."

"What's that?" I asked, thinking he was going to warn us about another, even larger, storm-front coming our way.

"I and my associates, along with schools of fish scattered all over this section of the ocean, have been noticing there is a mass movement of all submerged and surface warships from two particular countries, China and Russia, steaming back to one port, Shanghai, China. In the meantime, your country's Navy and Coast Guard vessels appear to be returning en mass back to your homeland. Soon enough all that will be left in the open oceans will be mostly commercial ships. Beyond that, there appears to be a scattering of coast guard ships and a rather insignificant number of other navies' ships on limited patrol around countries like Australia, New Zealand, Canada, Japan, Germany, Norway, Great Britain, France and Italy.

"It's almost as if these two largest navies are barricading this port against any outside intrusion and, more worrisome, as if they are preparing for some far-reaching conflict or conquest in the near-future."

"Why are you telling me this?" I stammered. "And, how did you know my name or where I was? What's going on here?!!" I exclaimed, almost shouting by this point. "I'm just a silly dog, for crying out loud!! Why don't' you tell this ship's Captain! Not me, I'm just a middle-aged nobody. Contact the news media, go online or create havoc in some large harbor, like say, in San Diego. But, whatever you do, don't start by telling me!!"

"On the contrary, you were exactly the one I was told to inform."

"By whom? How?" I retorted.

"By the warnings and instructions I got from millions and millions of our oceans' dwellers. And they, indirectly, by one, particular salmon, swimming up the Hoh River some weeks ago."

"What's this?!" Flo demanded, as she turned toward me. "What's this fellow saying?! Did you make contact with a fish when we were staying at

Willa's?! What have you done, Greg?!!"

"Well, it was certainly innocent enough, to start with," I replied, apologetically. "There was this salmon who I found stranded on the river's edge. I only nudged her back into deeper water, and then Ed, here, came along."

"Is that right, Ed?!" Flo, nearly shouting at this point, asked, as she spun around to face Ed.

"Yep. Greg, here, stood guard over the top of that fish as I swooped down to grab it for breakfast that morning. That's how we met."

"Did you realize what you were setting in motion by doing that?" Flo then asked, more puzzled than upset, as she turned back to face me.

"Well, honestly... no. After all, she was in distress. It wasn't like I was trying to eat her or create a global phenomenon of some sort."

Flo, still somewhat vexed, pressed on. "And did you give her your name?"

"I suppose I might have mentioned it. Why?"

"Greg!! Haven't you learned anything during our entire cross-country journey, and starting again with this voyage? You're not exactly just an aging, somewhat irritating at times, dog. You've got bits of Walt's wizardry coursing through your veins and out your pores. You should have told us back at Willa's when you made the contact with that salmon."

"I'm sorry," I replied, hanging my head down off the side of the ship.

"Well, anyway," the over-sized tuna resumed, "you need to be aware of this development and pass this information along to the appropriate people on this ship. I and my colleagues are prepared to provide you some escort to wherever you are going. That is really all I have to say at this time. Right now, I don't want to attract too much attention from the ship's crew. But I must add that you are not to sail much further with your ship painted the color it is and flying your country's colors as you are. You must camouflage yourselves and do it soon. You are in real danger, even now."

"But wait," Greg cried out, not wanting this messenger to disappear and not know how to get back in touch with him, in case Wally or Bernie needed to. "What is your name again and how do we get in touch with you?"

It was at that time Reg informed us of his name, who and what he was and that all I had to do was to come to this same spot, drape my front paws over the side of the ship, and he would resurface. He or one of his associates would always be in the neighborhood, watching out for us. But for the life of me I couldn't understand why. But I sensed, deeper inside me than I wanted to admit openly, that this was the beginning of desperate times for us and this ship.

No sooner had Reg finished his brief explanation of where and how to contact him, than he sank back into the gentle swells and was gone from view. It was at that moment the three of us had our first chance to look at each other and react to what we'd seen and heard. It was Ed who spoke first.

"If I was forced to guess, I'd say this voyage is not going to work out quite the way we envisioned. In fact, it looks like it might not even get more than just started, before it's over. I don't want to be the bearer of disappointing news, but, if possible, you both need to start sprouting some feathers and a wing or two. It doesn't feel to me like staying on this boat is the answer to a long and happy life."

"Those were almost my exact sentiments when we left Walt's cottage that day in New Jersey," Flo observed. "How about you, Greg? What's your sense of things now?"

"That we've got to tell the Captain immediately!! I don't know what else to do beyond that, except to also tell Bernie and Wally. And we've got to do it NOW!"

Both of them rolled their eyes at me, as if my response was to be expected, but only marginally appreciated. For Ed, he knew flight was his first class ticket off this ship of doom. For Flo, she was looking at the nearby lifeboat, like it was going to be her next home, until she landed somewhere that had lots of snow and ice and very few crazy people or talking fish.

Within seconds of that brief exchange, I took it upon myself to run over to LCDR Steele, who was busy inspecting some stored equipment, immediately under the stern's overhead crane. I informed her that we had an urgent message for her and the Captain and that we needed to deliver it as soon as possible. Again, I got an eye-rolling response. It figured. When she grudgingly agreed to take us up to the Bridge, where the Captain was, I then instructed Ed to fly around the ship and position himself on the Flying Bridge's railing. Once there, he was to wait for our arrival. Flo and I were to follow the LCDR to the Bridge.

When we got to the Bridge, I couldn't help but glance around at all the instruments. Actually, that was all I saw, other than shoes and pants legs. Dogs have such an inspiring, visual perspective sometimes. I then asked one of the Bridge personnel to please open the door and let Ed hop in. After that, Flo, Ed and I positioned ourselves in the middle of the room. Honestly, I compulsively wanted to ask someone to pick me up and let me see what the ocean looked like from this height, but I knew that would diminish the seriousness of our report. So, instead, I sat down at the Captain's feet, looked up at him and spoke.

"Captain, the three of us gathered at your feet have just had a brief conversation with a certain messenger. He has informed us of a serious threat to your ship and all our lives. The details of this are not clear to us, but we feel it most urgent that you come with us and hear for yourself what we just heard. We'd like to take you down to the stern, Topside Deck immediately."

Again, I got eye-rolling. What's with everybody, I wondered? Do I look or act like I'm having fun doing this, or reporting matters of doom? I don't think my getting respect is going to be one of my long-term, career goals. But fortunately, letting out a deep sigh, he just nodded his head and motioned for all of us to head out the door to the ship's stern.

It was at this point I began to have some serious doubts about what to do next. Obviously, I had no plan, beyond telling the Captain there was a problem on the near horizon. Beyond that, I was guessing. The only clue I had was that Reg, the tuna, did say for me to dangle my front paws over the edge of the deck to get someone to reappear, so I presumed that was what was next. I did ask that Flo stop by Wally and Bernie's cabin on the way down and request that they accompany us.

When all of us finally gathered around the spot where Reg's appearance occurred, I squeezed my way through feet and legs and asked for a little more room so I could lie down. Then I sprawled out and stretched my front legs as far out as I could over the side of the ship. You'll never know how foolish I felt, particularly if nothing came of this.

"What in heaven's name are you doing?" the Captain finally asked. "You brought all of us down here so you could bask in the sun? From the outset of this circus, I've had my doubts about the purpose and reality of this entire affair. I, for one, am fed up with all the illusions and fantasy. As soon as we get to the nearest port, all of you recently boarded oddities are departing this ship for good. AND THAT'S FINAL!!"

It appeared the Captain was feeling quite proud and in charge, for a change, when he pronounced that intention. As he looked out over the serene blue-green ocean and back onto his magnificent ship, you could sense his renewed sense of command, control and optimism. At least for those few precious seconds he enjoyed the resurgence of command and control.

"Not so fast, there, Captain," came that same deep baritone voice that we heard before, coming from the ship's waterline.

"Who said that?" the Captain called out, as if one of his crew was being insubordinate.

"I did," the voice, echoing across the water, replied. "Look down from where Greg is lying and you'll see me."

When the Captain looked down, sure enough there was Reg, or an exact likeness of him, with his oversized tuna head, poking out of the water. And with the Captain, LCDR, Bernie and Wally leaning over the edge of the railing, Reg proceeded to tell them what he had told the three of us earlier. But, because he knew there would have to be some additional "show and tell" to thoroughly convince this group, he added at the end of his message the following, "and now I want you to have some reinforcement of this from a few of my colleagues."

And following behind Reg, there followed a pair of Blue Fin Tunas, Humpback Whales, Sperm Whales, Grey Whales, Common Dolphins and Striped Dolphins. As they passed by, each pair raised enough out of the water to warn and offer support and protection for us. They said things like, "We're with you." "Don't be alarmed." "It's true." "Take precautions." "Listen to whatever Reg says." "Don't lose heart." "The world needs your courage and strength." and "Know we're always right beside you."

And finally, Reg reappeared and added, "You must now go to the nearest port, which I would suspect would have to be the naval base at Pearl Harbor in Hawaii. There you need to begin the process of camouflaging your vessel. There is no time to waste. Your adversaries are beginning to look for you as we speak. They don't know exactly what type of vessel you are on, but they know it will be the only one heading west rather than east back towards the U.S.A. homeland. All other of your country's fleets are being recalled home, and these stalking you know that. With each mile you travel westward, your risk of danger and discovery becomes greater. Take care. Much depends on the success of your mission."

With that said, all the deep water creatures disappeared from sight, leaving the onlookers, and most especially the Polar Wind's most senior leadership, transfixed, simply staring dumbstruck out over the ocean, which seconds before was boiling with huge, talking mammals and a blue fin tuna. No one dared speak, for fear they'd precipitate another burst of unimaginable events. The only sound was of the waves slapping against the side of the ship as she headed due west.

Shaking his head repeatedly, as if to clear his vision and refocus his mind, Captain Shriver turned and looked down at me, still lying partially extended over the ship's side.

"Right!" he began. "It's been made absolutely clear to me now that I owe you and your entourage the sincerest apology. I am truly sorry for doubting you. But what else should I have done? In my position I cannot afford to believe such things as I have witnessed over these last few days, starting with the last afternoon we were docked in Seattle. It's not at all easy for someone trained, as we commanders are, to just suddenly forego all reason and accept the reality of talking dogs, cats, birds and fish, nor of watching small children disappear and reappear large ships of sea, or of unrelated species parade in front of you in the open ocean, imploring you to be careful and to save the planet. You'll have to cut me a little slack on this. But I do most humbly apologize for my outbursts."

"It's perfectly understandable, Captain," I replied, looking up at him, as I rose to my feet. "Most days I, too, am stunned by what is happening around and to me. Like you, before all the changes and events started happening, apparently spawned by an entirely separate universe, I was content taking my daily strolls to the Atlantic City Boardwalk and snoozing on Howard's porch. I guess if nothing else, what you are experiencing now, and what I have been involved in over these past twelve months, teaches both of us that every moment we are given is precious and that occasionally intruding into any of them can be ones of true magic and wonder. You've now joined us in that realm."

"Yes, I see your point," he acknowledged. "And it's been made absolutely clear to me that we need to change our ship's present course and have everyone on board meet together as soon as possible.

"Marcia, I need you to go to the Bridge and instruct the helmsman on duty to make an immediate course change for Pearl Harbor. I would hope we will be there sometime tomorrow. Most importantly, we should not proceed further west than the Hawaiian Islands until we are disguised. Anyone tracking ship movement would expect traffic to go to and from the mainland United States to Hawaii. But any ship going beyond there, towards the South Pacific or Asia, would raise suspicions and need to be intercepted.

"Greg, I need you and your staff to go immediately back to your quarters, get the rest of your personnel and meet me in my Conference Room in fifteen minutes.

"In the meantime, I need to make contact with our various department chiefs and officers and tell them to meet us there as well. I will not make a general announcement to the entire crew until after our meeting in a few minutes. Now please, be quick and proceed with your assigned tasks."

NINE: PEARL HARBOR

As the Captain anticipated, by 2:30 p.m. on January 26th, the Polar Wind was making its way into Pearl Harbor's shipping channel. The afternoon clouds, as usual, were overhanging the hills surrounding Honolulu, giving the city's upper border a shimmering frame of white foam. Impenetrable blackness at their lower edges partially hid the hillsides' upper reaches. The lower portion of the hills had the lush green of tropical vegetation. It all combined to let you know you were entering paradise. In addition, the temperature was in the 70's, and the beaches were filled with swimmers, volleyball players, sunbathers, and surfers. Highlighting their presence were their brightly colored cabanas, beach towels, surf boards, out-riggers and kayaks.

It all left me no choice. As I stood transfixed, gazing at this lush vista, I began barking. It was as if I had been suppressing that urge for months, and the moment had come to express myself openly and honestly. As we passed in review of this sight, for the next fifteen minutes I raced back and forth along the deck railing and barked for the sheer joy of it. And to my surprise, the tourists, bathers, surfers, residents, business women and men began to wave back at us. It was grand. I hoped we'd stay here for a few months. The beauty was unmatched by anything I'd ever seen before. And I secretly wondered if there might be somebody here who'd take in a shaggy blue healer as a boarder. Maybe I could use Flo and Rita as references.

But all this foolishness stopped as we finally dropped anchor across from the main piers and docks. We were just south of the permanently moored Battleship Missouri, next to Hickam AFB on Ford Island. There were no more berths available for us. Recalling the Pacific Fleet had packed the Navy Yard with vessels of all types and sizes. And besides, who had ever heard of an ice breaker wanting to be berthed in Pearl Harbor. It was obvious to everyone we were lost, that we'd been blown way off course to end up here. We were a very low priority. Following stopping all engines and insuring the ship was securely in place, the Captain ordered our four zodiac boats to be lowered into the water. A crew of three was assigned to each boat, with Captain Shriver in the one heading to the Naval Yard's Headquarters and the other three, led by LCDR Steele, headed to the Yard's Supply Depot.

The Captain was carrying with him orders that had been fabricated between him, Bernie and Wally to indicate they were on an absolutely, need-to-know mission. Without these documents, there would be too many questions raised about what the Polar Wind's personnel were asking for and what they were doing with it, once they got it. Bernie and Wally had suggested to the Captain that they assist him in this matter. Likewise, they had prepared a requisition order for the necessary supplies that the three zodiacs would be getting at the Supply Depot. By 1730 hours all four of the boats were back and had lashed themselves to the Polar Wind. Immediately thereafter, most of the ship's crew began unloading enough battleship grey paint to cover the entire hull of the ship, from the black waterline to the deck railing. Along with the paint, the LCDR's party had secured eight boson's chairs and their required rigging. The next day these same three boats returned to the Supply Depot and brought back twenty gallons of red paint and enough white paint to cover over the just painted grey area, if the need should arise.

By dawn of the second day we were in port, the crew was painting the hull of the ship, dismantling and storing armaments from the stern, securing both helicopters in the hanger, removing all life-saving equipment from the top deck and, with Sophie's direction, making and installing curtains in upper decks' windows. The intent of all this activity was to give the appearance that this was no longer an official ship of the U.S. Coast Guard but instead was a tourist ship, one that specializes in taking passengers to Antarctica or to the Arctic. There was some discussion about which flag to fly, but it was finally decided it would remain the American one. Some things were not going to be compromised throughout this mission.

By the third day in port, Sophie's interior decorating supervision was no longer needed and she, along with our entire New Jersey Wagoner crew, decided to head into Honolulu and have a picnic in the Ala Moana Park, close to Waikiki Beach.

However, I must point out something quite disturbing at this juncture. We, as individuals or as a group, were not welcome ANYWHERE outside the continental United States. Word had gotten out, as would be expected, about what had happened in the Battle of Oregon and, most importantly, about who and what was involved. It created pandemonium throughout the rest of the world. We were somewhat immune to that fact, being isolated at Willa's. And with being on board the Polar Wind only added to that isolation. It was when Captain Shriver went to the Navy Yard's Headquarters that he became aware of this fact. Hawaii wanted nothing to do with trees, animals or birds having free speech or any kind of speech for that matter.

"Why?" you ask. Well, just think about it. The fact that humans have had the ability to speak for all these years hasn't exactly created the most ideal environment for rational discourse and peaceful co-existence. Democracy, at that moment, certainly wasn't flourishing everywhere, and even where it was fully established, human beings oftentimes couldn't agree on very much. And think how many decades it took, just in democratic societies, to give everyone the right to vote! Equal participation, up until recently by everyone with a voice, has been painfully slow; and for over half of the globe, it still was only a distant dream.

Now can you begin to imagine what the movers and shakers of humanity began to think when they heard of trees, animals, birds (and now fish) starting to have a say in things. It was viewed as a plague that had to be stopped at all costs, even in Hawaii. Whenever an odd, migratory bird might show up on the Islands who displayed this ability, every effort was made to isolate, contain and eventually remove it.

Captain Shriver immediately made us thoroughly aware of this atmosphere, but we still decided to take a chance anyway on slipping into the city and having a quiet picnic. It all seemed harmless enough to me. We even had the Captain arrange for Hickam Air Force Base to provide us a covered truck to use for transport. Frank, again, drove it. And I sat up front with Sophie, just like we did in the recreation vehicle on our cross-country trip. We packed a lunch and took some blankets. It was a beautifully, bright sunny day when we drove off.

Getting to the Park was no problem and soon we were unloaded and by noon had spread our lunches out on the ground beneath a huge Morton Bay Fig tree, whose limbs spread out at least thirty feet in all directions from its massive trunk. Throughout the park were Acacia Koa's, Hawaiian Ash and Ohia's. The Ohia trees were in full bloom with orange-red and yellow blossoms. It was a perfect setting. And to top it off, the fig tree had roots around its lower trunk, each with rather sharp ridge lines that meandered out along the ground like rivulets. Some of the smaller ones looked perfect for me to have a good scratch after we finished lunch.

Equally intriguing were the colorful birds that flew in and out of the surrounding trees. Particularly lovely were the bright red I'iwi's and Apapane's, along with the multicolored Monarch flycatchers. As later events unfolded, they were probably a little too curious.

And finally, the park was full of dogs…all kinds and breeds. And when they saw me, Flo, and particularly, Jennifer, it was clear that before long something unexpected was going to happen. And it did.

Almost simultaneously, three events occurred after lunch. First, I decided to have a scratch on the Fig tree root; second, Rita was caught unaware of a flycatcher swooping down to give her an investigative peck, and third, a particularly dumb, if you'll excuse my bias, boxer dog made a death-defying charge at Jennifer. All three of these respective species made contact with us or us with them, at the same time.

What followed is something Capt. Shriver never ceases to scold me about. The fig tree promptly accosted me saying, "Enough! I'm neither a hitching nor a scratching post. Take your itches elsewhere! I've had it with dogs taking advantage of me!"

The Flycatcher, upon making contact with Rita's tail feathers, cried out "Well, aren't you quite a ways from home. We don't see your kind around here. I see you keep your two larger friends (meaning Iris and Ed) around for protection. All gloss and glitter, but no fight. That's so typical of you outsiders," which, I might add, was not the way to introduce oneself to Rita.

And finally there was that Boxer dog. When Bubba, the name he apparently chose himself (...go figure...) was struck squarely on the nose by one of Jennifer's due claws, he exclaimed, "Golly, gee, what are you so sensitive about? I just wanted to have a little fun, playing with you." In reply, Jennifer was guardedly pleasant, but in no uncertain terms, told him where he might go to try and find it.

There soon followed, just at that magical moment in time: an afternoon breeze, which blew the outstretched limbs and leaves of the fig tree onto neighboring trees; the Flycatcher attentively made contact with his mate; and the Boxer ran mindlessly (how else do they?) from dog to dog, touching each of them in odd places. And with these nightmare encounters happening in unison, the Park soon erupted like a calliope. There was an explosion of cries, shouts, apologies, accusations and arguments. It was a Chamber of Commerce moment, I was sure. And we knew it was time we packed and left for the ship.

By dawn on our fourth day in port we had restocked our supplies, finished painting the ship's hull grey, cleared the top deck of any suspicious equipment and given the living quarters' windows a more festive look. It was time to leave Dodge. City fathers, mothers, children and pets were beginning to come to the conclusion that we were the culprits responsible for their newly transformed world. We had left our mark forever in that paradise.

Pearl Harbor was in our rear view mirror by 0700 hours, as the Captain gave orders for a course to Guam. We were now heading into enemy territory.

TEN: GUAM

Having to get used to ocean swells again was heart-breaking for me. I added Ala Moana Park to my list of places I wanted to eventually live nearby. In fact, I decided there and then, if Wally ever got really clever with that magical staff of his, that he, as a last favor to me, could transfer the Columbia River, Ala Moana Park and the Boardwalk to Willa's place. And I'd be ever-so grateful. After his and Walt's accomplishments of getting every creature on the planet, with either lungs or gills, to speak it didn't seem to me doing that would be that much of a chore.

Anyway, it was a satisfying daydream, and it kept my land-lubber spirits intact as I rested, completely unaware, with my front paws hanging over the sides of the Polar Wind.

And lying thus, it wasn't long before I heard a familiar voice yell out at me, "Did you have a nice stay in Honolulu?"

Shaken out of my reverie, I looked down and saw Reg bobbing along, about twenty feet away from the ship's side. Recognizing him was easy;

the ocean was in a pensive mood at that moment, with only lazy three to four foot long swells. Given this, he easily kept his head above the waterline. The trip had been basically this calm since we left Hawaii. And by now we were four days out from Honolulu, with one more left before reaching Guam.

"It was as close to heaven as this ole dog will ever get," I replied.

In response, the big tuna cautioned, "Well, it sure doesn't appear the likes of heaven is your destination now. From all we've been seeing lately, your ship seems to have set a course straight towards death's doorway. I'm afraid you're going to be greeted with untold misery, if not outright calamity, unless something beyond this world's usual pattern of conflict resolution does not occur soon.

"Do the folks in command of this ship and those leading your foray even begin to know what awaits them out here? Frankly, to be perfectly honest, from what all we swimmers out here have seen lately, you seem like a rather clumsy and odd lot. Have you recently just met one another? Is anyone really in charge?"

"Oh, yes," I answered; now feeling more confident that I could answer these questions and calm his doubts about our party's goals, plans and leadership. "Our group has traveled; well most of us anyway, all the way across the North American continent together."

"ON THAT SHIP?!!" The oversized fish shouted.

"No, no," I reassured him. "We traveled in small wagons and on tricycles most of the way."

"Did anyone think to suggest that maybe just riding in a motorized vehicle of some kind might be more practical? Even in my rather limited environmental condition, if I was making up a list of ways to cross a 3,000 mile landmass, using small wagons and tricycles would most likely never make the first one hundred options. So, I repeat, is anyone in charge of your band of voyagers?"

"Certainly," I hastily replied, beginning to feel a little out of my depth. "At this time there are two who are. They are Bernie and Wally."

"Weren't they the little girl and small boy who stood alongside you when the Captain came over here the day before you arrived in Hawaii?" he quickly asked with some wonder in his voice.

"That's right!" I shouted, relieved he was now fully aware of who provided our all-important and vital leadership.

Then shaking his immense head, the sleek swimmer sighed and muttered, "I think I feel a headache coming on. You're telling me that a somewhat scruffy dog, if you'll excuse my characterization, sets in motion the process of global conversations amongst all the world's bird and animal life, followed by the same phenomena occurring for all of the oceans' fishes and mammals. Then, what looks to me like two children, ages six and eight years, are now leading a mission to reset the course of humanity's self-destructive obsessions. But all this occurs during and only after both parties crossed a 3,000 mile landmass in small wagons. Might there be anything else of note that I've missed?"

"I don't think so," I said, somewhat puzzled by his further questioning. "Except that maybe you need to add that trees can also talk now, at least where we just came from; and that that you never met Walt, the Wizard, who came from the anteverse when he was quite young."

"And I guess he did magic tricks and cast spells."

"Oh, much more than that," I answered, more confident now about the course of this conversation. "He brought the evil Emissaries to their final end," I noted with some pride in my voice.

However, what I had failed to notice during this question and answer session was that there had now risen to the ocean's surface hundreds of fish and mammalian heads, all peering at me and either nodding or shaking their heads at one another. It was obvious they had been listening to what we were saying. I just hadn't noticed them.

And it was at that moment that Bernie and Wally walked up beside me. But in retrospect, I doubt that was by accident or happenstance. Nothing that occurred in those days seemed to be too random to me.

"We couldn't help but overhear your conversation with Greg, here," Bernie began. "And my brother and I thought it might be appropriate to come forward and help reassure you and then to give you some idea about what is ahead for all of us.

"We are traveling to Shanghai, China, by way of Guam. And from there we are going to four other ports in the next two to three months. They are in Pakistan, Kenya, Egypt and Venezuela. We will travel to each of these on this ship, which we did camouflage at your urging. And we are most grateful to all of you for that warning

"We will need your guidance and help throughout this entire voyage. As you are aware, there are forces being assembled, which are determined to sink this ship and all the crew on it, thereby preventing our completing this mission.

"And, as for your more immediate role in these upcoming battles, I must tell you that Wally will be doing more transformations of our various team members. At that point each of you will be a party to what happens next. I'd prefer not to tell you at this time what role that will be, but it will be pivotal to our eventual success.

"We know it seems nearly impossible to grasp who and what we've done, leading up to this very moment. Your questioning of Greg rightfully bears that out. But maybe if my brother gives you a little demonstration of what is possible, you'll be more inclined to believe both Greg and I.

Then to my amazement, as if almost on cue, Wally came forward and climbed up on the top rung of the ship's railing. Then, while holding his newly acquired staff, he balanced carefully, banged it once and intoned the words, "steak and kidney pie". Simultaneously, the staff then fell to Bernie's feet, while a transformed Wally lofted up into the blue, cloudless sky as a brilliantly white, winged horse.

He flew straight up five or six hundred feet, then dipped down, swooping over the tops of the waves, as the countless fish and mammal heads twisted around to watch him. Then he circled up to an altitude of one to two thousand feet and did a couple of summersaults, followed by a steep dive back towards the ocean. Skimming just over everyone's heads looking up at him, it was obvious there wasn't a mouth closed, either in that portion of the ocean or on board the ship at that moment. Finally he arched over in front of the ship's bridge and down onto the helicopter pad, where he immediately assumed his previous appearance as little Wally.

After that demonstration, I smiled my silly grin and looked down at Reg and asked, "Would you be having any other questions or comments at this time?"

Bernie quickly followed up with, "Please, everyone here, or as many of you as can, return to us in four days. We will be providing each of you with an additional ability at that time."

And certainly what happened next was simply astonishing. It was like the ocean's surface became a huge trampoline. Whales, dolphins, albacore and blue tunas, flying fish, seals, penguins and countless other varieties of fish and mammals began jumping, leaping, twisting and doing back-flips out of the water. There were shouts of joy everywhere. The ocean surface became alive with thousands of creatures reacting to Bernie and Wally's appearance. And, I imagined, wherever Walt was at that moment, he was dancing a bit himself, as well.

Remarkably, despite all the excitement that Wally and much of the ocean's wildlife created, the ship's crew was able to maintain our course and timeline, and we arrived, as anticipated, in Apra Harbor at the U.S. Naval Base on Guam. We stayed there three days, ones that were filled with non-stop relays involving lifting, sorting, stacking foodstuffs, medical and emergency supplies and extra fuel and lubricants for the helicopters. We had boxes and crates lashed down and secured in our rooms, hallways, conference room and auditorium. Everyone sensed that these supplies had to last us until our journey ended in the next three months.

Finally, at the Captain's insistence, a few crewmembers went to the local hospital and were able to plead long enough to get some white, medical uniforms for thirty of the crew. When I heard about this, it intrigued me at first, but then I became worried. "Was the Captain expecting a major emergency on board the ship?" I wondered to myself. And when I asked Bernie and later Sophie and Frank, they all just shrugged and said nothing. If there was a contingency plan or a major concern, they weren't telling me. But, because it wasn't like our group to keep secrets that might involve danger or harm, I eventually decided to add this development to my 'already worried about list'. I had worried about it, and now it was harmless and could be forgotten...Almost.

It was on our last day in Guam that the Captain gave all the crew shore leave, with strict orders for everyone to be back on board the Polar Wind by 0000 hours that night. We were to sail for Shanghai by 0600 hours that next morning.

A few of the ship's company went shopping for souvenirs, but everyone in the New Jersey Wagoners headed straight to the local beach. Flo and I ran up and down it, then in and out of the surf. Rita, Ed and Iris flew off to see if there were any unsuspecting, South Pacific delicacies swimming close to the ocean's surface that might provide them a nice lunch. But as good as they used to be catching fish; there was now a new order of things. Fish now talk. And it's true that birds still soar and hunt, but the odds are now in the fishes favor. They just dove a little deeper when word got around that Ed and Iris were in the neighborhood. So it was left up to Rita to pick up some nearby fruit. She was able to locate some figs, passion fruit, mangos and papaya for them to dine on that day. And despite Ed and Iris's being skunked, the afternoon passed in pure splendor and luxury for all of us. Guam was another paradise.

That next morning, under a threatening sky, we set sail away from Guam. There was a different mood permeating throughout the ship as we left. No U.S. ship should be in these waters, particularly if it was heading further west. Up to our arrival in Guam, at least since leaving Hawaii, it was assumed by the Captain that we were probably occasionally being tracked on someone's radar. But now the entire ship's company knew we most likely were coming under constant scrutiny.

That being the case, soon after we left port,

Capt. Shriver called Bernie, Wally and Po to his cabin for a conference. The gist of it, as Wally later relayed to me, was that the Captain was concerned that he had no one on board who spoke or understood either Chinese or Russian. They were the countries that possessed the largest oceangoing navies and who would most likely be monitoring our advance towards the Asian mainland. After some discussion, Bernie suggested that the Captain arrange to have all the assigned Radio Room personnel, as well as anyone who had Bridge duty, to meet Wally on the Bridge at 1000 hours.

At that time, eighteen crewmembers, including Capt. Shriver and LCDR Steele, assembled on the Bridge Deck, each lined up facing Bernie and Wally. Wally told me he was a little nervous, particularly after his mishap causing the disappearance of the entire ship in Seattle. He certainly didn't want to cast the Captain and all the ship's Bridge officers and crew off into a stellar dust cloud. And making his task even harder were the words chosen by Walt for him to use for this assignment.

It seems Walt, having lived for centuries in Europe, and more specifically in England for many of those years, had chosen key words or phrases Wally would use with his powerful staff that were associated with English cooking. It seemed logical to Walt that no foreign attacker or hacker would likely guess them and then would somehow prevent Wally from affecting his necessary changes. All that seemed well and good to Wally at the time, but keeping the list straight in his head was a nightmare in itself. Witness the disappearing ship as a prime example. But, being the ever-brave lad that he was, he forced himself to stand erect before the ship's present company, holding the magical staff in his right hand. Quickly, he banged it twice, intoning the words, "bangers and mash" and "bubbles and squeak".

When he had completed that very simple ceremony, he turned and smiled at Bernie. She, by now, was totally perplexed at this process, not having been drawn into Walt's confidence when he explained all this to Wally. Looking back at him in an almost vexed manner, she responded, "So, what do you do next? What happens now, Wally?" she snapped rather sharply. "That can't be all there is to this?"

"Yep, Bernie," he smiled and answered in a chipper, sing-song voice. That's it! I'm done!"

"Oh, me, Wally," she countered. "We're doomed if you can't do better than that. There must be more to it. You've forgotten something Walt showed you or told you to do. Have you? Think! What is it?!"

"Nope, Bernie. T...Th...That's all Mr. Walt sh...showed me," he stuttered in reply, now beginning to become obviously more nervous and upset.

"For crying out loud!! There has to be more to it than this!" Capt. Shriver then boomed out in flawless Chinese. And from that point on those transformed crew members comprehended and spoke flawless Chinese and Russian. And Wally, bless his heart, was now recognized as a true, budding wizard in his own right.

Soon thereafter, it was made absolutely clear that these two foreign powers were closely monitoring the advance of the Polar Wind. By mid-morning the next day, Bernie came up to me and asked if I would mind going to the Topside Deck and assume the position that would alert Reg or one of his cohorts to swim over to our ship.

When that occurred, I was to tell whoever came forward to spread the word that as many underwater creatures as could be assembled were to come to our ship by 5 p.m. that same afternoon. They were to be instructed that the meeting was vitally important and only by being physically present could the necessary message and directions be given to them.

Bernie then went up to the Bridge and asked the Captain to make sure there were no friendly nation ships in their vicinity. It was important that all of those vessels were either home-ported or on their way out of this danger zone. And by 1500 hours Capt. Shriver assured her that, indeed, no neutral or allied ships were in that region of the ocean.

After his confirming that this was the case, Bernie then found Wally and Iris, both of whom at that time were having a few laughs with Rita, Jennifer, Flo and I in our room. Pulling Wally aside, Bernie told him what he needed to do come 5 p.m. It caused him obvious distress hearing what she told him. He never returned to our room thereafter that day. That done, she then asked Iris to step outside our room and instructed her on what she needed to do at the time Wally was to perform his part of the upcoming operation.

At 4:45 p.m. Bernie knocked on our cabin door and told me to again go down to the Topside Deck and signal for Reg and his associates to rise to the ocean's surface and to make themselves visible. That, alone, concerned me. If the ocean was in an angry mood, you wouldn't be able to see those who came with Reg, due to all the turbulence and frothing of the waves.

To our amazement, when we walked outside onto the stairwell and looked out over the water, it was dead calm. Not even undulating swells were visible. The surface of the ocean was like a pristine mountain lake in midsummer. And, most stunning of all, when I lay down and dangled my front paws over the ship's side, up rose thousands upon hundreds of thousands of heads for as far as the eye could see. Big eyes, small eyes, huge eyes and heads of all sizes and shapes were everywhere. Mean fish, weak fish, small mammals, immense mammals, all were there and waiting silently for whatever was about to happen next.

It was at that point Bernie called Wally forward and told him to perform whatever he needed to do for any hostile ships of war to be neutralized. In addition, she told him the only ships of that description to be spared were ones of friendly or non-threatening navies. But if any of them ever appeared likely to engage in hostile acts, not of a defensive nature, they, too, were to become victim to the changes that were about to be initiated.

In addition, she instructed Iris to fly out into the midst of that assembled sea life and to hover over them, awaiting what happens after Wally's incantations.

Wally, despite all the power and majesty entrusted to him by Walt, just stood dumb-founded for a moment, looking unsure what to do next. And as he looked out over the hundreds of thousands of heads peering at him so intensely, he became progressively more nervous. Seeing this happen, I got up from my lying position and went up to him.

"It's ok, Wally. You can do this," I said in a soft, encouraging voice.

"I…I…I'm really sc…scared, Mr. Greg." he quietly whispered to me.

"So am I. And its right you should be," I reassured him. "But you've been given this ability, by Mr. Walt, to bring forth remarkable changes. And he must have known that you'd never fail to do it when that time came. He trusted no one else with your awesome powers."

"Yeah, but…"

"No buts, Wally," I interrupted. "This is your duty to do this. NOW!!!"

That outburst of mine so startled him that he lunged forward to the railing, staff in hand, banged it three times and yelled out, in a voice deeper, louder, and stronger than any I had ever heard before, "POTATO JUICE!!"

Nothing happened. And the tens of thousands of heads all turned and looked at each other and then back at Wally.

"Wally," I nudged him and said in my most

reassuring voice, "there is no such thing, to my knowledge, as 'potato juice'. 'Potato water' maybe, after someone has boiled a few potatoes, but not 'juice'."

"Oh, yeah! Thank you, Mr. Greg. I meant to say something else." And again he banged his staff three times and called out, "TOMATO JUICE!!! His voice, this time, seemed to carry even further, for miles across the placid ocean surface.

And it was like a halo of light began to radiate from Wally out over the miles-upon-miles of assembled ocean life. It shimmered over them and then down to the water's surface. And one creature after another, looked and nodded, as if they were being given unspoken instructions on what to do next. It was unquestionably clear that Wally had affected a multitude of life that afternoon with or by something. Likewise, it had a dramatic effect on Iris as well.

As we were to find out later, that 'something' was associated with their making contact with a hostile surface or submerged ship of war wanting to cause unprovoked harm. That particular vessel, once a transformed fish or mammal touched it, began to quietly, slowly and subtly to dissolve. It began at the topmost portion of the ship, beginning with its crow's nest, radar dishes, radio antennae, and smoke stacks. At the start of the process it might not seem too noticeable, but as crew members began to see dissolving metal, disappearing hardware or the shrinking of the ship's superstructure, they would realize something progressive and voyage-ending was at hand.

Apparently, Walt had not wanted to cause undue loss of life. He wanted this process to occur in a staged manner, so that a ship, if tagged in the open ocean, could make it back to a port before it was completely incapacitated and would eventually disappear altogether, like grains of sugar dissolving in a glass of water. The only catch was that once it was noticed that the changes were beginning, each ship had to make haste in their return to safety. There would not be time to dally, to pause or to interdict another vessel, like the Polar Wind. Any vessel that tried, would find themselves abandoning ship miles from landfall. And obviously, during these initial days of dissolving ships, there were ships' captains who did not heed their crews' warnings. And without exception, whenever this occurred, the only recourse the crews had was to seek refuge in their lifeboats. These craft were immune to the effects of this disappearing process. But when a willful command did attempt to pursue the Polar Wind, whether it was a surface or submerged vessel, soon enough all hands were finishing that tour of duty in a lifeboat of some kind. No warship was spared, once even the lightest brush was made against the surface of the vessel by the transformed sea life.

Within days of Wally's proclamation, hulls of once proud ships of war began limping toward ports along the Chinese, North Korean and Russian shorelines. Some actually made it to a port. Others had to scuttle their ships within sight of land and take lifeboats and makeshift rafts the rest of the way to shore. Fewer still were lost at sea, and their crews had to be rescued by commercial vessels who had heard their urgent "Mayday" calls. But, sadly, a determined handful, led by loathsome commanders who had a total disregard for their crews, were lost completely, with all hands on board. No one needed to lose their life in this transition period. That was one of Walt's primary objectives. The other was to simply eliminate these instruments of destruction, but certainly not the innocent or helpless individuals on board them. It was his intention to give everyone another opportunity to live a free and meaningful life. However, that goal was a world away at this time for the New Jersey Wagoners and the brave crew aboard the Polar Wind.

MISSION TIME

ELEVEN: SHANGAHI, CHINA

It was later that same day, right after our evening meal for that matter, when Bernie came around to each of our rooms and requested that the eleven of us Wagoners meet in the dining room at 7 p.m. She characterized the meeting as being urgent. But, by now, I was beginning to think that there was no other kind to have. We'd passed exciting, interesting, fun and enjoyable some time back, probably when we crossed the International Date Line.

There was a definite restlessness in the Conference Room as we gathered to hear what she had to tell us. Our trip cross-country was only a prelude to what was ahead. Each one of us was now certain of that fact. You don't baptize a half million sea residents and then charge headlong into hostile waters and not begin to sense that. The mood was grim as Bernie rose to speak to us.

"What I am about to tell you now is all that remains of what Walt told me that day at Willa's.

After you hear this, everything else that happens to us will not have been foretold and will be uncharted territory for all of us. Just the same, he did make it absolutely clear to me that we had to succeed in this mission we have ahead. All survival, as it hung in the balance at the Battle of Oregon, depends on it. And given that there is already a great search worldwide underway to locate us, we are already in the cross-hairs of all tyrants and bully's everywhere.

"My plan tonight is to initially address the common duties and preparations we'll need to perform before reaching each of the five separate regional centers. But there will be specific issues that will be discussed later, before we arrive at each separate city. In part, that's because each locale will require specific changes as we experience the unexpected at the previous locations."

Her use of the phrase, "experience the unexpected", had such a magical quality about it. Quite possibly, Experiencing The Unexpected, could be the title of my autobiography once all this traveling is concluded. Its subtitle might be, "While Trying to Avoid the Expected Experiences". And as I cast a weary glance over our assembled troop at that moment, I swear it appeared the same thought appeared to be coursing through everyone else's minds as well. Even Sophie appeared taut, possibly even bewildered. Seeing her, I knew it was time for an immediate lifeboat drill. What started those many months ago as a desire for an adventurous, cross-country trip was now verging on our own version of a suicide mission. And adding to my tension was when I looked at Wally. He was nervously fidgeting with his wand scabbard. Probably, I guessed, he was considering disappearing himself...if he could remember the right words. Bless his gifted and precious heart. It was my guess Walt probably thought he might have such thoughts and did not give him that avenue of escape. On that note, I'd sure like to have a mano-a -mano talk with Walt about now. But Bernie had cleared her throat, taken a sip of water and was about to resume the meeting.

"Before I discuss some specifics and any preliminary preparations that we will be undertaking, I need to inform you of those individuals who will always be going into each of these regional centers. Likewise, I need to outline who will be in the advance party, in other words those who will perform the preliminary duties before the core group arrives. The vanguard group will consist of Flo, Jennifer, Rita, Ed, Iris and Greg. And the party that will always meet with each of the five regional leaders will be Po, Frank, Wally, Greg and I."

'GREG! BOTH BEFORE AND DURING, EVERY TIME!!!' I screamed to myself. Why me? Get Capt. Shriver. He strikes a fine pose, even when his ship has just disappeared before his eyes. I'm a dog! Can't anyone get that straight!! Hearing Bernie announce this made me melt into the floor, with my head slumped over my front paws.

"And then," Bernie continued, "we'll enlist others of you, those I have not mentioned specifically, as for example, you Sophie, to go on succeeding trips into one or more of these five centers. This first one will require Iris to possibly make contact with some sea life in Shanghai's harbor, if there are still fighting ships left untouched when we arrive there. Any ships contacted by fish or mammals in there will experience a very rapid sequence of events. They will dissolve before your eyes in a matter of minutes, only allowing enough time for their crew members to quickly escape. Neither Walt nor I want any innocent individuals harmed. And, if it is at all possible, we especially don't want any of us in this room or any of the Polar Wind crew injured or killed.

"We will be wearing the clothes common to the country or region we enter. During this first stopover we will, of course, be dressed in typical Chinese attire. Just the same, given the globalization of dress, we probably won't be dressed too differently than we are now. However, our outward facial appearance will be changed. Each of us will appear Chinese and easily blend into the crowd.

"Frank will drive us to our destination, once we arrive on shore and secure a vehicle. He will carry Wally's staff to avoid having Wally appear too conspicuous. Wally, however, will always have his wand readily available to use. And it will be unsheathed and ready to fully deploy, if necessary in an emergency. Po will lead us, dressed like a local police officer. Both Wally and I will be dressed in typical school uniforms, and we will walk in the middle of our group whenever we are on foot. Frank will be dressed like a businessman. And Greg... well you all know... But, I will be leading Greg, with him on a leash."

A LEASH!! She'll have to drag me... And that's my final word on this matter.

"Those of us going will all need to be loaded and ready to enter the city at 8 a.m. on February 12th. Capt. Shriver hopes to have us slip, inconspicuously, into the harbor by midnight on February 11th. Iris, Ed, Rita, Jennifer and Greg will return to the ship by dawn on the 12th. We will be transported into shore on one of the zodiac boats, and it will remain there ready, at a moment's notice, to return us to the Polar Wind as soon as we've completed our business with whomever we'll eventually meet. Our plan is to spend only the time necessary in each regional center to effect the necessary changes and say what we need to say. Upon our return to the ship, we will immediately weigh anchor and leave the port, while there is still much confusion over what has and is taking place.

"The danger to this ship, its crew and to all of us increases daily from here on. The search will be frantic to find us, now that we will soon begin transforming certain people and most life forms in these regions. And it will become even more so, as it becomes evident we are also instrumental in making their implements of war disappear. Be vigilant! Stay brave and strong! We must prevail!"

Following Bernie's revelations that night, our ship traveled a twisting route after leaving Guam. We sailed across the Philippine Sea and up along the eastern coastline of the Philippines, Taiwan and the Ryukyu Islands. After hugging these territorial shorelines, we made a mad dash across the East China Sea. And the under cover of that night's nearly total darkness, except for any light provided by the myriad stars, we began the nerve-wracking approach into China's territorial waters.

Then at 9 p.m., while still fifty miles offshore, Bernie and Wally called Flo, Jennifer, and me to the helicopter pad, where Ed, Iris and Rita were already assembled. When we got there, we saw Wally, outlined by the pad's dim, emergency light, standing with Bernie, holding out his unsheathed wand. There was a brisk wind blowing in a westerly direction, indicating that a change of weather could be likely in a day or so.

Wasting no time, Bernie quickly informed each of us what our objectives were and how we'd be able to accomplish them. Flo was to be transformed into a Chinese Goshawk, Jennifer into a Red-footed Falcon, and I would become an Osprey. We were to fly as far inland as we could, in the time allowed, to get each of us back to the Polar Wind by 6 a.m. The ship, by that time, would be stationed somewhere in the Shanghai harbor. That timeframe gave us four and a half hours to fly one way into this vast land and begin our transformations.

Flo would transform large animals, Jennifer small ones and I would tend to the trees, as each of us did on our cross-country trip. Ed would see to inland fish, Iris was assigned to any saltwater fish she found still mute and unable to dissolve warships, and Rita was in charge of all birdlife she could contact. That said, it being nighttime, none of this assignment was going to be that easy. But it was safe to say that, if all went as hoped and planned, there was going to be a massive speak fest come the next few days.

I only wished I could have been in the neighborhood when a local Chinese herder or few North Korean and Mongolian farmers began to make their morning rounds these next few mornings, as migratory birds and animals made their way in all directions. Most likely, milking their once docile cows won't be quite the same, nor will saddling their rider-worn horses be as easy. There will probably be some new ground rules, work schedules, rest breaks, perks and meal times that will need to be discussed before much work will be done that particular day. As Ed noted that one day when we were getting acquainted along the Hoh River, giving free speech to everyone makes for some awkward moments, particularly after over 10,000 years of having your way with them. I can predict there might be some unresolved issues to settle come tomorrow's sunrise across this portion of eastern Asia.

Wally came forward to Flo, Jennifer and myself, as a few members of the ship's crew bustled about getting ready to make the final approach to Shanghai's harbor. Curious, they turned and then gasped in stunned amazement as Wally waved his wand before each of us and instantly we became the large birds that Bernie had foretold would occur. Obviously, I could not really see myself as others did, but I did sense there were some gasps, as I extended my six foot wing span to stretch and get ready to fly.

Jennifer fluffed her feathers, cocked her strikingly beautiful falcon head, and commented proudly, "How do you like my stunning red feet, Greg? Does my new attire suit me?"

"You look ravishing, my dear," I replied, which she did.

Flo, on the other hand, looked stern and determined. I worried that she was considering making a beeline north toward Siberia. But it must have occurred to her that without Wally's intervention, she'd remain a hawk and then would not be able to remain permanently at her dreamtime destination. Because then she'd know firsthand the downside of seasonal migrations.

Instead, as reality seemed to check in, she turned to me and said, "We probably should be on our way. Do you want us to fly as a group? The particular beneficiaries of my transformations are going to be near forested areas, which may be a different locale than some of you are going to. But we could at least start off together, maybe even do some aerial acrobatics as we prepare for our earthbound conversions. All of us that is, except for you, Rita."

"Yeah," Rita noted. "But I won't find many birds in flight at night. I'll have to catch most of them roosting. So, I can tag along with you folks most of the way."

"Hey! That sounds like a plan to me!" I hastily, and with great relief, replied. "I don't entirely trust my navigational skills. Jennifer, you might want to travel with us as well."

She agreed, and within a minute or two all six of us were aloft, circling the ship once, and then heading for mainland China. Who would have thought? Here I was, an aging blue-healer, just over a year ago occasionally sunning himself on the Boardwalk, and now I was skimming over the East China Sea, heading into China to bring the power of communication to trees, while my companions did the same for life forms of every description. Life, as Bernie said it would be, was certainly full of unexpected experiences. Wouldn't you agree?

We flew in a rather loose formation, minus Iris, who had swooped down over the coastline to investigate whether there were any stray sea life creatures not yet affected by the urge to talk and make large ships disappear. We agreed to meet up again just north of Shanghai in about eight and a half hour and then to fly over the city in to the Polar Wind, while in formation.

"Good luck, Iris!" I called out, as she swooped down, her awkward appearing waddle on land stunningly transformed into a ballerina in flight. Like an Olympic downhill skier, she could twist and turn effortlessly, and then she could dive and soar with unequaled grace. Pelicans get my vote as the world's most graceful of birds when in flight.

We met up with her at dawn, after she had surveyed Shanghai's harbor, made some necessary conversions there and then flew the remainder of her time along the coastline. The ships now affected by her fish transformations were disappearing quickly, and we saw none when we approached the Polar Wind after we were all done.

Soon enough, as we flew just over the treetops, we all began to see miles upon miles of rice paddies and scattered herds of cattle, sheep and goats. In the distance we noted land formations no doubt caused by the mighty Yangtze River. Ed called out that he was heading in that direction to check out any fresh water fish who might be surfacing unsuspectingly. And somewhere deep inside my multiple personalities, or now, my multi-transformed genes, I longed to go with him. The Seahawk in me was beckoning. A little midnight snack would be nice, those urgings signaled at that moment.

Instead, Flo, Jennifer and I flew on a few miles further. Seeing a rather large farming district appear over a wooded hillside, we divided up and each of us headed toward a group of large and smaller animals and me for a grove of cypress trees.

Landing in the branches of a rather stately cypress tree, I said out loud, with the utmost confidence and just a hint of cultural arrogance, "So this is China, eh."

To my amazement, there was an immediate response. "If you want to try getting ahead in life, it helps if you speak the local language and know some basic introductory customs. For starters, we speak Chinese in these parts, not English. Next, it's customary when introducing yourself to give your name and at least make a noticeable bow with your head or hat, if you will. It signifies your sincerity in requesting an audience. And it signals that you're asking the host country's representative's permission to speak. Maybe it's true the rumors I've heard that you are the bringer of unusual tidings and talents to the likes of me and my kind, but please show some class and courtesy in doing so. You need to understand that you yanks are not exactly the flavor of the month around these parts."

"Well, at least I got one out of four right," I managed to mumble in a subdued voice. "You can now at least talk, and you also now have the power to pass that ability along to your family and any of your associates. And if I may, I would ask that you do so with the greatest speed. The more of you that can speak right away, the more likely your ability will be sustained. If you slip and speak to an enemy of this change, you'll likely be cut down and will lose that ability."

Beyond telling him that, I sincerely apologized for my cultural ignorance and apparent rudeness. How was he to know I was really only a dog?

In the meantime, as I was so artfully fulfilling these duties with this particular tree, my other compatriots were busy making contact with a full range of fauna across this section of Eastern China. The only instruction any of us left with these initial contacts was to physically spread the word, especially in the direction of Shanghai or to anyone they knew heading in that direction.

Intuitively, each of us knew the potential success of this first regional venture depended on it. And as the hours passed and we reached the western most edge of our contact zone, we made sure we allowed enough time to make some additional contacts with other beings and trees in the city of Shanghai itself. Certainly, by the end of our nine hour foray, if someone had been keeping score, between the six of us, we made direct contact with hundreds of God's creatures. Relieved and exhausted, at 6 a.m. sharp our formation arrived back at Shanghai harbor, which we circled twice as Ed located the Polar Wind, and we quickly plunged earthward back onto the helicopter deck.

But while we were gone, the most amazing developments had been occurring in and around our ship. It seems as we were flying off to the mainland, Reg appeared alongside the ship and called out to one crew member. He told her to alert the Captain that he should reduce the ship's speed to 3-5 knots and allow it to be maneuvered, as if it were being assisted by harbor tug boats. But, and he was most emphatic about this point, it would not be any boats assisting, rather it would be Reg's associates. In particular, it would be Humpback and Sperm Whales. Other sea life was to form a channel to guide this procession through the blockade of gradually disappearing ships guarding the harbor's entrance. Under no circumstances was the Captain or any of the other crew members to attempt to pilot the ship during this time. They had to remain restrained throughout this transit period as the ship proceeding into the harbor and to our anchorage, where the final rendezvous point would be for the six of us returning at 6 a.m.

Apparently, but it came as no shock to anyone, with the advent of their mighty warships being dissolved, a frantic search was mounted for whoever or whatever was causing this unbelievable process to occur. All waterways were frothing with boats of every description frantically searching for the culprits. There was panic and chaos everywhere.

In response, after the six of us flew off, all lights were doused on board the Polar Wind. And the strictest orders were given for complete silence during this final passage. It was a terribly tense time for all on board. All the while Bernie, Wally and Sophie were crouched half-hidden on the Foredeck, ready to respond to any threat. If any ship, still seaworthy, approached them, Wally was determined to swiftly do a "Polar Wind", as the crew came to call it, and vanish it into the Eighth Sea, wherever in the cosmos that might be. Fortunately, for the crew and passengers of the Polar Wind, and those aboard any other vessel that night, his staff was not needed. The fish and mammals created diversions when suspicions were aroused, while others of their kind stealth fully maneuvered the blackened ship to its mooring in the Port of Shanghai.

Once the six of us arrived back on the helicopter deck, Wally did a quick retransformation, while Bernie grabbed and led me over to where a particular zodiac boat was being prepared to launch. But, here again, Reg had intervened, and he insisted that no one was to use the zodiac's engine. Instead, some of his band would power and guide us to a secluded docking area. And sure enough, by 8 a.m. Po, Frank, Bernie, Wally and I had landed safely on

Chinese soil. Previous to this, I had only been on Chinese tree limbs, doing my late night and early morning conversions.

It was apparent to me, once there was full daylight, that all my associates had been given a minor face lift by Wally. They all resembled anyone we might pass on the streets. Likewise, each of us had been given the pounding staff treatment by Wally and could speak fluent Chinese. Despite my grave misgivings, it was beginning to appear like this ruse might work. But, let me be perfectly honest at this point, I saw absolutely no reason why I was being dragged along. I even growled for the first time in years when Bernie first tugged at that leash. She scolded me in a variety of languages at that point, and I knew it would be best if I played along with this. I could see myself joining others at the Eighth Sea reunion, if I pushed my luck too far with Bernie and Wally.

Soon after reaching shore, Po did locate an idle taxi and convinced its driver, essentially by giving him a sizable amount of Yuan, to relinquish the vehicle for a couple of hours, with a promise we'd return it undamaged at that time. His police uniform gave the request the aura of authority and official business, and the money gave the driver the necessary incentive to comply. Within minutes of our landing, we were being driven through the streets of Shanghai by Frank.

However, and this was the trickiest part of the plan, no one, not Bernie, Po or Wally knew exactly where this all-important meeting was being held. All that Bernie was told by Walt was that something would be emitting a signal or force of some kind and that would lead Wally to their final destination, the place where all the regional leaders, scoundrels, warlords and bullies would be meeting. And to everyone's surprise, Wally's most of all, it was just after Frank drove off with the taxi that his staff began to tremble. Instantaneously, both Bernie and Wally knew it was to be their compass.

Over the next hour we weaved in and out of the loud and overly congested streets of Shanghai. Wally's staff would increase or decrease its vibrations as we twisted and turned. And by the time we finally stopped, it was actually pounding up and down on the floorboard of the taxi. It was clear to everyone, even me, that we'd arrived at the meeting place. It was a huge, ornate, bluestone building, partially hidden by a high red brick wall. Its main entrance was heavily guarded by both armed troops and large military vehicles. We had to find another entranceway into the grounds and building.

Frank suggested he drive around the nearly square mile compound to see if there was another entrance. Fortunately, on the opposite side to the front entrance, there was a less intensely guarded service entrance. It had an equally large portal, framed within a five-foot, thick wall. Two immense metal doors were used to seal it, but at the moment of our arrival one of them was open. Two armed soldiers stood on either side of the opening. And as luck would have it, they were busy lighting cigarettes when we drove past, not taking any notice of us when we did.

Noting that, Frank quickly turned up a side street and parked the cab. Po, picking up the cue, announced that all of us needed to get out and make our way over to the service entrance, which we did with surprising speed. He then added, as we got much closer to the rear entrance, as if being prompted by Walt, "Wally, you'll need to help these two fellows at the doorway become unaware of our presence, as we walk through it."

"Sure thing, Po," Wally cheerfully acknowledged. And in a deft move, he quickly moved his wand upward, while we walked briskly along the fortress-like high brick wall. Each guard was positioned about four paces in front of the wall, on either side of the entranceway. This allowed us to slip past them as they were now transformed, ever-so-slightly, to hear or sense nothing other than what was occurring immediately in front of them. They were presently experiencing a form of tunnel awareness and cognition, which as I thought about it, was not unlike what so many of our own elected, government officials seemed to exclusively govern by, once they were in office. Anyway, for these two guards, it was a spell that Wally hoped and expected would last at least an hour, but there were no guarantees. However, he failed to tell anyone of that possible complication.

Slipping inside the compound, Wally now took the lead, holding both his staff in one hand and the wand in the other. It was all such a contrast. Around me was this immense structure, with huge forbidding walls surrounding it. Iron doors barred any uninvited entrance to all but a relative few, determined individuals, obsessed with their intentions to crush, conquer and oppress as much of the world as possible. And before me stood this very small, stuttering and nervous little boy, along with his not-much taller sister to guide him. They, alone, could block the evil obsessions present in this auditorium.

How remarkable, I thought, that I was to accompany them there and elsewhere during this voyage. Probably even more remarkable, I concluded, was if we actually survived it all. And now look at me, I even got to eventually record these events. I digress again...

But it was just as I was having these thoughts that Bernie knelt down and unhooked the leash from my collar and quietly said, "Ok, Greg, now it's time for you and for me to take center stage. I'll give you the cue when you're to address the audience."

"But...," I stammered.

"Don't worry," she interrupted me. "You'll be prepared to speak, even though you don't realize it at this moment. Walt's last words were that you were to join me on the speaker's platform for each of these five groups that we address. You'll know what to say when the time comes. Just follow me." Then she patted me on the head and walked forward to be with Wally.

The small doorway into the hall was unguarded, and it opened onto the back of the stage. Remarkably, there were no guards, dignitaries or stagehands in sight. It was as if all the security was in and around the perimeter of this building. Only those with the proper credentials and invitations were allowed inside.

Wally led us to the side of the stage, which had a thirty-foot high, richly colored, burgundy curtain as the backdrop. In front of it was a raised dais, with a lectern and small table on it. Behind the table were two arm chairs, and on the table were neatly arranged piles of papers and notebooks. There were microphones on both the lectern and on the table, allowing a speaker to address the audience, either standing at the podium or sitting at the table; or, in my case, as it later turned out, by standing or sitting on the table.

Also, and by far the most disturbing, resting on that same table was a three-foot high, solid black, obsidian vase. The base was a good six inches in diameter, and it maintained its girth a good two-thirds its height. It then tapered gradually to a two-inch diameter neck. There did not appear to be any opening at its top. I did not see a cap, cork or lid to remove to open it. It appeared completely seamless and permanently sealed to me. And there was no inscription, lettering or markings of any kind on its surface. It was ominously blank and commanded the attention of everyone in that cavernous room.

It was as I was observing it that Wally turned to me and whispered, "That's it, Mr. Greg. That's what made my big cane jiggle and jump up and down. And you need to tell Po to take it with us back to the ship when we leave here."

After I turned and relayed Wally's instructions to Po, Bernie shushed me immediately thereafter. Turning back, I now saw an individual take his seat in one of the armchairs. Probably I should add at this point that the nearly two hundred people in the audience were standing. There were no chairs. The only furniture in that huge hall was tables scattered around its perimeter. And they were overflowing with exotic dishes of food and all sizes and kinds of beverages, along with plates, glasses, napkins, and various flat wares. It was 9 a.m. when the seated speaker started his introductions.

"Ladies and gentlemen," he began. "I realize all of us here are seriously concerned about what is presently happening to our various navies, both to ships in port and to those on the high seas. And I plan to address what is being done to combat this development at the end of my portion of this meeting. Likewise, I will speak to the issue of the outrageous reports that we are getting from some areas of North America about there being talking wildlife. It's all too preposterous to take seriously, even for a moment. But, anyway, I will address that matter as well. Obviously, it is some capitalist plot to delay our final and fully, operational plans, which will be implemented within the next few weeks.

"And it's that plan that I want to discuss with you now. After my review, we will need to hear your input and then get your consent to initiate it. All five of the nations represented here will participate in the mightiest show of force on land, sea and in the air that the world has ever witnessed. We will ultimately divide the world in half. All of Asia, Europe and Africa from one half of the Arctic

Circle to the tip of Africa and Tasmania will become part of our empire.

"Not included in this conquest will be Great Britain and Ireland, due to their being separated by the English Channel. Also excluded will be Iceland, Greenland, and the entire continent of North, Middle and South America, the other half of the Arctic Circle and Antarctica. But all the resources and nearly all the land between the eastern half of the Atlantic Ocean, west of the International Date Line, all of the Indian Ocean and Southern Ocean will be ours."

At that point a deafening roar of approval and appreciation erupted from the standing audience. Clapping, shouting, patting each other, shaking hands and hugging followed for the next two, uninterrupted minutes.

After the crowd began to quite down, the speaker, who I was later to assume was of Chinese descent, stood and stepped over to the podium to resume his speech. "And now, I'd like to address…"

But, that was when all humanity began to experience, step by step, Walt's persuasive powers, as now so gently exercised by Wally. Bernie, at that moment, motioned each of us to come forward onto the open stage. Po was to remove the vase and the speaker, while Wally performed some needed transformations. After which, Bernie and I were to address the audience. After first lifting me up onto the table top, she went directly to the podium. Frank helped with resetting the chairs and microphone heights.

A loud, cry-like gasp went up from the audience as we stepped forward into full view. Actually, that was the only objection heard that morning, because Wally tapped his staff one time, while simultaneously waving his wand, and pronounced loudly, "Yorkshire pudding". And as I stood completely transfixed on that table, staring out over the audience of startled people, they immediately transformed into an assortment of docile farm animals, distinctly divided according to their previous nationality. Anyone from Russia was now a horse, from China a beef cow, from North Korea a dairy cow, from Vietnam a sheep and from Burma a goat. And yet, each could understand what Bernie and I were about to say. And she spoke first.

"All your thoughts, plans, schemes and obsessing about conquest or territorial occupation have ended as of this moment," Bernie said in a voice, rich far beyond her years, to an audience of paralyzed animals. "To paraphrase the words of an old song, 'practicing war' is now, henceforth and forever, banned. Any thoughts or plans for such will insure that you will permanently be retransformed, as will anyone else not in this room who does, into your present state. Furthermore, your weapons of conquest are now in the process of being neutralized or eliminated.

"Briefly, let me outline a little history with you. For you gathered here that feel a strong sense of nationalism, I will first address you. The nationalism that each of your countries embrace originally arose in response to either or all of the following forms of colonialism: military, economic, cultural or religious. Historically, military colonialism resulted from conquests by invading empires or emerging nation states, e.g. Persian, Egyptian, Roman, Greek, Mongolian, and European. Economic colonialism was derived from unpredictable, and often devastating, influences by vastly richer countries or by certain powers through their surrogates. This process has evolved up to the present day, whereby corporations and government backed entities enjoying unfettered globalization of the market place. Cultural colonialism developed due to unwanted or undesirable social customs, trends and fashions that offended a more conservation peoples' ideals and mores. And last, but certainly not the least damaging, religious colonialism has occurred from conquests by particular religious bodies over cultures in the Middle East, Europe and Central and South America.

"Following these historically invasive developments over a people, the full development of nationalism was facilitated by some or most of the following conditions. It usually required there be a common language within the offended region, more often than not a common religion, and a populace with a common set of values.

"For communism, on the other hand, which again is or was a major influence in governing most of the countries represented here today, it originally was conceived in response to reverse the excesses of the Industrial Revolution. During this period a given society's capital was being centralized. As a result, a relative few individuals or groups were being rewarded with vast riches and status, while urban factory workers often lived in extreme poverty.

"Communism then was facilitated by the appearance of the state or a national authority becoming a willing partner in this disparity of income and social status.

"However, nationalism and communism, both of which represent the two major forms of government authority found in this hall at this moment, became a threat to all life when five conditions arose soon after they each appeared: a leader gained absolute authority; the system sought to destroy the unique fabric of its own and that of other societies and cultures; it restricted ideas and basic freedoms; it centralized power; and it used force on its citizenry and on others outside its immediate boundaries to an almost unparalleled degree in human history.

"Next, I need to advise you of two remaining issues. The first is that I and my companions mean none of you any harm, despite what you have schemed and hoped to accomplish after you left here today. On the contrary, we are here to help you and the citizens of your countries achieve a lasting peace. The other issue is that the black vase that was placed on this table harbors enough malevolent power to extinguish all life that exists on this world. It, along with any others we may find in the weeks ahead, must be collected and, somehow, neutralized. Quite honestly, we don't know anything about them, other than who they originated from. Even our efforts here today, and elsewhere, may come to nothing if we don't find a way to unlock and interpret their secrets. And if we cannot, even the prospect of your possibly remaining in your present condition pales in comparison to the horror that would await you and all of us on this planet, should these vases become activated.

"In conclusion, I want to now introduce you to one of our group's members. He will talk to you about your new responsibilities. Following his remarks, you will then become human beings again."

And at that moment Bernie turned to me and nodded for me to approach my microphone and begin. I came forward and stood a few inches from it, not knowing what to say. As I looked out over the room full of farm animals, I couldn't help but feel a little less intimidated than I would have otherwise felt, if it had been overflowing with generals, admirals and politicians.

Probably before what followed next, as reconstructed from what everyone at Willa's later told me, I need to back up a moment. There were a few noteworthy conditions or limitations associated with Wally's transformations of this audience. The most remarkable was that none of those gathered there were able to move their feet. He didn't want a stampede to ensue. Another aspect of his spell was that they were all mute. He decided he didn't want a lot of mooing, snorting, whinnying, baaing and such. It was important to him that they would be able to concentrate on what they were being told. And the other condition they still possessed, as mentioned before, was that they could hear and understand perfectly all that Bernie and I said to them.

And wouldn't you know, I only vividly remember saying one thing before I was overcome by a strange and overpowering sensation, like every pore of my hairy body was having pure oxygen infused into it. I felt as if I was being swept away by a power that extended throughout my being and was restructured by it. I thought I was going to be reconstituted, like a butterfly must feel just before it emerges from its chrysalis. Believe me, I certainly don't want to overdraw this event, but it reoccurred repeatedly each time I arose at Bernie or Wally's command to address those four other regional audiences. However, before this internal redefinition and rearranging of my cellular self occurred, I leaned forward and said in my most pronounced New Jersey accent, "I trust everyone here by now has met one another. If not, please make it a point to do so, before today's meeting in adjourned…"

Then, what followed shocked everyone in our little band and the entire assembly of livestock standing before me. In a voice that filled that gigantic hall, like claps of ear-splitting thunder, I began a declaration, which was unrehearsed, unfamiliar and, up to that moment, unknown to me.

"Each of you standing here at this moment and for the duration of your remaining, earthly existence will henceforth follow the path of a lawful and orderly transition. That transition will take place in yourselves, in your citizenry and

162

throughout your respective nations. You will, in short, FETCH! And by doing so, you will establish and enhance freedom, justice, civil discourse and representative governments wherever you go.

"Following this meeting, as you leave this hall, there will be a most unusual, scroll-like device laid out on tables at each exit. The scroll you choose up will become permanently embedded to you alone, once you pick it up. It will be non-transferable. And it will be unlike anything you ever saw or possessed before. Each has the ability to display new directives, to have previous messages supplemented and to enlarge upon what I say here today, as our party continues our trek across the planet, visiting other troubled areas. You will see additional directives become inscribed on it as time passes, and you are to follow each new item to the letter. I warn you to do this because this device has the power and ability to know what you are and are not doing to bring about these changes. But as I just said, each scroll will be specifically tailored for each of you individually, once you handle it. And anyone who tries to leave without one, will immediately and permanently become the creature you are now. Trust me when I tell you this. Furthermore, you cannot discard, destroy or deny their place in your lives, for the rest of your lives. Additionally, they will automatically transfer their power and permanent identification to whomever takes your place in the orderly evolution of your governments, countries and cultures.

Today, you will be told the meaning of 'F', the first letter of 'FETCH!' The other letters' meanings will subsequently appear to assist and guide you in the work you have ahead of you. In other words, no one in this place and at this time is to be harmed or forever transformed into your present state, unless or until you do not follow the commandments you are to begin receiving today. You will test the truth of my message at your peril, of that you can be absolutely sure.

"But before I give you the first letter's directive, I must share with you a final observation. All monuments, memorials, buildings, structures, statues, autobiographies, individual accomplishments or triumphs that you or someone else erects to celebrate your presence in this world are transient and fleeting. Any legacy, memorial or imprint you hope to leave to this world can only be eternal and everlasting, if it is selfless and essentially anonymous. Fame, personal recognition and glory will, over enough time, diminish and disappear altogether. Each of us is destined to be forgotten in the long and ever-patient, course of history.

"The only timeless gift or course any of us, anywhere, can give or take is to insure that all life in and on this world will not perish by each of us selflessly pursuing the straightforward, yet dauntingly challenging pathway, defined by the letters in FETCH! And for you here today that first commandment is: 'follow the path that leads to humility, goodness and laughter'".

Upon announcing all this, I felt the surge of energy leave me, and I backed away from the microphone. Bernie then approached the lectern microphone and announced to everyone that they would soon resume their previous appearance and be able to function normally. Further, she noted there would likely be those who would test what she and I had just told them. And when and if they did so, they would experience a permanent and final retransformation. Likewise, she informed them to expect other remarkable changes as they embarked on their new mission this day. As she said this, she looked at me and winked. The work of Flo, Jennifer, Rita, Ed, Iris and I would soon become apparent to all these dignitaries. Today will be one they could all tell their grandkids about, if they weren't in some livestock pen or munching on mixed grains and pasture grass somewhere.

TWELVE: KARACHI, PAKISTAN

Our departure from the stage in Shanghai was brisk, to say the least. No sooner had Bernie finished her last words, than we all fled behind the curtains. Wally had incorporated a time delay in the reappearance of the human forms, emerging from the audience of livestock. But I can just image the horror they all felt as they watched us disappear and still could not move, signal in some way or object to our leaving so abruptly without tending to them. For the next ten minutes they were to be transfixed, then as quickly as they became various animals, they were to become humans again. At that point a sense of panic no doubt took over, and they would try to make a mad dash through the doorways. But, here again, Walt and Wally's powers took center stage. No one exited that room without first picking up their personalized scroll. It was at that moment all the reality of what they'd been told by Bernie and myself would come spiraling down and around each of them. The process of Fetching would then begin.

For the five of us exiting the building, our

first obstacle was the two guards at the perimeter's Service Entrance. Wally's spell had worn off, and these two were not feeling like being nice by the time we returned. As we dashed out, with Po leading the charge, and me in the rear, the guards, angry as disturbed hornets, spun around just as Po clothes lined them. Certainly, their last conscious thoughts that morning must have been sheer confusion that a nearly seven foot, Chinese-dressed policeman would approach them in such a manner. Between being transfixed by Wally and run over by Po, it had been a poor beginning to their work week thus far.

Getting back to our borrowed taxi, Frank directed all of us inside it and drove like he'd been wedded to the streets of Shanghai for years. Twisting, screeching, dodging the snarled traffic, he was back to the owner of our cab at dockside in less than ten minutes, just before the first attendees exited their meeting room with scrolls in hand. Again, we ran down to the dock, where the zodiac was parked and immediately were racing through the harbor to the Polar Wind. By now it was 10:30 a.m. and the Port of Shanghai was in high gear. Boats, large and small, were zigzagging throughout the harbor. Interspersed were literally hundreds of Chinese junks of all sizes. But our passage went entirely unnoticed.

Once safely aboard the Polar Wind, arrangements had already been worked out that Reg's cohorts were to maneuver us out of port and into the open waters of the ocean. You couldn't help but notice we were leaving an atmosphere of turmoil due to the sudden disappearance of anchored warships and the continued appearance of those limping into port before they disappeared altogether. We were exiting a region, in the beginning stages of a great transformation. I say this because about the time we sailed from the outer perimeter of the port, the first seabirds were about to begin their discussions with various port authority personnel about some issues involving their roosting rights. And dogs, kept kenneled in high rise condominium apartments, citywide, were going to begin raising the issue of more regular early morning walks to their handlers, not to mention the whole issue of ownership and new canine citizenship rights, which was going to also have to be settled eventually. Welcome to "The New World of Equal Conversation Rights for All", Shanghai!! I had to smile as we left the confines of its harbor.

By the time we were beyond the territorial waters of China, Capt. Shriver put the Polar Wind in high gear and made a direct heading for one of the uninhabited Ryukyu Islands.

We arrived at a small, sheltered cove around 8:30 p.m. that same day, at which time the Captain had arranged for the entire ship's crew and the Wagoners to meet in the Auditorium for a full debriefing on what had occurred before, during and after our leaving Shanghai. There was no time to share that discussion while we were making our escape. Plus, the crew, and most of the rest of us on Bernie and Wally's team, needed to know what happens next. What's our next destination? And how do we manage to get there with over half the planet looking for us?

Capt. Shriver called the meeting to order and immediately turned it over to Bernie, who I might add, spoke and behaved like a seasoned veteran. She recapped what had occurred since our leaving Guam, what took place after those of us left the Polar Wind for downtown Shanghai, and what was said and done at that first regional meeting. Her final remarks involved letting us know that we were heading to Karachi, Pakistan, our second regional destination, and that we needed to arrive there in no more than fourteen days, but that danger would stalk us constantly all the way. She concluded with saying that sometime in the next six to eight days there would have to be another gathering of vast amounts of wildlife on or nearby our ship, but she didn't go into any further detail.

Once she concluded her remarks, the Captain then informed all of us that we would have to navigate close by any available shorelines whenever possible, sailing mostly at night, while always having Wally on hand near the Radio Room in case someone challenges us in a language the individuals on duty at the time didn't understand. It was important we appeared to be locals to anyone searching for us, as we were making our way, supposedly taking tourists to our destination in Antarctica. In that regard, during any daytime travel, some of us had to dress in bathing suits and appear to be sunbathing or playing shuffle board for anyone flying overhead. And when that charade became too obvious, we'd have to stop somewhere and change the ship's appearance, as well as its broadcasted mission.

It should be noted that the eleven of us in the Wagoners were emotionally exhausted by the end of this meeting. I felt particularly sorry for Bernie and Wally. In hopes that Wally would not be needed for a while, it was arranged that both of them could sleep and have meals brought to their cabin for the next two or three days. But for any daytime sailing, or if any reports of approaching aircraft were broadcasted over the intercom, all animals and birds on board the ship had to find instant cover. No prying eyes should ever see us on this ship.

Following the meeting, at about 2300 hours, the ship was set on a southerly course, traveling mostly at night, from our nameless cove in the Ryukyu Islands, north of Okinawa, down the East China Sea, and along the east coast of Taiwan. From there we entered the South China Sea, into the Luzon Strait, and through the Bataan Islands. We briefly sighted Laoag, Philippines, and sailed along the western coastline of the Philippines to Brunei and Sarawak.

It was in this region, five days after leaving Shanghai, when we had our first physical encounter with hostile forces. Up to that time there had been numerous radio challenges from other ships, planes and shoreline installations. But Wally's ability, which enabled the Radio Room personnel to respond immediately in the challenging dialect, diverted any further investigations. But that was not the case as we entered the waters near Sarawak.

On this particular day, we were traveling during daylight. The Captain believed that our present location was safe enough to begin some daytime travel. To do so would allow us to sail faster and make up some lost time. It was at noon that day when we were approached by three speed boats, each carrying five or six men armed with an assortment of heavy weapons. They obviously meant to pirate us, thinking ours was a tourist ship, as we had so-steadily broadcasted that it was to any curious inquires. As they zipped around us, someone yelled over a megaphone for us to come to a complete stop or they would begin firing their guns at the Bridge. The Captain had no choice at that moment but to comply. He brought the ship to a standstill.

In the meantime, I decided the only thing I could do was to run over to my spot at the stern of the ship and plop down with my paws hanging over the side. And as he had previously promised, up popped Reg.

"We have a problem, Reg," I announced as quietly as I could, without attracting the attention of these determined bandits, or worse.

"What's up?" Reg asked, looking around. "I see your ship is stopped. Has something mechanically gone wrong?"

"No," I answered. "But there are three boatloads of badly dressed individuals, who apparently intend to do us great harm, unless we follow their instructions. They have ordered us to stop our engines or they will begin shooting. Can you help us?"

"I believe I, along with some of my associates, certainly can," he replied, with what I swear looked, all-the-world, like a smile. "You might want to watch this, Greg."

As one of the terrorizing boats, brimming with terrorists, approached us, maybe about fifty yards or so from where I was lying, each of the six individuals on board pointing various weapons at us. And it was at that moment Reg and about seven of his larger friends rose out of the water, which up until that point had been absolutely calm.

"Having a nice day, out robbing innocent victims?" Reg asked as about a third of him rose out of the water at the bow of their skiff. "Have you done a lot of this kind of work?" he went on to ask, without waiting for a reply to his first question.

And, of course, you had to see the sudden jerking of these six heads to appreciate the drama that followed. I'm certain their first instinct, which most likely for people like these is their only one, was to pull the trigger on some weapon that kills. And, sure enough, they began firing. But Reg and his band had anticipated this, having had centuries of experience with whalers and poachers. So, without waiting for their verbal reply, as unintelligent and uninformed as it would have been, these very, very large fish and mammals upended each of the three boats, causing the men on board to tip backwards away from the Polar Wind. In that way, any shots fired sprayed harmlessly into the air.

For a while I believe there must have been an underwater game of tag going on around us, but soon it became quiet and Reg again rose up alongside me.

"That should do it." he announced, but not with any glee in his voice. "We let some of these marauders swim off. We felt that they had probably learned a valuable lesson from us. The others? Well..., they weren't so fortunate. It seems they had plundered and attacked more than just ships like yours. A few in our group recognized them as being involved in past acts of senseless violence against our kind. Today, some balance occurred in the give and take of life."

"We certainly want to thank you for your help," Bernie yelled out, as she ran towards the ship's railing. "You and your friends no doubt saved both our lives and those of countless others the world over. These raiders probably would have doomed our mission from here on. Thank you kind sir."

And soon thereafter, many others of the crew came forward to express their own gratitude. It was a time of great relief and thanksgiving. And before Reg disappeared, he and I had one last, brief conversation. I informed him of our plans after today, at least the best I knew about them. I, for one, didn't want him or his mates straying too far from us here on out.

However, already there was a dramatic change in our future on the horizon, following Reg's orchestrated rescue. It seemed that one of those speed boats had a radio on board and/or one of the survivors that made it all the way to shore was able to contact certain government authorities in the area. As a result, a more intensive search was launched to locate us. Little specific information was apparently relayed to these agencies, but because the spared pirate mentioned large, talking fish and a rather stumpy cruise ship, it created a region-wide heightened interest and narrowed the suspect list of possible Shanghai culprits.

It was Wally who, remarkably, first became aware of this development. Not coming as too great a surprise to me, I found out later that as he matures, he is blessed with multiple senses that are far superior and totally foreign to critters like me. For one, he could sense approaching danger, regardless of its origin or how far the distance. And soon after we had our encounter with the pirates, he ran to the Bridge, passing by Bernie as she was coming down the stairwell to where I was having my conversation with Reg.

Once inside the Bridge, Wally asked to speak with Capt. Shriver. Wanting to convey the urgency of his barging into this area, he quickly gave the Captain an unvarnished and disturbing forecast of what was ahead unless he got the ship to immediate safety. Upon hearing what Wally had to say, the Captain immediately revised our present heading and made a full-steam-ahead dash to a nearby shelter, surrounded by mangrove trees. Hurriedly, the crew, and any of us Wagoners that could, was ordered to cut limbs and branches to cover the top and exposed bow of the ship, which at that point was facing the open water.

And for the next two days and nights, there were boson chairs slung over the sides of our ship and scaffolding built along the Top Deck, allowing most of us to paint the ship's hull pure white and others to paint large red crosses on top of the helicopter pad and on both sides of the white superstructure, where the Bridge was and where all of us slept. After that was completed, the Captain issued the thirty white hospital uniforms to various crew members and instructed them they were to be their dress of the day until we reached Karachi and possibly beyond. Selected ones of them were to always be out on the Top Deck or the helicopter pad whenever an inquisitive plane or ship was in our vicinity.

Our announced mission, which was now broadcasted from the Radio Room, was emergency relief to disaster victims in any area we were in at the time of a disaster. Interestingly, that same mission was later adopted globally, by any nation that could convert some of their merchant ships to rescue and hospital ships. It's funny what occurs when nations no longer practice preparing for or engaging in war. For once, in the entire history of so-called intelligent life on this planet, beings were now entering a phase of helping and healing, not hounding and hurting one another. This was to be one of Walt's gifts to each of us.

But the Captain did not want to expend all our camouflaging efforts in unnecessarily exposed sailing, so he elected to have us sail only by night as we maneuvered across the sea to the islands south of Singapore, up the Strait of Malacca and north of Banda Aceh, Indonesia. By the time we were near Banda Aceh, we had only three days left to reach Karachi. Because of this narrow timeline, the decision was made to race full steam ahead, day and night across the open water of the Indian Ocean south of Sri Lanka and up the India coastline to the port of Karachi.

But, one more detail had to be attended to before we departed for the Indian Ocean's dangerously exposed waters. Bernie was the maestro again for another gathering of wildlife. It all started when she called Rita, Ed, and Iris together for a meeting the day before we reached Banda Aceh. It was not a meeting that the rest of us on the ship were privy to. And the details of it are still fuzzy to me, but as best as I can reconstruct it, here's what was planned.

Apparently, Bernie requested that Rita, Ed and Iris were to each fly off in various directions, making contact with all species of birdlife, e.g. saltwater, freshwater and inland birds. And they, in turn, were to make direct contact with as many birds as they could, obviously passing on the ability to communicate to each of them. All transformed birds were to continue making further contacts with their families and associates. The particular message that had to be passed along to them, as well as the ability to now speak, was that all these birds were to find and roost on or about our ship outside Banda Aceh, one day from then.

On the following day, at 6:00 o'clock sharp, Bernie came to the stern of our ship and called out. It was like in the Shanghai meeting hall, her voice was so forceful and commanding. It carried across all the desolate countryside, now so brilliantly transformed by those birds. "ARE YOU READY

TO MAKE SOME CHANGES...???!!" she called out.

"YEAH !!! YEAH !!! YEAH !!!", over and over came the reply, each time their voices were louder and richer.

"That being the case, my brother here will now perform a further transformation within each of you. Following his doing so, you are to fly as far as you can, beyond any limits you've previously traveled, and as you do so, continuously search for any warplanes. When you have found one, swoop down and land briefly anywhere on it. After doing so, fly on to the next one you find. Cover as much of an area as you are capable of doing, crisscrossing it a number of times. As you do this, also make physical contact with as many of your fellow brothers and sisters, who did not have the opportunity to be here today. You will pass this transformation along to them. It's vital that this process extend everywhere."

After she said this, little Wally came to attention and adjusted his staff. Now it was his turn. He boldly and purposefully banged it on the helicopter deck two times and called out in a voice that echoed, as well, across the ship's deck, up its rigging, over the water, and up the surrounding bird-covered hillsides.

"PRUNE JUICE !!!"

And, again, as with the transformation of the ocean's creatures, a visible aura swept forth from Wally up to Ed, sitting on the uppermost mast, and then it extended outward, enveloping the entire ship's exposed surface, the surrounding water and ultimately all the land facing us.

There followed a kind of chill throughout the assembled throng of millions. Birds were ruffling their feathers, shuddering and stomping their feet. It was like they were preening themselves, in preparation for a lengthy journey. At that moment, if they had come equipped with seat belts, I imaged they would be cinching them, as well, in preparation for lift off.

Then, with one giant sucking sound, the stationary millions launched themselves skyward. It blotted out the early morning sunrise, creating a false nightfall. And within moments the sky and ship were clear of any birdlife, aside from Rita and Iris standing beside me. Ed had apparently left, as well, along with all the others flying off in every direction scribed on a compass. Later we found out that Bernie had assigned him to search out any aircraft on patrol in our area. There was no way he could make contact with them, but he could identify where they would eventually land.

It was at that point that warplanes, when on the ground anywhere, were set upon by solitary or groups of birds. Following their contact with one plane, the flocks moved on to ones nearby or further off. And within seconds of that stopover, if anyone happened to be in the cockpit at the time, he or she would have noticed that the dashboard instruments and dials were beginning to appear as if they were melting, which, in fact, they were. After that, the wind screen and hand and foot controls began to disappear, followed by the entire cockpit and tail section and wings. The process continued until all that remained was a small midsection of the fuselage. Within ten to fifteen minutes, depending on the size of the plane, all that remained were the wheels. And no matter what efforts were made to stop this process, within thirty minutes of the first bird's contact on a particular airplane, it was gone forever. Only passenger planes were left untouched, with possibly a few exceptions. This was primarily due to some overly exuberant feathered troops who felt all future possibilities of flight should belong exclusively to them. For some, particularly so-called "game birds", it was, likewise, pay-back time.

It was only minutes after their mass departure that the Captain, standing in the hanger's doorway, was given the nod by Bernie to resume the ship's voyage. From there on, it would be day and night sailing. The hope, and eventual outcome, was that no flights of hostile intent were observed on the ship's radar or by way of any radio transmissions. The threat of planes stopping our journey was almost over. Certainly, there were other means of ending it and of creating unimaginable destruction in the hands of evil doers. But, by this point in our voyage, they weren't ones that sailed or were piloted.

And as hoped by all of us, come February 25th, we were within one hundred miles of the Port of Karachi. Everyone was a little less tense, knowing we'd crossed the open waters behind us.

It was then, as was the case prior to our arrival in Shanghai, that Bernie and Wally called Jennifer, Rita, Flo, Ed, Iris and myself topside.

Again, we were transformed and instructed to make contact with animals, fish, birds and trees throughout the region, as we had done in eastern China. Specifically, Ed was transformed into a Eastern Imperial Eagle. He insisted on this, feeling that his usual appearance made him too conspicuous, as did Iris and Rita. In fact, each of us opted to become local birds. It heightened the sense of adventure and made us feel we were more than just passing tourists.

Anyway, as mentioned, Ed became a most magnificent specimen. He had a pair of large, white markings on his back, separated by rich, dark brown feathers, which extended over the rest of his body. The crown of his head was tan, with that same coloration sweeping down to his shoulders. His eyes, of course, had the same intense look of determination. He looked regal and commanding. But, being Ed, he just winked at me. Emperors clothing didn't change that guy. He was a rare one, untouched by flattery or ogling crowds.

Iris became a local, Dalmation Pelican, the largest bird of its kind anywhere on the planet. She now sported a ten foot wing span. She and Ed strutted around the helicopter pad, pretending to give us the brush-off, while Rita, Jennifer and I underwent our Wally-generated changes.

Rita, not aware what was to be her fate, noticed Bernie whisper something to Wally. To her shocking surprise, she immediately thereafter became a Mute Swan. She now was an elegant ivory bird, with sharp black markings around both eyes that tapered down to her sharp beak. But, initially, she couldn't make any sound or speak. I had to chuckle; Rita speechless. To coin an often used bird expression, "it was a hoot!" seeing her in that condition. That was, until Iris reached over and gave her a peck. Then the old Rita was back again.

"You wait, Greg", she snorted. "I'm going to request Wally convert you into an emu."

But before I could reply, Jennifer became an Asia Paradise Flycatcher, Flo a Bohemian Waxwing and I took on the appearance of a Greater Hoopoe Lark. Wally probably heard Rita, but decided Emus don't fly too well, or at all. And even he couldn't reverse that state of things. Besides, Bernie and he needed me and everyone else in our troop, airborne right away.

Soon realizing the seriousness of our mission, we all flew off after Bernie updated us with last minute instructions to return to the Polar Wind by 6 a.m. tomorrow. She noted that our ship would be docked in the Port of Karachi by then.

From what I learned later, entering their harbor did not have the threat that Shanghai's had. And, of course, our ship now had a quite different exterior, one that passing commercial ships infrequently acknowledged. But that was not the case once Captain Shriver docked.

In addition, the assigned task Bernie gave Reg and his cohorts to clear the oceans and waterways of threatening vessels had been quite successful. That left the possibility of deadly air traffic to worry about. But by the time the Polar Wind was moored, there were essentially only commercial aircraft left in flying condition in that region.

Don't get me wrong. Those that meant to do great harm soon figured out that any aircraft left exposed on runways were destined to become tarmac dust. To prevent that from happening, they began hiding them in secluded locations until the time for their flights to lift off. However, you've got to give our birdlife associates credit. They just waited patiently nearby, quietly passing time until the warplanes began to make their exit. The fact remained: no matter how fast any aircraft could take off and fly, there still were those brief moments when it exited its sheltered confines that it moved slowly. That was all it took: a gentle peck here; a feather-like touch there. A momentary landing or contact by a diving bird's wing tip and the disappearing process began.

And, of course, this all just made the madmen of the world that much more crazed. Their deadly toys were dissolving. BUT, they still had in reserve one very big and deadly one left, along with all the smaller, up-close and personal ones. Nothing that Bernie and Wally had orchestrated to this point had any effect on the rockets, and their launchers, scattered everywhere. And most were mobile or hidden away in bunkers. The only drawback for their use was that no one knew who or where to direct them. Word quickly spread that everyone, everywhere, was experiencing this phenomena. Everyone that is, except for a few so-called allied forces. But their officials were denying they had anything to do with any of this. And they even noted that some of their ships and airplanes had experienced the same fate, which, in fact, they had. It was something Bernie had decided to implement, anticipating the possible threat to them that would result, if they appear spared.

All that said, it was important for each of us on board the Polar Wind to understand that very lethal instruments of destruction and death were still left in the hands of the most crazed and delusional amongst the planet's life forms. And we were about to reenter one of their lairs.

By 4:30 p.m., as the six of us flew inland and began our transformations, the Polar Wind was brought alongside a quiet, freight loading/ unloading pier, with its huge, poised, overhead cranes looming high above our ship. The dock area initially was bare of shipping containers, or any personnel, when our ship anchored. And Bernie didn't anticipate our being there more than sixteen-seventeen hours at the most. Located at the westernmost moorage in the port, it seemed a perfect location for a quick exit once our business was completed there.

Two developments altered that idyllic anchorage. The first was that not more than thirty minutes after docking an official government vehicle was seen driving through the vacant storage area, heading directly for our ship. Inside it were three individuals: the driver, one highly-place Pakistani government officer, and the Pakistani Red Crescent Coordinator for Disaster Relief. While we had thought our ship was passing quietly unnoticed through the intercoastal waterways, shipping lanes and on to our conveniently vacant, dock area, the emergency response officials had been abuzz with relief at our arrival.

Why? Because six hours previously there had been a massive earthquake in the mountains ten miles north of Turbat, Pakistan, northwest of our present position. Our radio room had been experiencing some intermittent breakdowns and had closed down completely for trouble-shooting and repair throughout the last ten hours before our arrival. The crew was still working on it as we docked. We had no idea there had been a natural disaster in the area.

Seeing the car approach the ship was seen as a potentially grave development. How many others knew of our ship's arrival? Stealth was absolutely necessary for Bernie and Wally to accomplish what they had to in the meeting tomorrow. Nothing could alter that. And as the official vehicle pulled alongside the Polar Wind, Capt. Shriver and LCDR Steele, who had been alerted just minutes beforehand, rushed down to the starboard railing.

The car pulled to a sudden stop about twenty feet away from the ship, far enough to allow the two gentlemen who climbed out from the rear seat to easily view the Top Deck without straining their necks. One individual was dressed in a military uniform and the other in a business suit. If Capt. Shriver had been closer, he would have noticed a small Red Crescent emblem in the one individual's jacket lapel.

Seeing the two Polar Wind officers standing on the Top Deck, and with no gangway extended from the ship as of yet, they were not able to ask permission to come aboard. Instead, they would have to conduct their business standing on the dock. Both of the ship's officers stood silently awaiting what might be said. This was not the time to offer greetings or to say something that might provoke further investigation.

"Are either of you this ship's captain?" the gentleman in the military uniform called out.

"Yes. I am," Capt. Shriver yelled down to them.

"Then, good afternoon to you sir", he began. "I need to let you know that our coastal installations have been tracking your vessel for the past five hours. We have been trying, unsuccessfully, to establish radio contact with you. To our repeated attempts, we've had no response from your ship. But because you kept making way to this location, we decided to let you come on, despite not answering our calls. Why didn't you reply?"

For some unexplained reason Capt. Shriver began to feel a little less tense after hearing this. "Our radio has been giving us problems for a few days, and we finally decided we had to shut it down for an overhaul, even while we were still at sea. Unfortunately, we still haven't worked out all the bugs. That's the main reason we had to come here. We hoped to get some needed parts to complete the repairs. And we certainly hope by entering your waterways in this manner we have not offended you."

"Not in the least," the officer replied, to the Captain's not giving an entirely truthful reason for our being in Karachi. "On the contrary, that is why my associate and I have hurried down here to greet you. And certainly, you may enter our city at will to get whatever supplies you need; because, in actual fact, it is you, your staff and your ship that we urgently need to be seaworthy as soon as possible. Let me have my associate explain to you why this is so."

Turning to the man in the business suit, that individual then stepped forward and addressed the two officers. And by now the entire crew, and the remainder of the Wagoners still on board the ship at that moment, were listening intently to what was being said. Over the next five minutes this individual, a high ranking official in the Pakistani Red Crescent, described what was known at that moment about the conditions in and around Turbat, Pakistan. An 8.3 earthquake had struck the area a few hours earlier. Because the Polar Wind, now appearing as a hospital ship, was seen entering their territorial waters, they were eager to enlist it in a massive search and rescue operation. To assist in this effort, he asked that they set sail, as soon as possible, 200 miles further north to Pasni. They were to dock there and begin their rescue flights fifty miles further away into the Turbat area. Their helicopters and crews were desperately needed, as were their medical personnel, which made the Captain wince when he heard that.

They questioned why a ship like ours was sailing in these waters, flying the United States colors. They noted there were few ships left in the region that did. The captain explained that it was part of their orders to simply be "on patrol", to be

186

ready to offer assistance wherever the need arose. Both gentlemen expressed their relief we were there. It was agreed we would depart Karachi no later than noon tomorrow for Port of Pasni.

And let me add that two significant developments soon occurred within the Polar Wind crew following that Pakistani, government car driving off. The first was like an electric charge was sent through the crew. While it's true, each of the crew members had seen unbelievable events associated with Bernie and Wally's transformations. But for all intents and purposes, for them, it was search and rescue missions, saving lives and providing life-saving assistance that inspired and drove these ladies and gentlemen to be the remarkable people that they were. They were heading into a disaster zone. And like all first responders, they were remarkably and wondrously calm and determined to help.

And the second one was to insure that there was a full complement of medical services available on the Polar Wind. To accomplish that, Bernie and Wally offered the Captain their transformation talents. He and the crew quickly agreed this was necessary and allowed Wally to give certain crew members the temporary ability to perform most needed medical procedures, if they were necessary. All total, there were twenty-three crew members who agreed to this. And as a result, by the end of that first day in the Port of Karachi, the Polar Wind now had six surgeons, two anesthesiologists, three internists, and twelve nurses who would accompany the rescue helicopters into the disaster zone. They were to stay there for the next two weeks.

Needless to say, by the time our vanguard of feathered ambassadors arrived back at the Polar Wind at 6 a.m. the next morning, we got an earful. The ship was alive with preparations and activities associated with their upcoming mission in and around Turbat. The atmosphere was electrifying. It was my kind of place. A slow pace is not me. Give me lots of energy and activity. I wanted so bad to start barking, just to let everyone know how supportive I was. But Bernie sensed this and repeatedly stared sternly at me. This was no time for silly, dog antics.

And, as orchestrated by Bernie, by 8 a.m. we were all assembled on deck to go ashore. Capt. Shriver and some of his officers wished us good luck, as did Jennifer, Flo, Rita and Iris. Ed was still making contacts around the area so that no sequestered airplanes would escape detection. He even had to swoop down himself and clip the wing of a plane just starting to taxi down the runway. He noted as he soared off and looked back that the pilot and copilot were throwing open their cockpit canopy and jumping to the ground within seconds of his touching the plane.

The one Wagoner going this time, who had not gone into Shanghai, was Sophie. When I found out, I got so excited. Immediately, I ran over to Bernie and told her because Sophie was going that blasted leash was not going to be needed...Period. I would trail behind Sophie until pigs could fly, which, on second thought given the way Wally was waving that wand of his around lately, might not be too far off.

As luck would have it, once we got beyond the perimeter of the loading dock, there was a cab parked by a large business complex. Po approached its driver and offered him a sizable advance, with the promise of more to come, if we could borrow it for a few hours. That agreed upon, Frank again drove, with Sophie and I joining him in the front seats. It was just like old times!

What I did not notice as we all got settled into the cab, and was only made aware of later, was that Wally had made the lightest contact with Sophie using his staff and whispering "sponge cake" as he did. None of this registered with me at the time, and Sophie was not made aware of it either until our entire voyage was essentially over. But, remarkably, what Walt had done was to empower Wally to give Sophie the power, through her breath, to make discrete contact with any male. And by her doing so, she would erase, convert, rearrange and implant the immediate impulse and will in that individual to welcome all women as equals, in every respect, to all men.

The distinction here is the use of the term "male", but not to confuse it with "men". Those who had already reached the stature of men did not need Sophie's transforming breath, a number which varied widely throughout the world. Additionally, all this conversion could be passed from each recently affected male to another unaffected one. It was perfect. No one was imposing this change as a law or mandate. It was occurring spontaneously, by their own hand or breath, as it were. No outside society, government or religious body was forcing it to happen. They only had themselves to thank, once Sophie had smiled and breathed on them, while giving each her hearty, full-sized "Good morning".

At the same time Wally was tending to Sophie, his magical staff began shuddering and vibrating. Our nervous tracking device had awoken and was starting to direct us to our destination in Karachi. On this day it didn't take as long for it to begin its customary pounding as we neared an intersection with a remarkable building ahead of us. Facing it, we could see it covered at least two or three city blocks. It was shaped in a wide arc, which bordered a busy intersection of three boulevards. It was a three story building with countless, one story, beige brick arches extending along the entire first floor. The building also had a three or four story dome, resting above the red tile roof line. We later were told it was the old Port Authority Building. And Wally's staff indicated to us that was where our second regional gathering was being held.

Frank was able to find a parking spot one block behind the building. But just before we got out of the taxi, Bernie and Wally had to make some last minute additional changes. Because we were going to be entering an auditorium filled with individuals from Pakistan, Iran, Iraq, Afghanistan and Syria, we needed to be able to converse in Urdu, Farsi, Arabic, Pasto and Dari. To do so, Wally tapped his staff on the floorboard of the cab once and intoned quietly, "pot roast", "fish and chips", "Cornish pasties", "meat pie" and "English muffin".

Then, looking at each other, we smiled and thanked him in these various languages. Now we were able to mingle easily amongst the assembled throng that awaited us. And everyone, except me of course, had decided before leaving the Polar Wind to dress in white robes and wear covered headdresses. We wanted to move without incident throughout the mammoth room.

It's true, I drew some strange looks and comments, but Sophie scolded me to keep quiet. She, in turn, had been told by Wally and Bernie to openly and warmly greet all the attendees she could, addressing them face to face, letting her breath bathe their faces. It seemed a curious request to her, but, being the energetic and welcoming person she was, she happily complied. Dress customs in the region restricted this type of behavior, but her transformations would be initiated before anyone could intervene and stop her. Being completely unaware of her powers, she began a world-shaking change that over time came to be called "Sophie's breath". It was a term later used, when someone might say or do something that would eventually lead to great changes in the future. I was so proud of her. I just followed her around that room with my eyes on her the whole time.

Our group circulated within that gathering of warlords, terrorists, psycho-military types, wannabe world conquerors, rabid rulers, and just plain secret types who schemed in solitude or with only a few others to kill and maim for no other reason than to kill and maim. In my mind, at that moment, it was very likely a gathering of the most dangerous people on the planet.

But I was to learn later that it was just one of several. It seemed to be spawning season for pitiless people. After about thirty minutes of our socializing, if you will, Bernie caught the eye of each of us and motioned for us to meet her at the edge of the front stage. Her timing was perfect, because it was becoming obvious that Sophie was being eyed suspiciously and coolly. Just the same, it didn't seem to stop her from approaching and speaking to everyone she could.

Once we were all assembled at the stage, Bernie and Wally were the first to climb the steps onto it. As my turn came, following behind Wally, I glanced up and saw that the same furniture was on the stage, set in the same manner, with the same sinister black vase on the table, just as it was in Shanghai. It was curious to me that it would all be exactly the same, but then I thought back to the Emissaries and realized, with a shudder, that this was no ordinary coincidence. The most evil of intentions and designs were manipulating these meetings and the attendees. And we were venturing into hell's foyer.

Bernie had chosen to address the audience before any other speaker had come forward. Led by Po, once all of us were on the stage, he preceded Bernie to the podium and took one of the chairs from the small table for her to stand on. I followed her, jumping from the remaining chair at the table onto its top, making sure not to come into contact with that awful piece of black pottery. The last thing I wanted to do was knock that over. To me it would be like breaking a mirror and having seven years, or centuries, of very, bad luck. And behind me was Wally, who eventually moved quietly between the podium and the table, facing the audience. Frank and Sophie stood on the other side the table, watching the rest of us.

Bernie spoke first. "May I have your attention, please," she announced in a voice so startling and urgent that heads snapped and twisted like she had just announced the building was going to collapse in the next five seconds. Which, of course it wasn't, but I couldn't say the same for their present ambition and determination to bring untold misery on so many. "My brother here needs to perform a small act of transformation before we proceed with our portion of your meeting here today. Thank you."

Immediately, Wally stamped his staff, calling out "bubbles and squeak" and then smiled as a once boisterous hall, filled with corruption, deceit and murderous rage was transformed into another, potential feedlot of farm animals. After the changes, I wasn't sure who was from where originally, because there were now only horses, beef and dairy cows, sheep and goats. And as before, they were unable to move their legs or to talk. But they could hear and understand what was said. With Wally's transformation completed, Bernie again addressed the audience.

"Now that I believe I have your undivided

attention, there are a few items that need to be discussed here today. Foremost among them is for us to announce that your careers of violence are over. To emphasize that point, you can turn your heads and gaze about you. If any of you, by the time this meeting is over, decide this was just a trick or a dream of some kind and elect to test my words, you will immediately become what you are now for the duration of your much shorter lives. But still, even then, you will be unable to speak. However, you will be able to understand everything said around you, just as you do now.

"Unfortunately, there are some in this room today who have already proven that you cannot be trusted to renounce your violent ways. For you, welcome to your new status. You will not be changed back into your former selves. You will remain as you presently find yourselves, which will be unfortunate for you I realize, because you will not be able to speak ever again. Thankfully, for the rest of life on this planet, that ability shall never be yours again.

"But all of you need to at least understand why we are standing here before you today. How did it come to this? To answer that, I need to explore with you three driving forces that led you to be here. It only seems fair you should know.

"Tribalism is the first of these three motivating forces or 'isms' that I want to discuss briefly with you. In the tangled process of life gaining a more secure and self-aware foothold on this planet, one that also fostered life-sustaining communication, tribal societies evolved. Two major factors had to influence this process: the threat of harm, starvation or extinction and the desire to be surrounded by others who would care for and take risks to protect you and those closest to you. Over time, this association of individuals and families would evolve into a tribal entity.

"This connection or desire to be so connected has remained intact, to a greater or lesser degree, in many of our various cultures since these earliest yearnings. Complicating the integration of this simpler approach into daily life has been the rise of the nation state. With it, often came a despotic ruler and so-called laws that were cruel and denied serving the will of the people being governed. In short, whoever or however the society or nation was controlled, it often ignored or was unable to incorporate the spirit and strengths of tribalism.

"This failure to incorporate the benefits of the tribal culture facilitated frustrations and despair, which eventually led to acting out through small scale violence. Not satisfied with that, this failure evolved into gang-style retributions and revenge killings. The long-standing attributes of tribal cooperation, of a supportive and long-standing community, each of which offered its members security and comfort, often not found in other of society's institutions, was lost. Certainly, religious and paternal bodies give a measure of this, but they lack the historical context of the tribe, unless they evolved with it.

"Ultimately, those of you assembled here who swear allegiance to this ism, one that is distinct from the nations' whose boundaries surround your tribe, now think violence is an acceptable method to advance your agenda. Wrong. Anarchy, or tyrannical rule by one individual, group or tribe, will no longer be an option. To protect citizens of every country, checks and balances will be forthcoming in every reformed or renewed government. Your time-tested attributes will not be ignored, but neither will your violent methods be permitted to control the framing of any new society or government.

"Further, I will not allow conquest and imposition of rule by jihadism. This ism will not supplant or overthrow any representative government or democracy anywhere. True, unlike the other 'isms' that I will address here today, or at the other four, regional centers like this one, jihadism is unique in that it has been linked by its followers to a religion. And, like all other religions, Islam, as revealed by God to the Prophet Mohammad and recorded in the Qur'an and as practiced by its sincere and compassionate believers, is a most beautiful faith.

For myself, I am particularly touched by the practice of formally praying five times a day. The concept of sin, to me at my age, is somewhat daunting. But for those who faithfully practice being a Muslim day-to-day, they are not confronted with that state of being. Instead for them, it is the issue of forgetting, not sin, that is uppermost in the minds of the faithful. And to reduce the chance of forgetting, believers must pray this often to strengthen, protect and bring themselves closer to

God.

"But there are those of you in this room today that have taken certain words and/or phrases from your holy scriptures and molded them to fit your diabolical schemes. And the methods of achieving your goals are anything but compassionate. Most notable is your use of the word, "jihad". While some disagreement exists as to that word's original meaning and ultimately how it became most commonly interpreted by the more theologically gifted in your religious centers, the simplest and purest meaning of it is from a combination of words from your Qur'an: "lahd" or "juhd" and "ihad". By combining these three words, the word "jihad" was formed; and it came to mean a spiritual quest throughout one's life, one that was to earn God's blessing by submitting to His will. Jihad is a spiritual battle, the one, truly Holy war. It takes place within oneself to achieve compassion and mercy throughout a faithful follower's life. What could be more blessed?

"Facilitating the emergence of jihadism, the so-called 'just war' over anyone not a believer, has been the drive for conquest and forceful conversions. Other, equally disturbing, reasons for its rise can again be laid at the feet of colonialism. More specifically, it has been the recent decades of cultural and economic colonialism. These two developments represent a global, non-violent invasion, practiced most often by governments and global corporations. And they have widened the economic gulf throughout the world, separating each of us by income, material possessions, isolationist nations, frivolous pursuits, and loss of what a truly representative democracy can and should do for all. We, even in my own country to this very moment, have had difficulty realizing the interdependence of freedom and democracy for all people, everywhere.

"But instead of you organizing and exposing the injustices of the colonial excesses, you have chosen to become killers. Today that ends. Any who leave this room today, as a transformed member of humanity, will speak with one voice and seek justice with a single determination. All of us are returning to our humble beginnings and remaking ourselves in the image of something better. You will too. That's not a threat. It's a demand and a promise.

"Finally, I must conclude this portion of my talk this morning by briefly mentioning terrorism, the last 'ism' being fostered by many of you in this auditorium and elsewhere. Anyone who has suffered from this horrific experience can readily define it. They would tell you it involves becoming petrified, through mindless intimidation and violence. There are those of you, both in this audience and scattered around the world, who feel this form of 'ism' is justified for any perceived unresolved issue, which has, to you, life-taking importance. The grievance can be a territorial claim, a social issue, a medical procedure, maintaining illicit drug trafficking or simply the lust for power and money.

Of all the isms perpetrated on peoples of this world, this one is absolutely unacceptable under any circumstance. It is a plague. It represents the lowest level that humankind has reached. From there, the doorway to hell is an arm length away. And those who practice it show no mercy, and for them none will be shown. As of today, you here in this room and elsewhere, as you are identified, which believe me can be done with greater ease than you ever imagined, will be forever transformed into beasts of burden.

"Our presence here this morning is to give others of you the motivation and tools to right legitimate wrongs and injustices."

Bernie then explained about the scrolls at the exits and how they were to be used. Then she turned to me and motioned for me to begin.

Naturally, I couldn't let the opportunity pass, once again. I leaned forward to the microphone and called out, "Is anyone here from New Jersey?"

To my surprise there was a vigorous shaking of heads throughout the assembled herd. In retrospect, I felt that I had stooped close to their level by asking that. I realized after what Wally had done to them and following what Bernie had told them, there was no way they wouldn't try to respond in some manner, our of panic, to any question asked. However, there were exceptions. And I figured those were the hard core, the bad actors, and the ones who would leave this place that day unlike anything they could have imagined. And as it turned out nearly a third of the audience did not return to their previous appearance. They ultimately were led out onto the street and distributed, free of charge, to poor farmers and herders scattered throughout the region. The wages of sin…, I thought.

Gathering my wits somewhat, I then experienced my own transformation and took on the mantle of Walt's presence. My speech, thereafter, like it was in Shanghai and in the other three regional centers, was always the same, except for the last couple of sentences. But for your review, let me repeat my last words to them.

"The only timeless gift or course any of us, anywhere, can give is to insure that all life on this world will not perish/ This can only be done by each of us selflessly pursuing the straightforward, yet dauntingly challenging pathway, defined by the letters in FETCH! The first commandment, as introduced by the letter 'F; is: 'follow the path that leads to humility, goodness and laughter'. And the second one is: 'Enact laws that are just and that protect all life.'"

Bernie then followed up with her concluding remarks and the meeting was adjourned. As the six of us left the auditorium through the stage door, Wally quickly turned and performed his retransformations of those who were to live to speak another day. Po led the way back to the taxi, carrying the black container. Once back at the Polar Wind, he placed it next to the first one we'd taken from Shanghai. What followed his placing them together were an almost imperceptible shudder and a faint odor of sulfur, both of which briefly coursed throughout the Polar Wind.

THIRTEEN: NAIROBI, KENYA

However, before Capt. Shriver gave orders to leave Karachi, Bernie and Wally called a private meeting with Iris, Rita and Jennifer to meet them at the stern of the ship.   In hushed tones, Bernie explained to them that they had another mission to perform and that they would have to meet us in Pasni tomorrow.   Her instructions were that the three were to revisit the region around Karachi and then make their way westward toward us.   During that time they were to make direct contact with all the smaller mammals and reptiles they could, ones that by now were probably able to talk, following Jennifer's previous mission twenty-four hours ago.

The objective was to convert these smallest of animals, be they chipmunks, mice, moles, lizards, snakes, geckos, or voles, and have them wait outside any buried, weapon repository or any hidden, rocket-launching facility and make contact with anything inside those areas when the opportunity arose.   Through Wally's transforming powers, Jennifer, Iris, and Rita again became the Pakistani birds they were before, but each now had a new power to pass on. And so they did for hundreds of miles. With each contact, each creature was told to pass this same power on to others indefinitely. All caches and rockets, everywhere, had to be dissolved as soon as possible. Evil doers of every description, in places near and far, were becoming frantic. Their urge to kill indiscriminately was becoming overwhelming.

And curiously enough, it was these smallest animals, the ones that most often caused humans to turn away in disgust or attack them, who gave their own lives, by the thousands around the planet, to accomplish this task. Within hours of this process beginning, there were stockpiles of weapons and war material being dissolved throughout all of Asia.

Meanwhile, as these three were flying off on their assignment, the Polar Wind slipped out into the Arabian Sea and made for Pasni. Preparations on board the ship were in full gear for the rescue mission ahead. Wally, especially, was in great demand by the recently converted medical, surgical and nursing staffs. Many supplies and instruments were needed for their demanding ordeal ahead. Only he could arrange for them to get them. And it was decided that tents would be used for surgical suites and hospital wards. The supplies, tents and staff would have to be transported to Turbat by truck and helicopter. And the Polar Wind would serve as the maintenance and refueling facility for the two helicopters and their crews.

It was dusk on February 27th, when we anchored in the small port of Pasni. Within minutes of doing so, there was a convoy of trucks pulling up alongside us. And for the next six hours there was a mad rush to get supplies, equipment and personnel loaded onto them and onto the helicopters. By dusk both helicopters and trucks had left for Turbat. It would be three weeks before everyone on board the Polar Wind was reunited again.

Apparently, the earthquake north of Turbat was so devastating that entire towns were destroyed and many perished who lived in them. Rescue and recovery operations took their toll on all the Polar Wind personnel involved. Without question, Wally's transformations of the crew to become surgical and medical teams were adequate for what they needed to do, but none of them had had the prior experience that would give them the professional detachment to perform these duties. His efforts had been a mistake. Certainly, lives were saved, bodies were repaired and families were reunited with their heroic efforts. But those twenty-three crew members were never the same again, even after their being retransformed by Wally.

Helping the animal, bird and fish life to talk and do deeds that required little thought was one thing but having untrained or unprepared humans perform repeated procedures that usually require years of study and preparation was another. This was a wakeup call for both Bernie and Wally. Their youth had given them boldness and uncommon courage. But now they began to sense the limitations of both the psyche of humans and the scope of the problems facing them in this world. And their second lesson, exposing this weakness, was soon to be upon them.

There was no way that the Polar Wind could sail on to Mombasa, Kenya, from Pasni anytime soon. Another method of transport for the New Jersey Wagoners to there had to be found. And as luck would have it, there was a Japanese container ship finishing its loading of containers berthed next to them. Capt. Shriver, Frank, Sophie and Po walked over to the vessel the next day, after the search and rescue helicopters had refueled and left for another day of flying over the mountains north of Turbat.

After some lengthy discussion, it was agreed that the container ship would be able to transport the New Jersey Wagoners both to Mombasa and then onto Djibouti, where they had another layover. And it was further decided that the Polar Wind would rejoin the Wagoners in Djibouti, three weeks from then, and then they would resume their trip together. In the meantime, the container ship had one layover in Mogadishu, Somalia, before docking in Mombasa. They were going no further south down the African coastline. From there they were heading back into ports around the Mediterranean Sea. The ship was loaded with containers of emergency food relief supplies, which consisted entirely of rice, powdered milk, sugar, tea, and flour.

Reluctantly, all of us gathered our belongings and were shown two large rooms in the ship's, crew quarters to sleep. One room was for Sophie, Frank and Po, Bernie and Wally. The other room was for Rita, Jennifer, Iris, Ed and I.

It was a much larger ship than the Polar

Wind, but most of it was inaccessible to everyone. We were pretty much confined either to our quarters, the chow hall or to the small auditorium where meetings were held or movies were shown. Or, once our mission in Nairobi was over, where we gave performances, almost nightly, for various crew members, depending on their different watches.

Our performances were just like the ones we did on our cross-country journey, and the crew loved them. For them we were a circus act, nothing more. There was no cosmic significance to what we did or what we said, and I liked that. I was tired of being seen or thought of as anything other than an aging dog. I'm not a good pretender. And I don't mind getting old or simply being a shaggy-haired dog. Walt, Bernie and Wally's objectives were noble and quite remarkable. I'm not. For me, the time onboard the container ship was a welcome rest. And given the trials and forces we were to face soon enough, it was a needed rest for our entire troop.

Landing at the Port of Mombasa on March 17th, all of us immediately sensed the heightened desperation about us. This was a place in turmoil. Whereas, Shanghai and Karachi had been centers of intrigue and fanatical plots and determination to conquer, this land and its people were not given to organized conquest. It was like a continental-sized volcano, ready to erupt and envelope the entire globe with poverty, starvation, wasting, premature death and killer viruses.

However, I was struck by the resilience of the people and with the magical beauty of the land. The tropical lushness of the coastal area, soon gave way to an expanse of arid grassland, punctuated with groves of stunted trees or outcrops of rock-strewn hills. It was like a land that had always been waiting for something or someone to come and find quiet solace there, someone who wasn't looking for trophies, investments, minerals, or unique peoples and animals. This land wanted those who were looking to bring it a lasting peace and to also insure some for its weary residents. Stretching out into the far horizon, far beyond the gradually uplifting flatland, was Mt. Kilimanjaro. It was a contrast that warned you this was no ordinary place.

But I get ahead of myself. The first thing we had to do, after establishing the date and time we needed to be back at the ship, was to find transport to Nairobi. It boiled down to two options: the train or a bus. The adults and children wanted to take the train. The rest of us said it had to be the bus. On the bus, at least, we could perch or lie on top of it and/or fly about as needed. The train offered us no such option. And as luck would have it, we were able to book passage on a double-decker bus all the way through to Nairobi, by way of Voi.

We had no time to waste in Mombasa. Once we decided on the bus, the one to Nairobi left one hour later, at 9:15 a.m. Even though the trip was about 250 miles, depending on any detours along the way, it was expected we would not arrive there until 4:30 or 5 p.m. It was actually 6:15.

Quickly collecting ourselves and saying temporary goodbye's to our Japanese hosts, we hurried two blocks to the bus terminal, through the congested streets. It was impractical for Iris, Ed and Rita to fly over, so we all either walked, ambled, pranced or waddled, as our various lengths of legs would allow us. We weaved through the often, seemingly log-jammed crowds, with Po in the lead. I, of course, brought up the rear. Before we had completed the torturous hike, I had lost my patience completely and began yelling in Swahili and Gikuyu, but with my head always pointed to the ground to avoid anyone identifying who was speaking.

What, you ask, did I dare say at a time like that? They were comments like: "Make way for injured dog.", "Watch it!! You're stepping on my feathers!", "Clear a path, wounded cat coming through." and "I'm rabid, and I bite." The last one usually gave us a little more space.

Both of these languages I was spouting were ones Wally had embedded in us before leaving the ship. Amazingly, there are over 2000 languages spoken throughout the African continent. Being conservative, he chose to have us only speak Amharic, Oromo, Somali, Kirundi and Kongo, along with two that I was perfecting, as we tried to hurry to the bus station.

We got there just in time to purchase our tickets and find some seating for the adults and children. The rest of us went topside. And it was a delightful surprise. The few travelers that were already seated on the upper deck were preoccupied with sleeping, and they were sitting in the rear area. We had the entire front of the upper deck to ourselves. Soon enough, Ed, Iris and Rita were launching themselves skyward to explore the city and countryside. Meanwhile Jennifer and I did some heavenly sightseeing. We'd been on or around a ship and various seas and oceans for months, it seemed, and to be beyond the sight of water was so therapeutic. I felt like the most privileged tourist alive. I loved Africa, every inch of it.

And, as I said, we had ample time to see it along the way. The bus did not travel far between picking up or dropping off passengers, and the roadway was heavily congested, at times, due to construction. But we didn't mind one bit. It was all like a hallucinogenic drug, especially before we reached the outskirts of Nairobi that evening.

Then about forty miles from its city limits we began to hear conversations about some kind of uprising taking place, but they were vague in detail or extent. We assumed it was probably some political or union matter and well contained within a small area. It was Ed who suggested that maybe he should fly ahead and see if he could determine its location. Rita suggested she should tag along, just in case he got into trouble. I agreed to it, given that Bernie and Wally were both fast asleep, as were the adults. That was a big mistake. Off they flew with our agreeing that they'd be back in ten minutes.

One hour later there still was no sign of them. And by then Bernie had come up to check on us. She was livid for my letting them go. I'd never seen her so mad. I was just hoping she wouldn't go get Wally and have him transform me into a roadside sign or some other inanimate object. Thankfully, just as she was about to call Wally, the two of them showed up. They were breathless and terrified. It was Ed who spoke, after catching his breath.

"Bernie," he began. "We've just witnessed the most gruesome of sights. And the further we flew into the city, the worse it got. There are food riots everywhere. The people are starving. People have been pouring in from the countryside, where the droughts have parched all the tillable land. Grazing herds of animals have all perished. Drinking water is non-existent. Stores are being looted and burned. Piles of tires are being set alight, as are cars, if they haven't already been turned over or wrecked. Windows are broken everywhere: on buses, cars, stores and offices. There does not appear to be any order whatsoever. Any uniformed individuals we saw were huddled together to protect themselves. It's an absolute madhouse. What's more, we saw countless bodies lying in the streets."

Hearing this news, Bernie promptly went down to the lower level and ordered our driver to stop the bus. When he resisted, she had Wally immobilize him and the other passengers for the time being. Panic was something she wanted to avoid at that moment. She then had Po, Frank, Sophie and Wally come back up to our level to discuss what needed to be done next.

After much discussion, the only option we were left with was for Wally to convert himself, and the rest of us, into a bird and then for us to make our way into the downtown area, somewhere we could stay undetected until we were ready to leave for the third regional meeting place. The conversions consisted of Ed becoming an African Fish Eagle, Iris a Pink-backed Pelican, Rita a Narina Trogon, Po a Banded-snake Eagle, Frank a Vitelline Masked Weaver, Sophie a magnificent Fisher's Lovebird, Bernie a Spur-winged Lapwing, Wally a Purple Grenadier, me an African Hoopoe, a cousin to the lark I was in Pakistan. And Jennifer became a Eurasian Spoonbill. She was simply mortified and dared anyone to make fun of her. It was so hard not to. But soon we were all aloft, heading into Nairobi.

As we flew over the turmoil taking place below us, Wally turned to me and said, "Oh, Mr. Greg, I don't know what to do. How can I ever help relieve that suffering? It's so widespread." (This was his second jolt of earthbound reality that I mentioned earlier was to follow.)

Later when we had landed and had gotten ourselves settled into a small pension, Wally followed that conversation up with me. This time Bernie was present as well.

"Mr. Greg," he started. "I've been thinking about what is happening in the streets of this city, and that I am unable to help. My powers do not enable me to correct everything like this. I'm primarily here to help combat evil deeds and evil doers. The issues of geological, climate and atmospheric changes, population density, resource management, food production, water distribution and the ramifications of ignoring ominous trends or misusing precious resources connected to them are beyond my control. The human drives to squander, waste, poach, pillage and plunder are totally foreign to me. Nowhere in the anteverse did this occur to the degree it has here.

"In short, there is an absolute limit to my ability and power to change and offer a bright future for this planet. People must help themselves. I can help make wildlife talk and make certain dangerous things disappear. But there is no way I can change the hearts and minds of seven billion people.

"What can be done? Mr. Greg. How do we help stop what's going on in the streets around us? I feel so helpless..."

In all my dog years I had never felt as bad as I did at that moment. How I wished Walt was there or that some Universal Force could undo what untold millennia of neglect and abuse had evolved into. "Greg's Plan" was some half-baked list of ideas for my homeland to try and get back on track. It had no application to what we were seeing and hearing outside at this moment. What was needed were "Stop" and "Rewind" buttons in wherever this world's Operational Headquarters was located. It was "Start Over" time. This attempt didn't work. But no such device or option existed for the hundreds of millions, or likely billions, of desperately poor and hungry souls in this world.

All I could think of was what great herds of animals do in such circumstances. They begin massive migrations. And some face extinction,

It was like the New Jersey Wagoners had a front row seat to view the most tragic story ever told. Why were we brought to this place? At this time? Was this also part of Walt's Plan? I only could think of one thing to do.

"Wally, you need to call Po in here to talk with us. We have got to see if there is anything he knows that you, Bernie and I don't. Maybe there is something in his experience or background that will help you."

"Ok," Wally said and then immediately got up and left the little room we were sitting in. In a few minutes he returned with Po following behind him. Once we had all sat down, I took it upon myself to take the initiative and spoke.

"Wally, Bernie and I have been agonizing about what we are seeing outside these walls today. All of us know this is only a glimpse of what the future holds for this world unless something can be changed. But that is another side of the massive problem these riots represent; there is no one thing that has to be changed. Humanity appears to have made it an art form to take a wrong turn at every opportunity for any change or upgrades that were offered them. We have sought your help and want to ask you what can possibly be done to prevent the total collapse of this precious world. Our band of Wagoners is in the midst of reducing, even eliminating, the evil forces that have gripped it for so long. But what do we do about the selfish, self-serving, and self-destructive ones?"

After a long silence, Po finally spoke.

"Mr. Walt used to talk to me about this issue, but he never offered any solutions that I can recall. He did say that nothing like this ever existed in the Anteverse worlds. It was something unique to this place. I think he always hoped that by conquering the Emissaries and restoring order, like we are attempting to do now in these five regions, somehow goodwill and a sense of righteousness would be restored.

"All I can suggest at this time is that there needs to be an urgent worldwide redistribution of food, supplies, equipment and wealth. But accompanying anything like that, there would have to be oversight and behavioral transformations of both the 'have's' and the 'have-nots'".

"Who would provide that?" Bernie asked, with an earnest concern in her voice.

"Everything else that is part of this world," Po replied. "The trees, animals, birds, fish, the plants, grasses, all vegetation, the wind, the sea, the rivers and the land itself. This world, as we are now witnessing outside this room, has become a small neighborhood. Whatever happens in one corner of it will affect those living down the street, as it were. We are interconnected, interdependent, and intertwined with one another. Irresponsible behavior is no longer just a social misstep, it is now a crime. For the next two generations there will be awesome challenges facing humanity and all life. Somehow we must begin to think and act with one voice and one purpose: to serve one another.

"I would hope and pray that each individual will seek within the core of their beings and their religious faiths to find the will and strength to do this. We must each go to that most private and precious location and find the strength to change, to care, to love and to cherish this world and all who live in it. United we can rebuild. Stay divided and selfish and no transformations or Power can protect or save this world from human extinction."

"Then what can we do?" Wally asked.

"Continue your transformations and battle with evil," Po answered without any hesitation. "I do believe the life forms that you have already altered will begin to have a significant influence on the populations of this world soon enough. Changes in priorities and behaviors will be forthcoming. And for now, I believe there should be truckloads of food supplies coming from our Japanese friends that we left at dockside. They should start distributing them today sometime. And maybe it wouldn't hurt if Bernie or Greg mentioned something about all this at the remaining regional meetings. I'm sure the contact you've already had with creatures in Asia will influence those other two regions soon enough as well.

"And lastly, I would support Wally immediately transforming himself into that winged, white horse, the one you became that day over the ocean. Plus, I would further suggest that you let Bernie ride along with you this time. Together, you could both soar over these local neighborhoods and people, as they are being issued food supplies today. People need an outward, visible sign of the needed changes to come. Let them see that the impossible is possible and that it is beginning to happen. And I might suggest that you do this periodically whenever we go or where we've been."

Well, I can only say that even more remarkable events started happening after that brief meeting. First off, Wally and Bernie did take a long and daring flight over and through the entire city of Nairobi. Wally even landed a few times to let the children touch him and talk to Bernie. At first there were shouts of fear, but when the word quickly spread of their landing and that they meant no harm, the crowds' welcomed them with shouts of joy. It didn't hurt that food from the Japanese container ship was being distributed at the same time.

Then, the next morning there was the customary transformations of Ed, Iris, Rita, Jennifer, Flo and I into the same African birds we were the day before. Following that, Bernie again gave us orders to empower most living organisms to speak. But, in addition, we were to pass along to any butterflies and moths we encountered, the ability to also cause large and small weapons to disappear by their touch. Included in this list were items like rifles, pistols, cannons, tanks, machetes, RPG's and machine guns. The days of the gun were to pass into history. They had contributed little to lasting peace. Instruments of death, no matter how they were used in any locale, were completely disappearing from this world. Walt had made up his mind about that, and so it was to be.

And, of course, all of these transformed creatures could pass their skills and talents on to their kin anywhere. Bernie gave us two days to spread these changes across as much of Africa as we could. She figured the normal flight and migration patterns of the wildlife, we transformed, would spread them elsewhere soon enough.

As an aside, I must report that Flo had the most stunning news to report back to us upon our return to Nairobi two days later. When she got into prides of lions, groups of giraffes, families of elephants, and massive herds of wildebeests, she noticed that their new-found ability to speak caused quite a stir. In fact, the animals in the Nairobi National Park, which bordered the city of Nairobi, instantaneously upon being able to speak, lost no time in marching toward the City Center proper. They had a few bones to pick, no pun intended, with the country's government officials. The new order of things was going to include equal representation by some very large and very tall newcomers. And who would argue with a pair of articulate, white rhinoceroses.

Likewise, the conversion of the butterflies and moths made for remarkable moments for military, police, poachers, terrorists and thugs everywhere. Whether they might have had their weapons holstered or at the ready, one quick touch by these beauties and their weapons were disappearing in seconds. Take away a killing instrument from a bad guy, and you are left with someone who becomes much less powerful. Now was time to shift the power to those who earned and deserved it.

And lastly, while all this was going on, right after our meeting between Wally, Bernie, Po and I, there was Bernie's transformation of Frank. Since we had begun this odyssey in Seattle, each of the Wagoners had been very concerned about what to do for the children in the regions we were heading into. The proliferation of child gangs, child soldiers, malnutrition, diseases, infant premature deaths and poverty that denied any hope for a better life, all combined to pose a heart-breaking future for the vast majority of the youth of this world. It was to be Frank's commission to begin the reversal of those sad fortunes.

And the really unique thing about all of this; was how it was to happen. It was to be by sniffing various fragrances. For too long the world had been losing its heritage of cleansed air and unadulterated scents. That was about to change, at least in so far as Bernie and Wally could affect it. Frank was given the ability to heighten the fragrances of any blooming plant, wherever he flew. As a Vitelline Masked Weaver he could simply skim over a field of blooming flowers and they would erupt in much more potent and powerful scents. Flowers were now on the front line of changes worldwide, no matter where they were. And these fragrances, once inhaled, changed forever the recipient's care and concern for any child. It didn't hurt either that the world was beginning to take on the aura of a spring garden, ever in bloom. And it all made me so happy to know that Sophie and Frank had played such a pivotal role in the reshaping of the world's ills. They would forever remain my best buddies, even if Frank didn't allow me to ride in the bed of trucks.

All that done, it finally came down to the morning of our having to go to our third regional meeting. Wally's staff directed us to the Kenyatta International Conference Center in Nairobi's Central District. It was a swank, modern building, but certainly less imposing than the previous two in

Shanghai and Karachi. And again there was the usual group of us, including Sophie, who went into their forum.

By this time we were entering an auditorium that was in a near riot of despair and anger. Why? Because so many of the world's destructive implements were disappearing. Gathered together in this place were the top levels of vile individuals, who did nothing but plot and execute plans to kill. They came from Somalia, Sudan, Uganda, Kenya, and Tanzania. They represented the forces of warped nationalism, tribalism and terrorism in this region. And they each got the Wally treatment, only this time he changed the audience into animals found on the African veldt.

Bernie had her usual speech, as did I. The only addition was when I outlined what "FETCH!" meant. I described the first two commandments of that word, then I added the third, "T": "teach others well and constantly, especially the young." It seemed to blend nicely into what Frank had been doing the last two days with the flowers. And I should probably add that the butterflies were ecstatic with Frank's transformations. There was an ongoing surge in the number of flowers and butterflies the world over.

And with these changes well underway, Bernie and Wally elected to have us all transformed back into African birds and fly back to Mombasa to the container ship. The one exception was Po. He had to travel by car, which he drove. The third black vase's size required it be transported over land. Po wasn't much for flying anyway, so he didn't mind. For the rest of us, it would give us an opportunity to see the countryside from above and bid this part of Africa a fond farewell. Our work here was done.

FOURTEEN: CAIRO, EGYPT

We reunited with Po the evening of March 10th, the same day as our regional meeting in Nairobi. He met us on the pier, and all the Wagoners requested permission to board the Aki Hoshi, our Japanese freighter, for our trip to Djibouti to meet the Polar Wind. On the dock, everyone was talking at once, but we settled back to being docile and dumb animal and bird life as we climbed onto the gangway. Word had not yet spread to the crew of what was occurring throughout Asia and Africa. Possibly the Captain or some Radio Room crewmember had overheard rumors of what life-altering events were occurring elsewhere, but the crew appeared unaware. To insure peace and quiet, we wanted to keep it that way. However, suspicions were raised when Po brought the large black vase on board. Anyone could tell it was not of this world. But no one asked about it or anything about us.

The next day was filled with the reloading and reshuffling full and empty containers. Rita, Iris, Ed, Flo, Jennifer and I perched or sat on a deckhouse balcony and watched this symphony of movement all day. The sun was bright, giving the cold-blooded creatures among us needed warmth, and we were all glad to have these moments of rest.

By sunup the next morning we cast off and headed back north along the coast of Somalia. The ship had picked up containers in Mombasa to deposit in Mogadishu, Hobyo, Bandarbeyla and Bender Cassim. And by the last stopover in Bender Cassim, we had entered the Gulf of Aden. Our rejoining the Polar Wind was to occur the next day, on March 18th.

We put on a final performance for the entire crew of our host vessel that last night. Wally even arranged to materialize a banquet of food and small gifts, in ways only he and, I suppose, Walt understood or could do. By the end of our performance I doubt there was anyone on board that ship who didn't know that something really strange was going on. There was way too much talking going on between various species, other than humans, to be simple trickery or fanciful magic. But they were polite enough to keep whatever questions they had to themselves.

By midmorning the next day we had docked in Djibouti and said our farewells. Among the items that Wally left for them were individually wrapped small boxes that were to be opened only after we had departed Djibouti on the Polar Wind. In them, for each crewmember, were fifty, one ounce gold coins. Wally and Bernie hoped they would be used for the crews' stake in a new and better life one day. Not that shipboard life is punishing, but everyone needs to have something set aside for dreaming, if it is at all possible. For me? It was returning one day to Willa's on the Hoh River.

Our transferring to the Polar Wind was met with a lot of whoops and shouts. But, beyond any doubt, both the ship and crew had the appearance of being in a place where a struggle for finding and preserving life had been fought, and the outcome, too often, had resulted in defeat. Even then, after being away from Pasni for almost a week, there were still signs of how taxing their rescue efforts had been. They had waged a localized war against the devastation caused by nature's fury. From Capt. Shriver to the helicopter maintenance crew, they all still looked haggard. Wally would soon try to fix that, however. With a couple of swishes of his wand later that night, some memories were erased, aching bodies relieved and spirits were uplifted. It was the least Wally could do for them, he later told me.

It almost appeared like their crew had missed us or maybe they were celebrating that our trip around the world was half over. With two regional centers left to find, it was probably their feeling that the worst was over. Even I felt the same way. We were both wrong.

And the reason I knew that was the case was the moment when Po placed the third black vase alongside the other two. There was no mistaking it that time. The entire ship rocked side to side, like we had been hit with a rogue wave, and we were stationary, tied up dockside. The rocking was so violent it dislodged the mooring lines from the pier posts. It was an instantaneous, but brief and violent, event. Then all was quiet and calm. No one but Po knew the cause of the violent motion, and he initially only relayed it to Bernie and Wally. For them, it was only too obvious our rescue and transforming voyage was far from over. And most disturbing of all to Po was, when everything else was falling with the jerking motions, the vases stood perfectly straight and undisturbed.

We spent all day on March 19th sorting materials, scrubbing the decks, our rooms and the hanger. Everyone pitched in, in some manner. I ran errands for anyone one who needed clean rags, bottles of drinking water or just a rambling conversation to keep their minds off the tedium of their job. The birds pitched in where they could, flying back and forth to the observation station aloft, taking other messages to anyone not in ear-shot range or ferrying sandwiches and snacks to someone needing a break. Jennifer and Flo were assigned to helping Sophie, Frank and Po. It was a busy day. Everyone aboard wanted the Polar Wind to look sparkling, even though she was still in her hospital ship attire.

Capt. Shriver called the ten of us together after dinner that night to discuss a matter that he felt warranted a closed-door meeting. It involved what he had observed during the last three weeks, both personally and via radio transmissions. Apparently, according to all he heard, the better part of Eurasia and half of Africa were in an unprecedented uproar about the volcano-like changes transforming their countries. It seemed everything, fixed or moving, was now talking, and quite purposefully. And for those in positions of power and privy to classified information it was becoming only too obvious that their stockpiles of weapons, be they ships, airplanes, missiles or small arms, were gone. All that was left, according to their most secretive transmissions, were their weapons of mass destruction. This was confirmed by the Radio Room personnel being able to decipher messages. And further, to make matters even more confusing for everyone in this massive land mass, there was some kind of societal transformation beginning to evolve. The word "Fetch" seemed to be associated with this somehow. He was curious as to whether our group could enlighten him on some of these developments that he wasn't already aware were happening.

It was Bernie who filled him in on the details he was not fully aware of; including our plans for the next regional meeting, along with the confession that none of us knew what was the significance or purpose of the three black vases now residing in Po's cabin. The meeting ended with Bernie telling the Captain that he had their permission to share all this information with his crew. They deserved to know everything that the Wagoners knew. And the meeting ended with a solemn warning to everyone there that the danger facing them had not diminished. Indeed, if anything, with the black vases aboard, it might be increasing. No one really knew.

That done, we had an exhausted night's rest and left at sunrise the next morning, bound for the city of Suez, with our next extended stop in Cairo, Egypt.

It was during the following day, around mid-morning, as I was later informed, that Bernie and Wally asked Po to join them in their cabin. He was to be the next instrument of change. And it seemed an appropriate assignment, when you consider the centuries that Po accompanied and protected Walt. His task was to conclude the transformations that had been given to each of the Wagoners by Bernie. Anything else that Po did, it was theorized many years later, must have been prearranged with Walt, particularly if Walt was not around to advise and direct him. No one will ever really know how much the prosperity and harmony our world now knows is the result of Po's lifelong commitment to Walt, then to Bernie and Wally. I can only guess.

From the discussion these three had that morning came another decision as to how this sensitive matter was to be handled. All three of them decided that Sophie had to be involved as well. Her voice was absolutely essential to the ultimate success of this last transformation. And, finally, they had to enlist Capt. Shriver, LTCR Steele and the Radio Room crew's help to implement it. All that decided, over the rest of the day each person was briefed on what had to be done and at 6 p.m. the transforming process was to begin.

At that time Sophie and Po were escorted to the bow of the ship, and as a magnificent sunset was unfolding behind them, they began to sing a song of such beauty and meaning. I had had no foreknowledge or warning about this happening, and I began to cry uncontrollably. Po's magnificently rich and full baritone voice seemed to carry across the Red Sea, beyond the borders of any surrounding countries. And Sophie's...I never knew. Maybe it was something Wally did with that wand or staff, but her singing was different now. It was as pure a soprano voice as I ever dreamed of hearing. Even those nights on Howard's porch back in Atlantic City when I'd watch old TV movies or PBS Specials, I never heard anything like it before. And combined, their singing must have made the angels in heaven weep, as our ship rocked gently and eased westward into the setting sun as they sang.

And all the while, the Radio Room crew was busy beaming, videotaping, cell phone recording, radio and shortwave broadcasting their singing. Then once their performance, which lasted a good thirty minutes, was concluded, the crew transmitted it on the Radio Room's computer by way of the internet to all the various sites that were accessed worldwide. Additionally, copies of the videotape were sent to the region's television networks for broadcast. Then over the next four days we stopped in the Ports of Jiddah, Saudi Arabia; Marsa Alam, Egypt and Safaga, Egypt, where the ship's crew escorted Sophie and Po to the local radio and TV stations for them to perform the same song each time. The last time they had to give the same performance was right after we docked in Suez, just before the six of us left for the fourth regional meeting in Cairo.

What did they sing, you ask? What were the

words? Now see, there you go. I warned you at the beginning of this long tale, I have no memory. I bet you forgot that as well. And I honestly don't remember what words they sang. But, do I remember the haunting melody. And, most important of all, I remember the aftereffects for anyone who heard them. Which, by the time it was broadcast and rebroadcast over all the media available to everyone on the planet, there was no one not touched and transformed by their message. That was Bernie and Wally's objective: transformation through music.

So, you ask then, what happened? Well, it wasn't a matter that after hearing them that the blind could see, the lame walk, the aged return to their youth or the less aware becoming fully functional. But it so happened that afterwards everyone, everywhere, recognized for evermore after those magical moments, the beauty and value of all life. There was to be no more solitude, shunning or subtle hostility and condescension of the elderly, the disabled, the sorrowful, the lonely or the poor. No more fellow workers, family members, neighbors or strangers acting like they were somehow filled with the knowledge of the ages and others were too slow to grasp it. Humility, before God and all living creatures, was to be the order from that moment anyone heard their song. Walt had had it with the centuries of arrogance, pseudo-intellectualism and self-pride that he had witnessed throughout our world. If humanity wasn't able to mature properly on its own, he was going to give it a kick-start. And in the process he did a little rearranging and cleansing of the niceness and compassion genes in each of us.

But don't get me wrong. There were still going to be diseases, disasters, disabilities, accidents, tragedies, births that are too premature and death. But what would also occur was a worldwide consciousness that all the world's creatures deserve to live and to do so meant that reproduction is one of life's most important decisions. No species could wantonly reproduce itself. All living creatures had to become caregivers of one another. No moment, no day, no decision could be made in a self-absorbed box, as if it was yours' alone to live or to make. After hearing Sophie and Po's singing, we were all joined together in their everlasting, haunting melody of preciousness of life.

That left one final transformation and Bernie and Wally would be free from any further tampering with the matrix of humanity and the world's life forms. Or at least so they thought at that time. And besides, they realized there were still the last two regional centers that were to be addressed in Cairo and Caracas. But this final transformation was, by far, the most complex and dangerous of them all to date. It involved deactivating and then eliminating the possibility of some particular agents ever being reconstituted again. It involved radiological, biological and chemical compounds that were reconstituted into weapons of mass destruction.

And given the complexity and universality of actually accomplishing it, Bernie decided to give the entire effort to Wally. At the time she felt she was shirking her responsibility, but after repeated attempts to come up with a solution to the problem, she finally gave up. That really surprised me. Bernie had become someone I thought would never do that. But, being who I am, recognizing your limitations has always been a hallmark of mine, as it was when I actually accomplished something. It's only by realizing both these spectrums in one's life that you can rightfully claim the mantle of having lived a mature and successful life. Even I, a dog, know that.

So at 4:30 a.m., the morning of March 23rd, the day when the Polar Wind was supposed to dock at Port in city of Suez sometime mid-day, it was a complete shock to me when Wally came into our cabin and shook me awake.

"Mr. Greg," he whispered, "I need you to wake up. I need you to come with me... NOW!!!"

Shaking the sleep off as much as I could and being only half alert, I mumbled, "Why me?.." "What time is it, anyway?"

"It's early. We have to be there at sunrise. Come on, HURRY!!"

"But why me?" I pressed.

"Because Walt made you the Scribe," was all he would say. "Now, COME ON!"

At least, I didn't have to shave or put on any make-up. That's one advantage to being who I am: I always look my best, which in certain social circles may look somewhat on the scruffy side. But at least it is just that; it's my best.

Wally led me quietly down the narrow

ship's hallways, out the stern-facing, deck door, and down the steps, past the helicopter hanger and up onto the helicopter landing pad. In the dim light of the two stern deck lanterns I could just barely see him turn and face me.

"Stand back a little ways from me, Mr. Greg," he said in a muted voice.

And as I moved backwards four or five steps, he unsheathed his wand, waved it back and forth, the way I'd seen him do when he...transformed himself into THAT FLYING WHITE HORSE!!!

Then, of all the unimaginable things in the world I EVER expected to hear anyone or anything say to me, Wally, or what used to be Wally, turned his huge, white alabaster-colored head toward me and said in a voice so commanding and direct, "Ok, now I want you to jump up on my back. We have some traveling to do before sunrise."

As he said this, he moved effortlessly over to a step-stool, and I promptly, without any argument, jumped from it onto his back. After all, would you argue with a mammoth, winged horse, if it told you to do something? Well, anyway, I didn't. But, then I did ask how do I hold on?

"It's not necessary. You'll be safe. Just lie down," the newly-customized Wally replied.

And just the second I had settled down, he lifted off the quietly, sailing Polar Wind and headed due east into the Sinai Desert. The air was chilly and the scent of broiled sand, from it being scorched eon after eon, filled the air. It was a cloudless, star-studded sky, with just a hint of light breaking on the horizon. The only sound was the flapping of his wings, which was not rapid but like the sound of a sail on a small boat in a light breeze. Besides being scared witless, it was actually quite nice... as long as I didn't look down.

Finally, after about five minutes of flying, I asked rather formally, "Do you mind if I ask where we are going?" Remember, this was a side of Wally I didn't really know. Wouldn't you feel the same under the same circumstance?

"To Mt. Catherine in the Sinai," he replied.

"Can I know what's going to happen there?" I asked with some hesitation.

"No. Just watch and remember what you see and hear." And that was all that was said for the remainder of the flight.

In about thirty minutes we swooped down in a lazy spiral and Wally, or whatever he called himself under these circumstances, landed on top of this very rocky hill. At least that's what I'd call it, after seeing the Rocky, Cascade and Olympic Mountains back home. Once we landed, I was directed to stand off to one side, about twenty paces from where he or it now stood.

And now I have to rely on the most untrustworthy part of me, my memory. But as best as I can recall, as the first rays of sunlight broke over the surrounding hills, Wally solemnly and in a hushed tone uttered a prayer, seeking help and guidance for what he was supposed to do with these last, most dangerous weapons left on earth.

And within seconds of his finishing his praying, a light so bright I could not look into it burst forth in front of Wally. It was spontaneous in appearance. And accompanying it was the sound of serene music, with a lush fragrance permeating the area. Soon the light enveloped Wally and he stood silhouetted in its brilliance. Above the sound of the music I could barely hear words being spoken, most of which were unintelligible to me. But I did hear something to the effect of "suffer the little children unto me...", and "...it will be so..." Following hearing voices, there was a period of pure silence, with Wally still bathed in that light. At that point I realized this was some kind of heavenly event. This wasn't Walt's magic, Wally's wand or his thumping staff creating some atmospheric pyrotechnics or the Anteverse visiting the Universe. This was the Supreme Being over all the verses paying Wally a visit. It took the soulful prayer of a child to complete this world's needed transformations.

Gradually the light faded, as the sun rose higher. And within a few of minutes of its disappearance, Wally shook his head, as if coming out of a deep sleep, and called out to me to climb back on him and we should return to the ship.

Later that day, when I caught up to Wally, after our ship had tied up to the wharf in Suez, I asked what was going to happen after our trip to Mt. Catherine. He told me that the electron bonding of our world's most dangerous weapons was forever broken. Plutonium, Uranium-235, hydrogen bombs, TNT, anthrax, smallpox, VX nerve agent, serine and mustard gas and a host of others were never to be bonded together again. They were now inert and would forever be so throughout the Universe.

These compounds were history, in those particular formulations.

And then Wally smiled and said, "Don't forget to record all that you saw and heard this morning, Mr. Walt. And don't give me any credit for what happened. And make sure you note how precious life on this world, the only one of its kind left in the Universe, is to the God of all Creation. You will do that, won't you?"

And I assured him that I would. And you see now, I did. It was probably at that moment when I realized, as never before, how important Walt, Po, Bernie and Wally's mission had been. And my guess was that in the days, weeks, months and years that followed, throughout the planet, others would feel the same.

And by 11 a.m. we had secured the Polar Wind's mooring lines in Suez's Port Ibrahim. It was a bustling port, actually the busiest we had visited since leaving Shanghai. Being at the southern end of the Suez Canal, it served as the entry portal, for ships heading north.

Bernie wasted no time getting the usual gang of us outfitted in Egyptian, bird uniforms for our flights throughout the region. We had to complete them by the usual time tomorrow morning. Ed became a Goliath Heron; his eagle days were interrupted for a change, at his request. Flo was transformed into a White Stork; Iris into a African Silverbill; Rita into a Cirl Bunting; me into a Dunn's Lark, a variation of which now seemed to be my M.O.; and Jennifer, to her stunning surprise, into a Greater Flamingo. She couldn't stop looking at her reflection in the ship's windows before we flew off. I think Bernie and Wally found her alter ego at last. And again we were commissioned to spread the spoken word and various other transformations, as we all had been given powers to do, across the region. Obviously, we concentrated most of our efforts along the sea shore and the Nile River. One look at the expanses of desert to the west and south convinced me to stay in the immediate vicinity or head east. Of course, by then, there had been a significant cross-section of these regions already transformed by birds, Sophie's breath, Po and Sophie's singing, delicious fragrances, mice and other small creatures, moths and butterflies, fish of every description, and through Wally's supplications on top of Mt. Catherine. At that, Bernie still reminded us to return by 6 a.m. the next day.

Upon our return, there was the usual hustle and bustle to get ready and dash off into Suez. The plan was to ride the train from Suez to Cairo, about 60 miles away. We got to the train station in Suez by 6:30 a.m., with the others in our party dressed, as usual, in native garb. I guess you could say I was too. How else does an individual like me dress? We wear hair, of course. Unless, you think it proper to dress your canine companions like those dandies Flo and I saw that morning in Hagerstown, Maryland. People who do that to us should have to reciprocate and wear full-length, imitation, dog-hair coats as they parade their mortified pooch.

Anyway, our party was inconspicuous, particularly when we separated ourselves into three groups: Po; Frank and I; and Sophie and the children. We all sat within sight of one another, but we didn't communicate until we arrived at the Ramses Train Station, in mid-town Cairo. And as Sophie later reported to me, Wally's staff, even though it was telescoped for travel, began to vibrate inside his jacket about three miles before we arrived at the station. From that, she and Wally knew the fourth regional, meeting site must not have been too far from the railroad terminal.

We all reassembled in the main entrance hall of the station. Po then told us it was important that we secure a private vehicle to travel the rest of the way to the meeting place. He had a premonition that our departure from this fourth site was not going to be easy or unnoticed. Word had no doubt spread far and wide about what was happening to all armaments and their supplies throughout the continents of Asia, Europe and Africa.

While on the train it was obvious that the conversations and newspapers were filled with nothing else but the colossal changes we Wagoners had instituted everywhere. Wally had arranged for each of us to understand and speak both Arabic and Berber for this fourth meeting. By doing so, we understood the train passengers' conversations, and why they were both excited and anxious about what was going to happen next. It was obvious they were very unsure what the future held for them. The stabilizing and rebuilding phase of this global transformation process and the immediate effects from Fetching, as outlined in the first three regional meetings, had not yet been seen, even though they had had their immediate, intended effect. Lawlessness and violence had all but disappeared in those areas. And gradually, the ramifications of the FETCH commandments were starting to be seen and felt in wider circles.

Given all this, Po rightfully insisted on getting our own transportation. To do so, he asked Frank to go over to a car rental booth and arrange for us to hire one for the day. It was anticipated we'd have to use it both here in Cairo and to take us back to the Polar Wind. Unsure exactly what to get that would accommodate all of us and the black vase, Frank arranged to hire a panel van. And soon enough, we were all picked up on a side street by the train station, after Frank completed the rental agreement. To this day I have no idea how he managed to pay for that. My guess is that he had an old credit card stuck in his wallet. Who knows what he used for identification. I'd never seen either him or Sophie with a passport.

Luckily, we were all safely and secretly hustled into the van, and Wally got his staff fully deployed for an accurate determination of where the next meeting was to be held. It was clear to all of us it was to be close by. Frank turned onto Shana Ramses, the main boulevard in front of the train station, and headed southwest. With each block we traveled, the staff became more active, until we were stopped at a large, very congested intersection, facing the Egyptian Museum, which bordered the Nile River. Without a doubt, the staff was telling us the fourth black vase was inside that museum.

Frank, by now, was becoming an expert

driver in any circumstance and soon found a loading zone, parking spot at the rear of the museum. A couple of museum staff members came out to inquire what his business was, and when all of us began to pile out, they were told we were the guest speakers for the highly secret meeting to be held at 10 a.m. That took care of that. No one was supposed to know about that meeting, unless they were important, and then they were to be given full latitude and any help they might request. Po simply asked that the two watch our van until we returned in about an hour. At that moment it was 9:50 a.m.

Hurriedly, we wove our way into the museum, following the directions the two staff members gave us to the rear stage area. Wally's staff, likewise, clearly indicated the direction for us to go. He could hardly keep it from jumping out of his hands. Oddly, once he got on stage with the vases, the staff became completely docile.

We were able to position ourselves behind the auditorium curtain with a few minutes to spare. It was just a few minutes before the first speaker mounted the stage to speak. And what we could overhear in front of us was sheer pandemonium. There was yelling, screaming, shouting, and curses. The effects of our transformations were all too evident to this assembled crowd. Their instruments of death and destruction were gone. They were insanely mad at this point. All they could do at that moment was vent their rage to each other and at us. It was clear, given a chance; each of us Wagoners would have been eliminated in seconds. There were rewards and bounties posted everywhere for our arrest or capture, dead or alive.

Into that fury, each of us stepped out from behind the curtain. And, as usual, the stage was set up as always. The black vase was on the small table. No one had yet stepped forward onto the stage. We were the first, and that was unfortunate for this crowd, given their unspeakable intentions.

Without any explanation, Bernie signaled to Wally to do his animal transformations of the audience, which was comprised of individuals from Algeria, Palestine, Lebanon, Saudi Arabia, Morocco, Libya and Egypt. Following Wally's incantations and staff banging, there stood before us an assortment of camels, donkeys, goats, sheep, horses and cattle. In an instant the hall was quiet. And then Bernie climbed up on the chair Po had placed behind the podium and spoke to them about nationalism, jihadism, tribalism and terrorism and their soon-to-be-ever-present, personalized scroll.

When my turn came, I gave my usual speech about what they should do henceforth and added the fourth commandment to the other three in the FETCH list: to "champion life, liberty, compassion and the pursuit of wonder, discovery and happiness." At that point it became quite clear to me: there was to be a fairly large number of farm animals, presently gathered in that room that would be sold at auction later in the day. This was not a group easily motivated to see governance in terms of 'give and take'. This was, by and large, a 'take all you can', 'as often as you can', 'anyway you can', crowd. But, with a great sigh, as Po gathered up the vase, we nodded to each other and knew the worst of this region's miserable excuse for leaders had been dealt with. It was time for us to leave.

Our trip back to the Polar Wind was fraught with near-misses. People everywhere, it was evident, were unsure how to react to all the changes in their lives. If you have too much change, too fast; panic sets in. All you could hope for was that the combined voices of all creatures would enrich the dialogue and begin to allow these abused and tormented souls a chance to live a productive and happy life. Leadership had to arise from their midst, from whatever life form was most willing and able. Humans had not done such a hot job. Maybe, I thought, it was time to let that pair of white rhino's take the gavel for a while.

With a great sigh of relief, we arrived back at our ship at 2 p.m. We cast off and immediately began our passage through the Suez Canal. But just so you knew, Po did not place the fourth black vase in the same room, with the other three. He left it in the helicopter hanger. But even bringing it on board the ship caused it to rock back and forth again. It was time for Bernie and Wally to try to understand the mysterious meaning of all this. If it was up to me, I'd thrown all of them overboard. Of course, it would have been precisely the wrong thing to do, as we later learned.

FIFTEEN:CROSSING THE ATLANTIC OCEAN

Passage through the one hundred mile long Suez Canal was fascinating, to say the least. There were no locks, unlike what we later experienced passing through the Panama Canal and from what I recalled hearing was necessary for anyone wanting to travel up my Columbia River back home. The sea water just passes unimpeded from the Mediterranean to the Red Sea, without any coaxing or stopping. Most amazing of all to me is that the canal's builders dug down over fifty feet along its course. And they did that in the middle of drifting, desert sand. Apparently, the plan now is to begin the process of digging it even deeper, to over seventy feet, which would allow passage of the world's largest, commercial ships! That would be like having a basement over seven stories deep! I just couldn't see how they'd keep it from filling back up in that shifting landscape. It was a marvel.

But besides that, our passage was uneventful. That's not to say that what was going on around us was as well. We had set in motion, throughout these continental landmasses, social and political earthquakes and tsunamis. And soon enough, despite our best efforts, it would become common knowledge who and where we were and how we were traveling, once we exited the Suez Canal. And to confirm that premonition, a surprise awaited us once we were about to leave the Mediterranean Sea, for the open waters of the Atlantic Ocean.

In the meantime, we had three days of uninterrupted sailing. It was on that third day, after both the ship's crew and the Wagoners had had a chance to rest up following the exhausting, preceding weeks, when Bernie and Wally asked me again to come to their room for a chat. I was beginning to feel like I needed a court-appointed stenographer and a legal representative present for these meetings. They were getting too complicated and involved for me. If what they said was true; they had more faith in me, than I did in myself.

Bernie, as usual, opened the discussion, "We asked you to come here because you are one of our most-trusted companions, you and Flo. Remember? It was you two who rescued us from the Emissaries in Atlantic City, so long ago. We trust your judgment, as did Walt. So please bear with me as I outline what Wally and I have been observing and are now very concerned about. It involves the black vases.

"As you are no doubt aware, with each additional one that we bring on board the Polar Wind, it creates a more violent reaction within all the rest. We believe these dark and sinister containers are like lighthouses and magnets, with each one having these functions fused inside them. They appear to have brought together, in each of these four regions we've visited so far, the worst of the worst. They did inadvertently, however, allow us to quickly identify the most dangerous individuals in these regions. Wally and I are now convinced that the Emissaries placed them in these venues. And if Walt happened to be successful in defeating the Emissaries in the Battle of Oregon, they were to be automatically activated or be deployed in some manner.

"They were also to serve, and still may be doing so at this very moment, as messengers, beaconing anyone who would or could to embrace evil and terrorize everyone around them. Even now, we worry about members of our ship's crew. Any of them could fall under their spell. And for that reason, we are going to ask Capt. Shriver to call a meeting of all the ship's company to allow us to explain our concerns. We'll need to have him post guards at both locations where the vases are stored, and everyone will have to monitor one another for any signs of increased unrest or aggression.

"In particular, we are additionally concerned what happens once all of these vases are collected in one location. It appears they gain strength as they are reunited. What does that mean? Are we in danger at this moment? Wally and I believe so. And we're going to assign Po as the primary guard for the three vases in his room and you and Flo as such for the one in the helicopter hanger. If you feel the need to enlist the others in our group to help you, please do so.

"One thing is clear, we cannot lose track of them. If one of them were to disappear or be thrown overboard, it would no doubt cause unending turmoil for this world. We must eliminate all five of them simultaneously. And from all indications, that is the total number we now assume there are.

"These containers brought together the worst amongst us, in each of these regions. And they probably have goaded and facilitated the worst behaviors and activities within and between us. Wars, assassinations, kidnappings, drug trafficking, gang activity, slave trading, all these and more have been part of their demonic legacy. They are part of the Emissaries backup plan. And until they are somehow destroyed, our world is vulnerable and unsafe. Guard them, as if your life depends on it. Sadly, in fact, it does."

Well, so much for my lazy days of springtime after that meeting. I didn't want to trust myself to protecting all life on this planet to just me, so I called together Flo, Rita, Jennifer, Ed and Iris to join me. Together, we all stationed ourselves, in shifts, around the fourth vase in the helicopter hanger. And to phase Po, we each helped relieve him, as did Frank and Sophie. And somehow, we felt the vases were aware what we were doing. It was all too creepy...and deadly.

But, somehow we managed to sail undetected, or at least unrecognized, until we were about twenty miles east of the Straits of Gibraltar. At that point the passage narrowed down to a nine mile gap between the Sea and the Ocean. And it was then that we began to observe, both by way of radio traffic and visually, the presence of people coming to and lining the shorelines on both sides of us. Life forms from Europe and Africa were migrating down to this narrow gap to wish us a safe journey. Our secret passage was over. Everyone who came knew who we were and how we were traveling. Animals, birds, people by the hundreds of thousands, if not millions, were gathered on both continental promontories. Their shouts of joy and gratitude for being released from the bondage of terror and abuse were overwhelming. It was a roar of affirmation. Life on this planet was fighting back, taking back its rightful heritage.

Each of us on board the ship hugged and waved back to the hosts of life on each side of us. It made what lay ahead bearable, even possible.

Finally, upon reaching the open waters of the ocean, feeling spent from all the recent excitement, I again assumed my posture over the ship's stern railing and up popped Reg.

"Hey, there," he called out to me. "You've been a busy fellow, I understand."

"Where'd you come from?" I asked, stunned to see my Pacific, tuna contact over here in the Atlantic Ocean.

"I, and a few of my colleges, decided it was best if we took the long way around and met you here, provided you made it safely through your last two meetings. We couldn't travel undetected through that Suez Canal area, besides it was too congested for us anyway. But we're relieved to see that you did make it. However, I have some disturbing news for you, I'm afraid."

"Like what?" I asked, thinking he was going to tell me a bad storm was brewing ahead of us.

"Like where you are heading next is not going to welcome you. The word is that they're planning a big surprise for you. Seems that whatever changes and transformations you made back home, on your cross-country journey, didn't migrate as far south from there as you might have hoped."

"How do you know that?" I exclaimed, wondering just what exactly this all meant.

"News and transformations appear to travel faster underwater than they do by way of air transport. Once we fish-types got the privilege of talking, we spread it as far and as quickly as we could. However, you can't say the same for the birds of North America, especially the ones you made contact with in the areas of your travels. You probably should have spent more time in the Southwestern part of your country, where more birds migrate further south into Middle and South America. In summary, your ship is heading into an area still patrolled by aircraft that means to do you great harm. We did take care of any ships that might. Just the same, it has been widely circulated in this region what you are, who and where you are, who you are traveling with and that you are coming there next. In fact, I'd give you about five or six days in the open ocean before you start to run into real trouble."

"Are you sure?" was all I could ask.

"Yep. I verified it myself through my

various contacts with some porpoises and a few of my shirt-tail, tuna relatives who regularly travel along the South American coastlines."

"Oh, me...could you wait here a few minutes while I go get Bernie, Wally and Capt. Shriver?" I asked, as I began to feel that this ordeal was never going to end or if it did, it would not be in our favor.

I decided right there and then if anyone thought cleaning up humanity's 10,000 years of abuses and poor choices was going to be quick and easy, they were delusional. And, furthermore, I was sure that I was, just by being there. What chance does one child wizard, one child herald, two talking dogs, one talking cat, and three talking birds have to reverse what thousands upon thousands of years have created? Look around you. What would you think at that point? If I could have bought a one-way ticket to Howard's porch at that moment, I'd have done it in a heart-beat. I would have started walking back to Atlantic City, if I could have. As I thought about it, for all intents and purposes, time was up for humanity to be the sole party to bring peace to this world. It had its chance. Now it was all of life's creatures' time as well. We certainly couldn't do any worse.

Eventually, I found everyone who needed to talk to Reg, and I bid farewell to my roost at the stern of Polar Wind. I must confess I didn't return there again the remainder of our voyage. Call it battle fatigue. Call it cowardice. I did not want to be the bearer of bad news any longer. From then on Flo and I began to hang out together at the bow of the ship, sheltered by the zodiac boats when we were in rough seas. We both wanted to be the first to see friendly landfall and know we were about home. Both of us were desperately homesick by this time. As Bernie was to announce later in this voyage, we'd had "enough".

After the discussion with Reg, Capt. Shriver sent urgent messages out to the U.S. Naval Fleet Operations Center for the Atlantic Ocean. Without detailing the reason in too much detail, for fear others with deadly intent might intercept them, he simply announced that our ship was in need of help, that we were on a life-saving mission and that all available ships in the region needed to respond. He further noted that radio silence was of utmost importance.

It wasn't until five days later when we were southwest of the Canary Islands that we spotted the first U.S. Naval Ship. It was a cruiser. But within minutes of seeing her, we saw countless ships on the horizon, including three Nimitz-class aircraft carriers and their accompanying battle groups. All told there must have been forty or fifty ships come to our aid. It was thrilling.

To show our appreciation it was decided by all the Wagoners that we would give three or four performances each day on each ship for the next three days. Word had spread about us, while we were on our round-the-world voyage, so it wasn't necessary to pretend we were anything other than whom and what we were. But we wanted to give the sailors and marines a real show, full of the magic and mystery that lay ahead for everyone on the planet. There were Wally transformations and appearances/disappearances; Bernie dialogues; singing and banjo/fiddle playing; dancing, acrobatics and comedy skits by Flo, Jennifer, Rita, Ed, Iris and myself. Each performance was three hours long. We brought the house down each time. This renewed my spirits as nothing else could.

It was three days later that we had our first encounter with a hostile intruder. Actually, it was a flight of them. Various countries in that region had banded together to launch a coordinated air attack on our ship. But, as they approached the armada, they realized the air and sea cover made it a suicide mission and quickly turned back.

In the meantime, Bernie and Wally had decided that we needed to spend a good three days in these still hostile countries, spreading the word and transformations. They arranged to have all of us transferred to one carrier and then have them fly us into various areas. But before that happened we had to address the issue of the black vases.

They were becoming more active, the closer we came to the fifth one. They had to be separated. In conversations with the officers of the Polar Wind, it was decided that the four vases would be confined in separate, secure quarters. There would be no access to these areas, except by Bernie and Wally. The vases were beginning to have a disturbing effect on various crew members. The taunts and alluring temptations they emitted were too tempting. Separating the vases would at least buy us some time before there would be a mutiny of some sort. It was clear to each of us that time was running out. The Emissaries could very easily win after all.

But I need to shift back to our being flown into the various countries of South and Central America. Each of us, even Bernie and Wally, were made birds again, and most interesting of all, each of us now were endowed with all the transforming powers that individual ones of us previously had. For the next three days I felt like everything I touched got sprinkled with some fairy dust. Seriously though, Bernie wanted us to spread our good news and all the various transformation quickly and as far and wide as we could. It worked.

Ed, at this point, wanted to remain looking like his true self, as did Iris and Rita. They were each getting closer to home and didn't want to pretend they were someone else. That left the others of us to become local bird species. Bernie became a Chaulk-browed Mockingbird, Wally a Rufus Throated Hummingbird, Sophie an Indigo Bunting, Frank a Macaw Parrot, Po a Buff-necked Ibis, Jennifer a Striped Cuckoo (which only encouraged more theatrics), Flo an Amazon Kingfisher and I became a Scissortail Flycatcher. With the eleven of us flying in all directions for those three days, we were able to quickly make up for lost time. We had 95% of the birds, trees, animals and humans throughout South and Central America tap dancing to a brand new tune by the end of that third day.

To get started we had to be ferried over to one of the carriers by our own helicopters and then Wally transformed each of us and himself. From there we were flown by carrier planes into the various, surrounding countries. Upon landing on remote runways, scattered over this huge area, we were quickly released and told to return to the same spot in three days. I ended up in southern Mexico. Wally also had us transformed to speak Spanish, given that it was the sole language spoken in the majority of the countries that we were assigned to. The exceptions were for those going to Peru and Bolivia, where the indigenous languages of Aymara, Quechua and Chiquitano were spoken as much as Spanish. Wally went there. His young lungs could more easily handle the mountains' high altitude, as well as the jungles' high humidity.

At the end of those amazing, three days we were returned to the Polar Wind, which by this time had sailed past the Trinidad and Tobago Islands and its capital, Port-of-Spain. By then we were approaching La Asuncion. It was at this point that the Naval Armada protecting us veered northward into the more open waters of the Caribbean Sea, but they always had aircraft patrol the skies above and beyond us. We were entering enemy territory. And to provide the Polar Wind additional security, she was to maneuver back into the more open waters of the Sea, once Po, Frank, Bernie, Wally and I, along with the four black vases in separate zodiac boats, were deposited on shore.

Our destination at 3:30 a.m., that last night before the regional meeting the next morning, was a deserted beach area five miles southwest of the coastal town of Barcelona, Venezuela. Everything had been done to protect us these last few days and to give us the best chance of succeeding in Caracas. All anyone, other than the five of us, could do after we were safely on land, was wait. The next two days were an eternity for everyone. The planet held its breath.

SIXTEEN: CARACAS, VENEZUELA

Because of the darkness, we could not see that we had chosen a spot barricaded by a high bluff, separating us from the main highway. It passed east-to-west along the Venezuela coastline. Behind the highway rose steep, mountain cliffs, but again none of that was evident until daybreak. Landing at high tide, the surf's rhythmical booming made any conversation impossible. Luckily, we had all been instructed what to do before leaving the Polar Wind. And as good fortune would have it, our Coast Guard shipmates landed us in a sheltered cove, protected from the most violent waves. Little did we know at the time but an almost unheard-of severe, Atlantic-driven storm was heading in our direction, given the hurricane season wasn't supposed to start for another few months. As an afterthought, some years after all this happened, I was convinced that storm had something to do with the black vases.

Carefully, Po and the zodiac boats' crew carefully lifted and carried the four vases to separate locations and stored each of them 150 feet apart, well above the reach of the highest tide. Following the crews depositing us, the zodiacs hurriedly took off and headed back to our mother ship. The highway was adjacent to where we were huddled, and it was streaming with vehicles, most of which were heading west. We could only guess why, but I figured it was not part of a welcoming party for us.

By 7 a.m., on that April 7th day, the flow of traffic had dramatically decreased. That convinced us that what we heard earlier was a mass movement of individuals toward Caracas. It filled each of us with dread. We now anticipated we'd be greeted with throngs of people. No one knew what their mood would be like. We hadn't been able to completely cover the entire region with our transformations. There just wasn't enough time and too few of us.

Realizing our mood was becoming deeply despondent, Wally, of all people, piped up and asked, "Ok, I need two of you to carry my staff and wand into the city. Who will volunteer?"

"Do I have to walk all the way with it?" I replied.

"No, Mr. Walt," he giggled and answered. "You and the rest of us are going to fly there."

"In that case, I'll carry one, but if I'm to be a flycatcher or a lark, as has been my customary way up to now, I'll only be able to carry one of their empty sheaths."

"Oh, don't worry about that," Wally reassured me. "You and one other of us will become Andean Condors for this trip. And in case you didn't know, they are the world's largest birds.

You'll easily be able to carry them in your talons."

"Then count me in," I volunteered, anxious to be the biggest bird of the flock for once.

"So will I," Frank offered. "Being a parrot was ok, but I'd like to gain some altitude and see a little more of the landscape this time. Condors soar."

"That settles it then," Wally said with some relief. "Po, you'll still be an Ibis, Bernie a mockingbird and I'll be the same hummingbird. I think it is time we change over and head off. Is everyone ready?"

With a nod of heads and a swish of Wally's wand, we were all left standing on the seashore looking at each other and ruffling our feathers. Frank and I went over and picked up Wally's wand and staff, and then we all lifted off into the morning air. Coastal clouds had begun banking into the mountains rimming the shoreline. It reminded me of Hawaii. It was a lush landscape. Why such evil lurked in these places confounded me. Why didn't humans ever learn to get along and stop wanting to hurt one another? Maybe someday a geneticist will identify a DNA strand that causes all this meanness, and someone can shave it off. I'd like to think much of the harm we've caused one another can be linked to the Emissaries and their manipulations. But, somehow, that doesn't quite explain it all. Humanity bears much of the responsibility. The Emissaries were just so pleased to assist and help direct its evolution.

Our flight into Caracas took two and a half hours. And by the time we reached the outskirts of that huge city, the staff I was holding in my feet was beginning to shake. As we circled over the Central District, it was jerking me up and down as I flew. It was obvious we had to land, and I called out to Wally and Bernie that we had reached our destination.

It was to be at the oldest, city park in Caracas, the Parque El Calvario. It had a very large grass-covered area, a small lake and an ornithological museum, among its most obvious features. And within its boundaries, the surrounding neighborhood and the bordering streets, there were thousands upon thousands of angry, desperate and vile individuals. There were gang leaders; drug traffickers and warlords; assassins; kidnappers; torturers; intimidation, shakedown and protection mobsters; and criminals of every variety, in uniforms and without.

It was a gathering, mustered together by this fifth vase, of the very worst of the North, Central and South American continents. Many had traveled thousands of miles to get there. And they meant to demonstrate, by their angry presence, that no one, whether through a so-called War on Drugs or War on Terror or War on Crime, was going to stop their eventual conquest of all society. They had in their hands the final, ultimate weapons of mass destruction of civilization: drugs, crime and terror. And they relished the thought of spreading them everywhere..

The five of us swooped down onto an elegantly decorated, vaulted stage laid out before this mass gathering of madness and murderers.

Again, the setting on the stage was like the other four, with the black vase placed on a small table and the podium set off to the side of it.

No sooner had we alighted, then Wally reconstituted us; and Bernie signaled for Wally to perform his crowd-control changes. Taking the staff I had laid at his feet, he pounded it loudly three times, repeated the phrase "Pigs' knuckle soup" and approximately 50,000 shouting, knife waving, gun shooting, feet stomping, loud swearing and raging low life's were changed instantly into nicely trimmed out, feedlot piglets. Hog futures in the months and years to come were going to be weak I imagined. A small part of me felt like maybe I should have forewarned the brokers at the Chicago Board of Trade. Instead, I just smiled.

And, of course, the same conditions applied, as before, to their transformations. The rapt audience could hear and understand every word spoken. However, for now, they couldn't even 'squeak', 'oink' or move. Party time was over. Bernie and Wally had arrived on the scene. How proud Walt must have been at that moment. So instead of a brewing riot of would-be killers, we now had a sullen, if not surprised, audience of piglets. "My, my," I thought, "fortunes can rise and fall in an instant." Now it was Bernie's and my time to talk.

And as was the custom, Po lifted Bernie up onto the chair to speak.

"It was not our intent to shock or harm you, but we had no other choice but to transform you, for your own safety and certainly for ours and the rest of life on this planet. As you are now realizing, you understand what I am saying and that will remain the case throughout the remainder of your lives. And you will be able to move again, but you will remain mute. Our intent has not been to take life but simply to transform it. And so you have been. We trust your lives will be safe and relatively comfortable ones. Certainly, they will likely be more so than the poor souls you have tormented with your schemes, crimes and chemical compounds over the ages. Those days, as of a few moments ago, are over. And those of you assembled here, each of whom plied your terrorist acts so methodically and destructively, have now officially retired. The rebuilding of communities, cities, societies and countries can now commence without your controlling influences.

"And to complete this transformation process, I am going to ask my brother to step forward and perform one last act here today."

At that point Wally stepped up, between the podium and the small table that the black vase and I were resting on, and waved his staff in a manner I had not seen him do before. Immediately, a light radiated from the end of it and shot upward the then it spread out beyond the staff, like an immense canopy, high above the park and city of Caracas. Soon it passed over the countries surrounding Venezuela, the Caribbean Sea, the Gulf of Mexico, where the Polar Wind was anchored, the Pacific and Oceans, all the countries of Asia, Africa, Australia, Europe, Central, South and North America. Every continent, city, village and township, worldwide was covered by this veil of light. It remained in place for an hour, I was later informed. During that time it allowed its presence and power to seep into every crack and crevice that might harbor people like those that had been standing before us in that park. And when it faded, the only reminder of its presence was an amazing outbreak of mute piglets throughout the globe.

Once the aura of light faded Bernie nodded at me to begin my portion of the agenda. But with all that had gone before, I wasn't too sure what needed to be said. Be that as it may, the powers of Walt again took over and I spoke.

"Usually, at least in cities we've previously been to, I instruct the audiences about the use of scrolls that are left by the exits. In your case, there are none. You are not going to have any successors, as some who attended the previous meetings were to have. You are the end of the line. But I would like to at least conclude today's encounter with each of you by enlightening you on what will be the last working commandment, as outlined in the word 'FETCH!'. It is the letter 'H', and it commands everyone to 'honor that which is good and merciful in each of us'. Maybe you could see if you can practice a measure of this in your new circumstances, at least to the degree that it is practical…as a piglet.

"As we leave today, you will also be free to leave. My guess is that you will be welcome guests in the homes of families everywhere. I would encourage you not to panic. Let those closest to the exit ways and streets leave first. You have all the time in the world now at your disposal. Your previous commitments have been cancelled. Good day."

Wally and the others of us wisely waited behind the stage until Po was able to locate an empty limousine, which was still idling, with two piglets squirming in the front seat. My guess was that they used to be two of the attendees guards. Po opened the doors and shooed them out. Afterward, Wally performed the necessary wand movements to energize the audience.

As we drove off, Frank saw in his rearview mirror a surge of animal life pour into the streets behind us. That left just one more obstacle to overcome before this world-circumventing mission was over. And it was to be our most dangerous one.

Po had the fifth black vase beside him in the rear seat of the limo. Wally and Bernie were in the front seats with Frank and I. Before we drove off, Po had instructed us to ride back that way. And by the time we reached the outskirts of Caracas, the storm front was hitting us full force. If it had not been daylight, I'm sure Frank would not have been able to see his way clear enough to drive. The rain was blowing horizontally, coming directly from the Caribbean Sea. Quite likely, if our vehicle had not been so heavy, we would have been blown off the highway.

The closer we got to our landing site, south of Barcelona, the more concerned Po got that the surf may have risen so high it would have swept the other black vases into the sea. If that had happened, our entire voyage these last few months would have been a waste, to say nothing of our cross-country trip we took earlier. He urged Frank to drive as fast as conditions would allow. I simply had to shut my eyes. It had been a long day, and I knew there wasn't anything more I could do. At that point, I curled up on the floorboard, with Wally's feet swinging just above me. It seemed to comfort him to have me close at hand. Every now and then he would reach down and scratch me behind my ears. What a lad! With a dear friend like him petting me, I knew then I was the luckiest dog alive.

Being asleep, I wasn't aware of the struggle that Po was having in the back seat with the fifth vase. The closer we got to the other four, the more erratic and violent its shaking became. Finally, Po asked that Frank turn on the back compartment overhead light so he could better control the vase. When he did, Po let out a gasp.

"There is writing appearing on the side of the vase. It's incomplete at this moment, but I can just make out some of the markings. Oh, me...it's written in the language of our previous world, back in the anteverse. It's been so long ago, I'm not sure I can read it. How I wish Walt was here now."

Hearing this, Bernie leaped up, pushed the limo's dividing window further apart and climbed over her seat back into the rear compartment with Po.

"Let me see if I can translate some of it for you, Po," she urgently whispered.

Kneeling down in front of the three-foot high vase, resting on the back seat, Bernie saw that indeed cuneiform-appearing letters were visible at the point where the widest portion of the vase began.   And the message did appear that it was incomplete, that it was still revealing itself.   Her knowledge of such writing was limited to what Walt had imparted to her during their evenings together on the cross-country trip.   And as best she could translate it, all it said thus far was:

"Whether apart or together,
The time has come.
We would have waited forever;
But now, it's too late to run.

Come sunset on April Seven,
Our work here will be done.
And you…"

"Oh, Po," Bernie cried out, "These vases and this message are from the Emissaries.   They planned all along to end all life on this world today, no matter what had happened that afternoon we battled them in Oregon.   These vases are their backup plan.   What can we do? Something terrible is going to happen whether these vessels are all together or apart.   It was all a hoax, having these five regional meetings.   They were meant to throw Walt and us off their trail.   All along it was the vases that were the immediate dangers.   And what if one of those vases has already washed into the Sea from this terrible storm?   Oh, I fear we've failed, Po."

It was then, with all this commotion going on, I climbed up on the seat and looked back at Po and Bernie.   For the first time since Flo and I rescued her and Wally, I saw her sobbing.   It made me so sad and very, very afraid.

Then I saw something else and yelled out at Po, "Look! There is a crack appearing at the top of the vase. Is it going to shatter or something?"

Po quickly turned the vase toward him and saw for himself that there was indeed a crack now visible at the vase's sealed top.

"Frank!" Po shouted, "We must hurry! Faster!...Oh, mercy! Didn't we agree to have the four zodiac boats waiting for us at the shoreline in front of those other four vases by 2 p.m.!!?"

Frank yelled back at him that it was his understanding that was the plan, but that he had brought ashore one of the ship's hand radios, in case there were any changes. He followed up by asking Po if he wanted him to try to reach the Polar Wind and to relay any further instructions.

"Most definitely!" Po loudly replied. "Tell Capt. Shriver to have each of the four zodiac crews proceed as previously instructed to the four vases, but instead of waiting there for us to come, they are to each carry their assigned vase to a central point in the middle of their landing zone. They are not to worry about what may happen when the four vases are assembled together. But they are to be sure that the area is well above the crashing surf. Then they are to take their boats far away from that area. It would be best if they returned to the Polar Wind, and immediately set sail further offshore as well. No one is to be in the area once the four vases are united. Can you make sure to tell him all that?"

"Sure thing, Po," Frank answered. "And where do you want me to drive us in the meantime?"

"Estimate where the midpoint would be that they might place the four vases, and drive us there," Po quickly replied.

At that moment, as Wally unsheathed his staff and held it upright on the limo's floorboard, he reassured Frank he'd know exactly where that spot would be. The staff would show them the way.

And by 5:15 p.m. Frank pulled to a stop at a small turnout, along the ocean highway. Wally's staff had faithfully shown them the exact spot to park.

Stunned, Bernie called out to everyone, "I can read the rest of the message on this vase now! And it's clear there are no more words to be revealed. It says,

"And your pitiful dreams of heaven,
Will die, like an exploding sun."

"We'll see about that," was all Po said, as he wrestled the churning and twisting vase out of the back seat into the howling gale. By now the crack had extended half way down the vase, splitting the first words of the message. He then turned to Wally.

"Follow me, Wally!" Po snapped, not meaning to be curt with the boy, but obviously now obsessed with trying to do the impossible, under absolutely horrific, weather conditions.

"Time is running out!" Po continued. "We only have about thirty minutes before these vases begin something that will destroy this world. Bring your wand and staff. You will need both, and you need to be brave and believe everything Walt ever told you that you could do. Now is your moment of truth."

Sliding down the steep hillside, both Po and Wally wove their way down to another sheltered cove where the Polar Wind's zodiac crews had piled the other four vases. And despite Bernie's warning calls to me, I trailed behind Wally. I remembered how he had asked me to be with him in Oregon. And, besides, he was my buddy. I wasn't going to leave him alone now.

Once the three of us were down at the beach level, the noise was deafening. You could not hear each other speak, even if you yelled. Methodically, Po approached the pile of vases and placed the fifth one on the very top. It was clear to me that the same message had appeared on all of them and that they were all cracking in the same way as the one Po was transporting. Something final was about to happen.

Once Po got the vases together, there was only five minutes left, until the time he anticipated would be sunset. Coming over to Wally, he cupped his hands over Wally's ear and yelled something to him. Wally then nodded and motioned for me to come alongside him. Unsheathing his wand and staff, he had me hold the staff in my teeth, while he had to take both hands to wave his wand. This was followed by him then taking the staff from me and waving it in the same manner. All the while he was saying something that I didn't understand. I figured it had to be in some anteverse dialect.

And while he was doing this, with our now

being some distance from Po and the vases, the most remarkable thing I have ever seen before or since happened. Po was transformed a final time into the tall, erect and powerful Centurion he was in Walt's home that day in New Jersey so long ago. He was dressed immaculately in a Roman officer's uniform. And before him was a large chariot, now loaded with the five vases. And harnessed in front of the chariot, most stunning of all, were four pure white, winged horses. They were spaced far enough apart so that their wings could be easily extended.

Aghast, I could also see that the vases were beginning to now break apart and expose a deep black chasm inside each, and coming out from them was a roaring sound, louder than anything the storm was producing. And it was creating a vortex, around which sand and rocks were beginning to be drawn into it. With each passing second, the noise and suctioning were becoming louder and stronger. It was the sound of rage, unlike anything you'd ever want to hear again.

And in an instant, Po took the reins and snapped them one time, and the chariot lofted off the beach. As he began to rise off the beach, he turned to both Wally and I and shouted, in that booming baritone voice that I loved so much, "Farewell, my dear friends. I join Walt now. Our blessings will be upon you dear ones always."

And in a flash of light he was gone from view. It was later reported that astronomers around the world noted an uncommon flash, in the southern sky, light years beyond our solar system. It occurred that same evening Wally and I stood, so stunned, on that beach. They theorized it was a black hole swallowing a nearby galaxy. Wally later told me that Po had said the vases probably contained dark matter, which at a designated time would become so heavy that a black hole would begin forming within them. It was the same method used to destroy his and Walt's world so many eons ago.

Frank later contacted the Polar Wind, and two zodiacs picked us up by 9 p.m. that same, stormy night. And for the first time in almost two years the New Jersey Wagoners, once we got back to the Polar Wind, slept soundly and peacefully the remainder of that night. However, each of us would remain ever-mindful of Walt and Po's absence. It was because of them, all of us slept peacefully that night, and every night since then.

SEVENTEEN: EPILOGUE

There was no question about it; the loss of Po had a dramatic effect on all of us. His life-sacrificing heroics were certainly not out of character, but his absence left us without that immediate contact with Walt. Now the two members of our group who were vital for its eventual purpose and very existence were gone. We were rudderless for some time thereafter. Actually, until a few days after we finally arrived back at Willa's, we were still in a state of shock.

While it's true that we did find sleeping easier after leaving Caracas, we were left with many images of the darker side of existence. Maybe that was the price anyone pays who tries to combat the worst in humanity, whether it is crime, war, drugs or disease. I know it took a lot of the silliness out of me. I was not the chase-my-tail, bark at passers-by from-the-bed-of-a-truck, kind of critter anymore. I even asked Flo if she thought I should be in therapy. Her reply was who would provide it? Dogs with black, depressive moods, as a result of seeing and personally experiencing the upheavals and transformations we had, were not the hallmarks of the average shrink's clientele. She jokingly advised me to consider starting to smoke or drink. Nice. We work diligently to rid humanity of its deepest, ingrained vices and my best friend advises me to sample two of its more addictive ones to face reality. I chose talking to my other best friends instead. It was Wally, Bernie, Jennifer, Ed, Iris and Rita who pulled me through. Later, I realized Flo was indirectly, but effectively, pushing me in that same direction.

So for hours upon hours we all spent time on board the Polar Wind talking, rehashing and reliving the experiences of the past months. Even Hope, the Polar Wind's mascot, came in handy during that period. True, she had stayed completely out of our way throughout the cruise, but her naiveté and sweetness made for good company in itself. We invited her to come to Willa's anytime she had leave from the Polar Wind, which of course meant Capt. Shriver would be coming along as well. He had certainly earned that right. And the invitation was always there for him and all his crew.

The trip through the Panama Canal on April10[th] was electrifying. It was nothing like the Suez Canal. Seeing the jungles, the mountains, the locks, and realizing the diseases and hardships those who built this structure endured made me both sad and truly impressed.

And from there, we simply sailed non-stop past the Columbia River entrance into the Pacific Ocean. It was at that point that Frank and Sophie approached the Captain and asked if he could drop us off at the Grays Harbor Port town of Westport, Washington. That would save the Wagoners the trouble of trying to find a way back to Willa's from Seattle. Eager to please the weary guests, Capt. Shriver agreed. Sophie then used the ship's telephone and called Willa to let her know we were being discharged in Westport. She was very relieved, not knowing what had happened to us over these last three months. At her age and with her background, news had a way of being repetitive and disheartening. She had a good idea what we were charged, by Walt, to do; but she knew nothing about what we had actually accomplished. She was eager to have us back home, as was I, to be sure. In response to Sophie's news, she said she would get Jimmy and Diane to drive the bus down Hwy 101 to Aberdeen and then take the cutoff to Westport. They should arrive there in about three hours.

Rather than attempt to maneuver into the Grays Harbor ship channel and then try to berth in Westport, Capt. Shriver gave orders to have two zodiacs transport us to shore. The Polar Wind, given the calm waters, could stand fast a few miles offshore, while we were ferried in. There were no long looks when we made our final preparations to leave. The ship's crew had been diligent and professional during our voyage, but they wanted to go home to be with their families. We had robbed them of their earlier shore leave when we commandeered their ship in Seattle. They realized that something rather stunning had been accomplished during this cruise, but sailors for all time, the world over, long to be reunited with their loved ones back home when their cruise is over.

Bernie and Wally, despite their age, knew this. And interestingly, ever since the traumatic events on the stormy shore outside Barcelona, Venezuela, they both appeared to me to be losing their Walt-transforming presence and powers. In a word, they were becoming children again, just like any other, anywhere. But the one last act of wonder that they generated was just before we departed the Polar Wind. They had Frank lug a heavy trunk into the ship's Auditorium and place it in the front. Following that, they gave the Captain instructions to call all the crew together before their leave began in Seattle and to issue to all of them what was inside it.

Only some months after our trip was over did Wally confide in me what was inside that trunk. Apparently, as a last act of creative transformation, Wally had struck large one hundred percent, pure gold medallions, with the Polar Wind's image on the front and a likeness of the twelve of us Wagoners on the back. He told me they weighed at least five pounds each. Additionally, there were smaller gold pieces with the same images on them for each family member. They were the only ones of their kind and were each nearly priceless.

Our departure was quick, with some waves and shouts of "good-bye", and we were off. Ed, Iris and Rita chose not to fly over, but rode in the zodiac with Jennifer, Flo and I. Sophie, Frank, Bernie and Wally rode in the other zodiac. Once we docked, there were some stares, but before we attracted a crowd, Jimmy pulled up in our converted bus. We all climbed aboard and were off before the zodiacs had time to reverse their engines and head back out to sea.

There wasn't the shouting and antics we performed on the trip to Seattle. Having firm ground underfoot, heading to our home, rejoining family after brushes with danger and death left us reflective and relieved. We were just thankful to be alive, and very sad to have lost Po. Jimmy and Diane were kind enough not to ask questions and left us ride quietly back to Willa's. We pulled into the front gate of her farm on April 15th, late in the afternoon.

And for the next few days we slept, roamed through the pastures and woods, soared above the firs and hemlocks and sat by the rushing Hoh River. None of the returning veterans of the Global Voyage, as we came to call it, were ready yet to talk much about our experiences.

Until we got word on April 22nd that the United Nations was convening a special session of the General Assembly in their New York City Headquarters. It was Sophie and Willa who saw it announced on a national news channel. And it was both of them who informed the other nine of us that we had to be there on April 25th for that meeting. At first, it seemed a little far-fetched to me, but after everyone discussed the possibility of our going, the importance of it was evident to each of us.

Immediately, Sophie and Frank began to book airplane reservations out of Seattle and contacted their relatives in Brooklyn where we would stay. Their relatives would offer more secluded and private lodging, away from the press and cameras. We knew there could be intense interest in us after our appearing at that Assembly. But we each knew we had to go. It was to be our last official act as a team.

The trip to Seattle, the flight to La Guardia Airport and shuttle ride to the Brooklyn Transit Center were a blur to me. All I was focused on was that meeting on the 25th. It was like I was holding my breath the whole time, since we first heard about it going to be convened.

Frank had arranged for one of his family members to hire a van to transport us to the United Nations Building on the 25th. The issue of getting inside the General Assembly building was solved by Sophie, who had prearranged with the security officials to let us drive the van into the service area. We were to be an International Welcoming Body, made up of animals and birds that recently had been given the ability to speak. And because that was one of the main reasons for calling this meeting, the Security Staff approved our backdoor arrival, as it were.

Upon our arrival, we were spirited quickly into the back of the General Assembly Hall. A fabric partition had been erected to block our being seen by the audience, until the time when we were to be introduced. At least that was the agenda that Sophie outlined for the Security personnel. Everyone was very obliging, especially when Ed and I made it a point to thank them for their help and courtesy.

Hurriedly, we all collected ourselves behind the screen and listened to the mammoth hall fill with Heads of State and dignitaries the world over. One hundred ninety-two countries had sent their highest government officials. What had been happening, worldwide, these last four months had prompted this assembly. The liquidation of war materials, killing instruments, harmful chemicals, dreadful biological concoctions and illicit drugs, to say nothing of the ability of most living organisms' ability to communicate, had turned the world upside down. If for no other reason, they had come here to commiserate and seek each other's advice on what to do next. For many, it seemed the world had gone absolutely mad and impossible to control.

As the Auditorium had reached its capacity and the General Secretary was about to mount the dais to open the meeting, Sophie motioned for the ten of us to walk and waddle around the protective screen and approach the speaker's microphones first. This we did with some precision, I might add. And, as was noted in the regional meetings, there was again a lectern and a large table with numerous chairs around it and microphones on it. Like clockwork, Sophie and Frank marched up to the lectern and Bernie, Wally and us animals and birds climbed onto the chairs and table.

It was a sight to see. Here was Ed, with his feathers just recently pruned and groomed, Rita with her yellow sash resplendent over her gorgeously white body, Iris stretching out her six foot wingspan and arching her head and neck, Flo standing powerfully erect with her husky features facing the audience and Jennifer and I at the other end of the table, glaring, unblinkingly. And each of us was wearing Willa's colorful ribbons around our necks. Bernie and Wally, dressed in the uniforms Willa gave them, stood at attention on two chairs behind the table. Sophie and Frank, also dressed in their uniforms, stood at attention behind the lectern.

It was Sophie who spoke first.

"Ladies and gentlemen, let me introduce you to the New Jersey Wagoners. It is we who you have suspected have brought you here, so to speak. It is both us standing before you now, and two of our members, who have died in the course of our missions, who have attempted to bring this world back into some balance. But I am not here to make a speech, nor is anyone else in our troop. But I do want to introduce one amongst us who will share a final word with you, and then our work, as a team is completed. We will not be available for questions or interviews. Understand and respect that. Now, if you will, please let me introduce to you, Greg, who will have our final words for you."

Then Sophie turned, smiled, nodded and gave me one of her now famous winks. She knew she had caught me completely by surprise, and it thrilled her to do so. Worse still, there was no Walt magic coursing through my hairy body. I just stood there, simply as Greg, the middle aged dog that I was. No claps of thunder, no heavenly lights shown down from above. And everyone on the planet was looking at me at that moment. Swallowing hard, I began.

"There has been enough oratory in recent months about what has and is happening around us. Maybe it's time to ask a few questions, leaving the answers to them up to each of you. And maybe just a couple of quick summation comments are in order to send you on your way.

"Why did it take wizardry and magic to bring sanity back into this world? Why were the multitude of life forms, other than the biased selection of humanity, denied some kind of representation in this Assembly Hall? Why has the contribution of living creatures, whether in the oceans, the forests, jungles, mountains, savannahs, or in your own homes been denied a voice? How did evil and terror take such a stranglehold on the majority of life on this world? Are the Emissaries solely to blame? I sincerely doubt it. Who, then, is? How are we to keep this world safe from now on? Who will be responsible for keeping it so?

"Everyone here in this place and every individual life form beyond its perimeter is responsible from this moment on. You have in your hands the scrolls that we left in various regional centers and others that were transported to major capitals around the world. And on them are inscribed the FETCH! Commandments: follow, enact, teach, champion and honor. Nowhere is it commanded that you lead. That insatiable urge has led to disaster, century after century.

"We must become interdependent as nations and as individuals. And, foremost, above all else, we must DO NO HARM! Maybe one day, soon, you can add the invocation to do good. Right now, it's enough to avoid harming one another. That's as good a starting point as one can hope for at this moment.

"And let this be enough said. You are the last inhabited world in this Universe left intact. And it is a magnificently beautiful one. Treasure it. Care for it and for yourselves. We are finished."

There followed a stunned silence as the ten of us climbed or hopped down from the table and walked out the rear exit of the Auditorium. By the time the exit door was closed there was an uproar of clapping, shouts and whistles. It seemed to me like the beautiful sounds of a rich, new beginning.

Prior to our leaving Sophie and Frank's relative's home this morning, we all decided not to take the van home after our appearance at the General Assembly. Instead, we wanted to just mingle with everyone, being unafraid and ourselves, and take the subway back to Brooklyn.

Once we arrived at the subway station, after waiting a few minutes, the train arrived that was to take us back to Frank and Sophie's relatives. Eagerly, we all boarded it and began our search for seats. But that's when a surprise of never-ending proportions struck all of us New Jersey Wagoners.

Surrounding us, everywhere in that subway car and in all the others on that train, were countless animals, birds and humans, all engaged in animated conversations and laughter. It was the sound of joy.

Walt and Po must have known at that moment, seeing it through all our eyes and hearing it through our ears that the anteverse had at last been reborn in this universe and that it was thriving.

Sitting between Wally and Bernie, Sophie leaned around them and said to me, "Listen, Greg. We are surrounded by the sounds of rebirth and

276

renewal. See what you have done, my sweetest and dearest of friends."

And looking around at her and at all my other cherished companions, I was filled with such happiness at that moment. Each of them nodded, knowing what was going to happen next. In response, I arched my head back... and barked and barked and barked and...

Polar Wind's Around the World Voyage

The Individuals Mentioned in Fetch!

Name	Species	Function	Place of Origin
Greg	dog	Sage*	Atlantic City
Rita	bird	Performer*	Atlantic City
Jennifer	cat	Performer*	Atlantic City
Flo	dog	Performer*	Atlantic City
Bernice	child	Herald*	Atlantic City
Wally	child	boy Wizard*	Atlantic City
Sophie	adult	Nurturer*	Atlantic City
Frank	adult	Nurturer*	Atlantic City
Walt	?	Vanguard**	Anteverse***
Po	?	Protector*	Anteverse
Emissaries	?	foster evil	Anteverse
Willa	?	Guardian	Anteverse
Big salmon	fish	Harkener	Hoh River
Ed	bird	Harkener	Hoh River
Iris	bird	Harkener	Hoh River
Margaret	adult	Hostess	Hoh River
Helen	adult	Hostess	Hoh River
Jimmy	adult	Bus driver	Willa's farm
Diane	adult	Bus passenger	Willa's farm
Sparkie	dog	Security	Polar Wind
Capt. Shriver		Ship Captain	Polar Wind
LCDR Steele		Ship XO	Polar Wind
Trees/ animals/ birds		facilitate change	Worldwide

You, the reader.

*Most characters have Harkener duties as well.

**In the Anteverse a Vanguard is a Wizard.

***A place where life existed, prior to the creation of our Universe.

www.ingramcontent.com/pod-product-compliance
Lightning Source LLC
Chambersburg PA
CBHW031257170626
46807CB00001B/182